CAMILLE

Also by Pierre Lemaitre in English translation

Irène
Alex

Pierre Lemaitre

CAMILLE

Translated from the French by
Frank Wynne

MACLEHOSE PRESS
QUERCUS · LONDON

First published in the French language as *Sacrifices* by Editions Albin Michel in 2012
First published in Great Britain in 2015 by

MacLehose Press
an imprint of Quercus
55 Baker Street
7th Floor, South Block
London W1U 8EW

ROYAUME-UNI

This book is supported by the Institut français (Royaume-Uni)
as part of the Burgess programme.

ISBN (HB) 978 0 85705 276 6
ISBN (TPB) 978 0 85705 277 3
ISBN (Ebook) 978 1 78206 621 7

10 9 8 7 6 5 4 3 2 1

Designed and typeset in Minion by James Nunn
Printed and bound in Great Britain by Clays Ltd, St Ives plc

For Pascaline

To Cathy Bourdeau, for her support.
With my affection

We only know about one per cent of what's happening to us.
We don't know how little heaven is paying for how much hell.

William Gaddis, *The Recognitions*

Translator's Note

The judicial system in France is fundamentally different to that in the United Kingdom and the U.S.A. Rather than the adversarial system, where police investigate, and the role of the courts is to act as an impartial referee between prosecution and defence, in the French inquisitorial system the judiciary work with the police on the investigation, appointing an independent *juge d'instruction* entitled to question witnesses, interrogate suspects, and oversee the police investigation, gathering evidence, whether incriminating or otherwise. If there is sufficient evidence, the case is referred to the *procureur* – the public prosecutor, who decides whether to bring charges. The *juge d'instruction* plays no role in the eventual trial and is prohibited from adjudicating future cases involving the same defendant.

The French have two national police forces: the *police nationale* (formerly called the *Sûreté*), a civilian police force with jurisdiction in cities and large urban areas, and the *gendarmerie nationale*, a branch of the French Armed Forces, responsible both for public safety and for policing the towns with populations of fewer than 20,000. Since the *gendarme*rie rarely has the resources to conduct complex investigations, the *police nationale* maintains regional criminal investigations services (*police judiciaire*) analogous to the British C.I.D, they also oversee armed response units (*R.A.I.D.*).

Glossary

Brigade criminelle: equivalent to the Homicide and Serious Crime Squad, the brigade handles murders, kidnappings and assassinations, the equivalent of the British C.I.D.

Commandant: Detective Chief Inspector

Commissaire divisionnaire: Chief Superintendent (U.K.)/Police Chief (U.S.) has though he has both an administrative and an investigative role

Contrôleur général: Assistant Chief Constable (U.K.)/Police Commissioner (U.S.)

G.I.G.N.: "Groupe d'intervention de la *Gendarmerie* nationale": a special operations unit of the French Armed Forces trained to perform counter-terrorist and hostage rescue missions

Identité judiciare: the forensics department of the national police

Inspection générale des services (I.G.S.): the French police monitoring service equivalent to Internal Affairs (U.S.) or the Police Complaints Authority (U.K.)

Juge d'instruction: the "investigating judge" has a role somewhat similar to that of an American District Attorney. He is addressed as *monsieur le juge*

Préfecture de Police: the local police headquarters overseeing a district or arrondissement.

Procureur: similar to a Crown Prosecutor in the U.K. He is addressed as *magistrat* in the same way one might say "sir", or "your honour"

The Périphérique is the inner ring-road circumscribing central Paris, linking the old city gates or *portes*, e.g. porte d'Italie, porte d'Orleans

DAY 1

An event may be considered decisive when it utterly destabilises your life. This is something Camille Verhœven read some months ago in an article entitled "The Acceleration of History". This decisive, disorientating event which sends a jolt of electricity through your nervous system is readily distinguishable from life's other misfortunes because it has a particular force, a specific density: as soon as it occurs, you realise that it will have overwhelming consequences, that what is happening in that moment is irreparable.

To take an example, three blasts from a pump-action shotgun fired at the woman you love.

This is what is going to happen to Camille.

And it does not matter whether, like him, you are attending your best friend's funeral on the day in question, or whether you feel that you have already had your fill for one day. Fate does not concern itself with such trivialities; it is quite capable, in spite of them, of taking the form of a killer armed with a sawn-off shotgun, a 12-gauge Mossberg 500.

All that remains to be seen is how you will react. This is all that matters.

Because in that instant you will be so devastated that, more often than not, you will react out of pure reflex. If, for example, before she is shot three times, the woman you love has been beaten to a pulp and if, after that, you clearly see the killer shoulder his weapon having chambered a round with a dull clack.

It is probably in such a moment that truly exceptional men reveal themselves, those capable of making the best decisions under the worst of circumstances.

If you are an ordinary man, you get by as best you can. All

too often, in the face of such a cataclysmic event, your decision is likely to be flawed or mistaken, always assuming you have not been rendered utterly helpless.

When you have reached a certain age, or when a similar event has already destroyed your life, you suppose that you are immune. This is the case with Camille. His first wife was murdered, a tragedy from which he took years to recover. When you have faced such an ordeal, you assume that nothing more can happen to you.

This is the trap.

You have lowered your guard.

For fate, which has a keen eye, this is the ideal moment to catch you unawares.

And remind you of the unfailing timeliness of chance.

Anne Forestier steps into the Galerie Monier immediately after it opens. The shopping centre is almost empty, the heady smell of bleach heavy in the air as shop owners open their doors, setting out stalls of books, display cases of jewellery.

Built in the late nineteenth century towards the lower end of the Champs-Elysées, the Galerie is made up of small luxury boutiques selling stationery, leather goods, antiques. Gazing up at the vaulted glass roof, a knowledgeable visitor will notice a host of Art Deco details: tiles, cornices, small stained glass windows. Features Anne, too, could admire if she chose, but, as she would be the first to admit, she is not a morning person. At this hour ceilings, mouldings, details are the least of her concerns.

More than anything, she needs coffee. Strong and black.

Because this morning, almost as if it were destined to be, Camille wanted her to linger in bed. Unlike her, Camille is very much a morning person. But Anne did not feel up to it. Having gently fended off Camille's advances – he has warm hands; it is not always easy to resist – and forgetting that she had poured herself some coffee, she rushed to take a shower and so by the time she emerged and padded into the kitchen towelling her hair, she discovered that the coffee was cold, and rescued a contact lens that was about to be washed down the drain . . .

By then it was time for her to leave. On an empty stomach.

Arriving at the Galerie Monier at a few minutes past ten, she takes a table on the terrace of the little brasserie at the entrance; she is their first customer. The coffee machine is still warming up and she is forced to wait to be served, but though she repeatedly checks her watch, it is not because she is in a hurry. It is an attempt to ward off the waiter. Since he has nothing to do while he waits for the coffee machine to warm up, he is trying to engage her in conversation. He wipes down the tables, glancing at her over his shoulder, and, moving in concentric circles, edges towards her. He is a tall, thin, chatty guy with lank blond hair, the type often found in tourist areas. When he has finished with the last table, he takes up a position close to her and, hands on hips, gives a contented sigh as he stares out the window and launches into pathetically mediocre meteorological musings.

The waiter may be a moron, but he has good taste because, at forty, Anne is still stunning. Dark-haired and delicate, she has pale green eyes and a dazzling smile . . . She is luminously beautiful, with exceptional bone structure. Her slow, graceful movements make you want to touch her because everything about her seems curved and firm: her breasts, her buttocks, her belly, her thighs . . . indeed everything so exquisitely shaped, so perfect it would unsettle any man.

Every time he thinks about her, Camille cannot help but wonder what she sees in him. He is fifty years old, almost bald and, most importantly, he is barely four foot eleven. The height of an eleven-year-old boy. To avoid speculation, it is probably best to mention that, although Anne is not particularly tall, she is almost a whole head taller than Camille.

Anne responds to the waiter's flirtation with a charming smile that eloquently says "fuck off" (the waiter acquiesces and returns to his work) and she, having hastily drunk her coffee, heads through the Galerie towards the rue Georges-Flandrin. She has nearly reached the exit when, slipping a hand into her bag to get her purse, she feels something damp. Her fingers are covered in ink. Her pen has leaked.

For Camille, it is with the pen that the story really begins. Or with Anne deciding to go to a café in the Galerie Monier rather than somewhere else, on that particular morning rather than another one . . . The dizzying number of coincidences that can lead to tragedy is bewildering. But it seems churlish to complain since it was a dizzying series of coincidences that led to Camille first meeting Anne.

The pen is a small dark-blue fountain pen and the cartridge is leaking. Camille can still picture it. Anne is left-handed and holds her pen in a tortuous grip, writing quickly in a large, loping hand so that it looks as if she is furiously dashing off a series of signatures yet, curiously, she always buys small pens which makes the sight the more astonishing.

Seeing the ink stains on her hand, Anne immediately worries about what damage has been done. She glances around for some way to deal with the problem and sees a large plant stand, sets the handbag down on the wooden rim, and begins to take everything out.

She is quite upset, but her fears prove unjustified. Besides, those who know Anne would find it hard to see what she might be afraid of since Anne does not have much. Not in her bag, nor in her life. The clothes she is wearing are inexpensive. She has never owned an apartment or a car, she spends what she earns, no more, but never less. She does not save because it is not in her nature: her father was a shopkeeper. When he was about to go bankrupt, he disappeared with funds belonging to some forty associations to which he had recently had himself elected treasurer; he was never heard of again. This may explain why Anne has a rather detached relationship to money. The last time she had money worries was when she was single-handedly raising her daughter Agathe, and that was a long time ago. Anne tosses the pen into a rubbish bin and shoves her mobile phone into her jacket pocket. Her purse is stained and will probably have to be discarded, but the contents are unaffected. As for the handbag, although the lining is damp, the ink did not bleed through. Perhaps Anne decides to buy a new one, after all an upmarket shopping arcade is the perfect place, but it is impossible to know since what happens next will make any plans superfluous. For now, she dabs at the inside of the bag with some wadded Kleenex and when she has done so sees that both her hands are now ink-stained.

She could go back to the brasserie, but the prospect of having to deal with the same waiter is depressing. Even so, she is steeling herself to do so when she spots a sign indicating a public toilet, an unusual facility in a small shopping arcade. The sign points to a narrow passageway just beyond Pâtisserie Cardon and Desfossés Jewellers.

At this point, things begin to move faster.

Anne crosses the thirty metres to the toilets, pushes open the door and finds herself face to face with two men.

They have come in through the emergency exit on the rue Damiani and are heading towards the Galerie.

A few seconds later . . . it seems ridiculous, and yet it is true: if Anne had gone in five seconds later, the men would have already pulled on their balaclavas and things would have turned out very differently.

Instead what happens is this: Anne pushes open the door and she and the two men suddenly freeze.

She looks from one man to the other, startled by their presence, their behaviour, by their black balaclavas.

And by their guns. Pump-action shotguns. Even to someone who knows nothing about firearms, they look daunting.

One of the men, the shorter one, lets out a moan or perhaps it is a cry. Anne looks at him; he is stunned. She turns to the other man whose face is harsh and angular. The scene lasts only a few seconds during which the three players stand, shocked and speechless, all of them caught unawares. The two men quickly pull down their balaclavas, the taller one raises his weapon, half turns and, like an axeman preparing to fell an oak tree, hits Anne full in the face with the butt of his rifle.

With all his strength.

He literally shatters her cheekbone. He even gives a low grunt like a tennis player making a first serve.

Anne reels back, her hand reaching out for something to break her fall only to find empty air. The blow was so sudden, so brutal, she feels as though her head has been severed from her body. She is thrown almost a metre, the back of her skull slams against the door and she flings her arms wide and slumps to the ground.

The wooden rifle butt has smashed her face from jaw to temple, breaking her left cheekbone, leaving a ten-centimetre gash as her cheek splits like a ripe fruit, blood spurts everywhere. From outside, it would have sounded like a boxing glove hitting a punchbag. To Anne, it is like a sledgehammer swung with both hands.

The other man screams furiously. Anne only dimly hears him as she struggles to get her bearings.

The taller man calmly steps forward, aims the barrel of the shotgun at her head, chambers a round with a loud clack and is about to fire when his accomplice screams again. Louder this time. Perhaps even grabs the tall man's sleeve. Anne is too stunned to open her eyes, only her hands move, flailing in an unconscious reflex.

The man holding the pump-action shotgun stops, turns, wavers: firing a gun is a sure way to bring the police running, any career criminal would tell you that. For a split second, he hesitates over the best course of action and, having made his decision, turns back to Anne and aims a series of kicks to her face and her stomach. She tries to dodge the blows, but she is trapped. There is no way out. On one side is the door against which she is huddled, on the other, the tall man balancing on his left foot as he lashes out with his right. Between salvoes, Anne briefly manages to catch her breath; the man stops for a moment, and perhaps because he is not getting the desired result, decides on a more radical approach: he spins the shotgun, raises it high and starts to hit her with the rifle butt as hard and as fast as he can.

He looks like a man trying to pound a stake into a patch of frozen ground.

Anne writhes and twists as she tries to protect herself, she slithers on the pool of her own blood, clasps her hands behind her neck. The first blow goes awry and lands on the back of her head, the second shatters her interlaced fingers.

This change of tactic does not go down well with the accomplice, since the smaller man now grabs his arm, preventing him from continuing. The tall man, unfazed, goes back to the more traditional method, aiming brutal kicks at her head with his heavy military-style boots. Curled into a ball, Anne tries to shield herself with her arms as blows rain on her head, her neck, her arms, her back; it is impossible to know how many, the doctors will say at least eight, the pathologist says nine.

It is at this point that Anne loses consciousness.

As far as the two men are concerned, the matter has been dealt with. But Anne's body is now blocking the door leading to the arcade. Without a word, they bend down; the smaller man takes her arms and drags her towards him, her head thumping against the tiles. Once there is space to open the door, he drops her arms which fall back heavily, her languid, broken hands coming to rest in the oddly graceful pose of a painted Madonna. Had Camille witnessed the scene, he would immediately have noticed the curious resemblance between the position of Anne's arms, her abandon, and a painting by Fernand Pelez called "The Victim", something he would have found devastating.

The story could end here. The story of an ill-fated incident. But the taller of the two men does not see it like that. He is clearly the leader and he quickly weighs up the situation.

What is going to happen to this woman? What if she regains consciousness and starts to scream? What if she runs back into the Galerie? Worse, what if she manages to get out through the emergency exit and calls for help? Or crawls into a toilet cubicle and phones the police?

He puts his foot against the door to hold it open, bends down and, grabbing her by the right ankle, he leaves the toilets, dragging her behind him with the same ease, the same casual indifference with which a child might drag a toy.

Anne's body is bruised and battered, her shoulder slams against the toilet door, her hip against the wall of the corridor, her head lolls as she is dragged along, banging into a skirting board or one of the plant pots in the Galerie. Anne is no more than a rag now, a sack, a lifeless doll leaving a scarlet trail that quickly clots. Blood dries fast.

She seems dead. The man drops her leg, abandoning her dislocated body without a second glance; he has no more use for her. He loads the pump-action shotgun with swift sure movements that emphasise his determination. The two men burst into Desfossés Jewellers yelling orders. The shop has only just opened. A witness, had there been one, would be struck by the disparity between their fury and the empty shop. The two men bark orders at the staff (two petrified women), and immediately lash out, punching them in the stomach, the face. The Galerie echoes with the sound of smashing glass, screams, whimpers, gasps of fear.

Perhaps it due to being dragged along the ground, to her head being bumped and jolted, but there is a sudden pulse of life and in that moment, Anne struggles to reconnect with reality.

Her brain, like a defective radar, tries desperately to make sense of what is happening, but it is futile, she is in shock, her mind literally numbed by the blows and the speed of events. Her body is racked with pain, she cannot move a muscle.

The spectacle of Anne's body being dragged through the Galerie and abandoned in a pool of blood in the doorway of the jeweller's has one positive effect: it lends a sense of urgency to the events.

The only people in the shop are the owner and a trainee assistant, a girl of about sixteen, thin as a leaf, who wears her hair pinned up in a chignon to give herself some gravitas. The moment she sees the two armed men in balaclavas, she knows it is a hold-up; hypnotised, sacrificed, passive as a victim about to be burned at the stake, she stands, her mouth opening and closing like a goldfish. Her legs can barely hold her up; she clutches the edge of the counter for support. Before her knees finally give way, the barrel of the shotgun is slammed into her face. Slowly, like a soufflé, she sinks to the ground. She will lie here as events play out, counting her heartbeats, shielding her head with her arms as though expecting a shower of stones.

The owner of the jeweller's stifles a scream when she first sees Anne being dragged along the ground, skirt rucked up to her waist, leaving a wide, crimson wake. She tries to say something, but the words die in her throat. The taller of the two men is stationed at the entrance to the shop, keeping lookout, while the shorter man rushes her, aiming the barrel of his shotgun. He jabs it viciously into her belly and she only just manages not to vomit. He does not say a word; no words are necessary. Already she is working on automatic pilot. She clumsily disarms the alarm system, fumbles for the keys to the display cases only to realise she does not have them on her, she needs to fetch them from the back room; it is as she takes her first step that she realises she has wet herself. Her hand trembling, she holds out the bunch of keys. Though she will not mention this in her witness statement, at this moment she whispers to the man "Don't kill me . . ." She would trade the whole world for another twenty seconds of life. As she says this, and without having to be asked, she lies down on the floor, hands behind her head, whispering fervently to herself: she is praying.

Given the viciousness of these thugs, one cannot help but wonder whether prayers, however fervent, serve any practical purpose. It hardly matters: while she prays, the two men quickly open the display cases and tip the contents into canvas bags.

The hold-up has been efficiently planned; it takes less than four minutes. The timing is perfectly judged, the decision to enter the arcade through the toilets is astute, the division of roles between the men is professional: while the first man ransacks the cabinets, the second, standing squarely in the doorway, keeps one eye on the shop and another on the rest of the arcade.

The C.C.T.V. camera inside the shop will show the first robber rifling through cases and drawers and grabbing anything of value. Outside, a second camera films the doorway and a narrow section of the arcade. It is on this footage that Anne's sprawled body can be seen.

This is the point at which the meticulously planned robbery begins to go wrong; this is the moment on the camera footage when Anne appears to move. It is an almost imperceptible movement, a reflex. At first, Camille is hesitant, unsure what he has seen but, studying it with care, there can be no doubt . . . Anne moves her head from right to left, very slowly. It is a gesture Camille recognises: at certain times of the day when she needs to relax, she arches her neck, working the vertebrae and the muscles – the "sternocleidomastoid", she says, a muscle Camille did not know existed. Obviously, on the video the gesture does not have the tranquil grace of a relaxation exercise. Anne is lying on her side, her right leg is drawn up so the knee touches her chest, her left leg is extended, her upper body is twisted as though she is trying to turn onto her back, her skirt is hiked up to reveal her white panties. Blood is streaming down her face.

She is not lying there; she was thrown there.

When the robbery began, the man in the doorway shot several quick glances at Anne, but since she was not moving, he focused his attention on watching the arcade. Now he ignores her, his back is turned, he has not even noticed the blood trickling under the heel of his right shoe.

Emerging from her nightmare, Anne struggles to make sense of what is going on around her. As she looks up, the camera briefly captures an image of her face. It is heartrending.

When he comes to this moment on the tape, Camille is so shocked he twice fumbles with the remote control before he manages to stop, rewind and pause: he does not recognise her. He can see nothing of Anne's luminous features, her laughing eyes in this bruised, bloody face swollen already to twice its size, in these vacant eyes.

Camille grips the edge of the table, he feels an overwhelming urge to weep because Anne is staring straight into the lens, gazing directly at him as though she might speak, might beg him to come to her rescue; he cannot help but imagine this, and imagination can be devastating. Imagine someone you love, someone who relies on you for protection, imagine watching them suffer, watching them die and feel yourself break out in a cold sweat. Now, go one step further and imagine in that moment of excruciating terror, this person crying out to you for help and you will wish you could die too. This is how Camille feels, staring at the video monitor, utterly helpless. There is nothing he can do save watch, because it is all over . . .

It is unendurable, literally unendurable.

He will watch this footage dozens of times.

Anne behaves as though her surroundings do not exist. She would not react if the tall man were to stand over her and aim the barrel at the back of her head. It is a powerful survival instinct even if, watching it on the screen, it seems more like suicide: scarcely two metres away from a man with a shotgun who only minutes earlier made it clear that he was perfectly prepared to put a bullet in her head, Anne is about to do something that no-one in her position would wish to do. She is going to try to stand up. With no thought for the consequences. She is going to try to escape. Anne is a woman of great courage, but confronting a man with a sawn-off shotgun goes beyond bravery.

What is about to happen arises almost automatically from the situation: two opposing forces are about to collide and one or other must prevail. Both forces are caught up in the moment. The difference being that one is backed up by a 12-bore shotgun, which unquestionably gives him the upper hand. But Anne cannot gauge the balance of power, cannot rationally calculate the odds against her, she is behaving as though she were alone. She musters every ounce of strength – and from the flickering images, it is clear she has little left – draws up her leg, hoists herself laboriously with her arms, her hands slipping in a pool of her own blood. She almost falls back, but tries a second time; the slowness of her movements lends the scene a surreal quality. She feels heavy, numb, you can almost hear her gasping for breath, you want to heave her up, to drag her away, to help her to her feet.

Camille wants only to tell her not to move. Even if it takes a minute before the tall man turns and notices, Anne is so dazed, so out of it that she will not make it three metres before the first shotgun blast all but cuts her in two. But several hours have passed, Camille is staring at a video monitor, what he thinks now is of no importance: it is too late.

Anne's actions are not governed by thought but by sheer determination which knows no logic. It is obvious from the video that her resolution is simply a survival instinct. She does not look like someone being threatened by a shotgun at point-blank range, she looks like a woman who has had too much to drink and is about to pick up her handbag – Anne has clung to the bag from the beginning – stagger to the door and make her way home. It seems as though what is stopping her is not a 12-bore shotgun, but her befuddled state.

What transpires next takes barely a second: Anne does not stop to think, she has struggled painfully to her feet. She manages to stay standing, her skirt is still hiked around her waist. She is scarcely upright before she begins to run.

At this point, everything goes wrong and what follows is a series of miscalculations, accidents and errors. It is as though, overwhelmed by events, God does not know how to play out the scene and so leaves the actors to improvise, which, ineptly, they do.

Anne does not know where she is, she cannot get her bearings, in fact in attempting to escape, she heads the wrong way. If she reached out a hand, she would touch the tall man's shoulder, he would turn and . . .

She hesitates for a long moment, disorientated. It is a miracle that she manages to stay upright. She wipes her bloody face with her sleeve, tilts her head as though listening to something, she cannot seem to take that first step . . . Then, suddenly, she tries to run. As he watches the video, Camille falls apart as the last pillars of his stoic courage crumble.

Anne's instinct is fine in theory; it is in practice that things go wrong. She skids in the pool of blood. She is skating. In a cartoon, it would be funny; in reality it is agonising because she is slipping in her own blood, struggling to stay on her feet, trying desperately to run and succeeding only in flapping and flailing dangerously. It looks as though she is running in slow motion. It is heart-stopping.

The tall man does not immediately realise what is happening. Anne is about to fall on top of him when her feet finally reach a patch of dry ground, she regains her balance and, as though powered by a spring, she begins to lurch.

In the wrong direction.

Initially, she follows a curious trajectory, spinning around like a broken doll. She makes a quarter turn, takes a step forward, stops, turns again like a disorientated walker trying to get her bearings, and eventually manages to stumble off in the vague direction of the exit. Several seconds pass before the robber realises that his prey is attempting to escape. The moment he does, he turns and fires.

Camille plays the video over and over: there is no doubt that the killer is surprised. He is gripping his gun next to his hip, the sort of stance a gunman takes when trying to hit anything within a radius of four or five metres. Perhaps he has not had time to regain his composure. Or perhaps he is too sure of himself – it often happens: give a nervous man a 12-bore shotgun and the freedom to use it and he immediately thinks he is a crack shot. Perhaps it is simply surprise, or perhaps it is a mixture of all these things. The fact remains that the barrel is aimed high, much too high. It is an impulsive shot. He does not even try to aim.

Anne does not see anything. She is still stumbling forward through a black hole when a deafening hail of glass rains down on her as the ornamental fanlight above her head is blown to smithereens. In the light of Anne's fate, it seems cruel to mention that the stained-glass panel depicted a hunting scene: two dashing riders galloping towards a baying pack of hounds that have cornered a stag; the hounds are slavering, their teeth bared, the stag is already dead meat . . . It seems strange that the fanlight in the Galerie Monier, which survived two world wars, was finally destroyed by a ham-fisted thug . . . Some things are difficult to accept.

The whole Galerie trembles: the windows, the plate glass, the floor; people protect themselves as best they can.

"I hunched my shoulders," an antiques dealer will later tell Camille, miming the action.

He is thirty-four (he is precise on this point; he is not thirty-five). The stubby moustache that curls at the ends looks a little too small for his large nose. His right eye remains almost entirely closed, like the figure in the helmet in Giotto's painting "Idolatry". Even thinking about the noise of the gunshot, he seems dumbfounded.

"Well, obviously, I assumed it was a terrorist attack. [He apparently thinks this explains matters.] But then I thought, that's ridiculous, why would terrorists attack the Galerie, there's no obvious target," and so on . . .

The sort of witness who revises reality as fast as his memory will allow. But not someone to forget his priorities. Before going out into the arcade to see what was happening, he looked around to check whether there was any damage to his stock.

"Not so much as a scratch!" he says, flicking his thumb against his front tooth.

The Galerie is higher than it is wide; it is a corridor some fifty metres across lined by shops with plate-glass windows. In such a confined space the blast is colossal. After the explosion, the vibrations ripple out at the speed of sound, ricochet off every obstacle sending back wave upon wave of echoes.

The gunshot and the hail of glass stopped Anne in her tracks. She raises her arms to shield her head, tucks her chin into her chest, stumbles, falls onto her side and rolls across the glittering shards, but it takes more than a single shot and a shattered window to stop a woman like Anne. It seems incredible, but once more she gets to her feet.

The tall man's first shot missed its mark, but he has learned his lesson; he takes the time to aim. On the C.C.T.V. footage, he can be seen reloading the shotgun, staring down the barrel; if the video were sufficiently high resolution, it would be possible to see his finger squeezing the trigger.

A black-gloved hand suddenly appears; the shorter man jostles his shoulder just as he fires . . .

The window of the nearby bookshop explodes, splinters of glass, some large as dinner plates, sharp and jagged as razors, fall and shatter on the tiles.

"I was in the little office at the back of the bookshop . . ."

The woman is about fifty, an archetypal businesswoman: short, plump, self-confident, expensive make-up, twice-weekly trips to the beautician, tinkling with bracelets, necklaces, chains, rings, brooches, earrings (it is a wonder the robbers did not take her with the rest of their loot), a gravelly voice – too many cigarettes and probably too much booze, Camille does not take the time to find out. The incident took place only a few hours earlier, he is in shock, impatient, he needs to know.

"I rushed out . . ." she gestures towards the arcade. She pauses, clearly happy to be the centre of attention. She wants to make the most of her little performance. With Camille, it will be short-lived.

"Get on with it," he growls.

Not very polite for a policeman, she thinks, must be his height, it's the kind of thing that must make you bitter, resentful. Moments after the gunshot, she witnessed Anne being hurled against a display case as though pushed by a giant hand, bouncing back against the plate-glass window and then crumpling on the floor. The image is still so powerful that the woman forgets her affectations.

"She was thrown against the window, but she was hardly on the ground before she was trying to get up again! [The woman sounds amazed, impressed.] She was bleeding and disorientated, flapping her arms around, slipping and sliding, you get the picture . . ."

On the C.C.T.V. footage, the two men seem to freeze for a moment. The shorter one shoves the shotgun aside and drops the bags on the floor. He squares up, it is as though they are about to come to blows. Tight-lipped beneath his balaclava, he seems to spit his words.

The tall man lowers the gun, one hand gripping the barrel, he hesitates for a moment, then reality takes hold. Reluctantly he watches Anne as she struggles to her feet and staggers towards the exit; but time is short, an alarm goes off inside his head, the raid has taken far too long.

His accomplice grabs the bags and tosses one to him; the decision is made. The two men run off and disappear from the screen. A split second later, the tall man turns back and reappears on the right-hand side of the image, grabs the handbag Anne abandoned when she fled, then disappears again. This time he will not be back. We know that the two men went through the toilets and out onto the rue Damiani, where a third man was waiting with a car.

Anne barely knows where she is. She falls, gets up and, somehow, manages to make it out of the arcade and onto the street.

"There was so much blood, and she was walking . . . she looked like a zombie." A South American girl, dark hair, copper skin, about twenty. She works in the hairdressing salon on the corner and had just stepped out to get some coffees.

"Our machine is broken and someone has to go out and get coffee for the customers," the manageress, Janine Guénot, explains. Standing, staring at Verhœven, she looks like a brothel madam, she has the same qualities. And the same sense of responsibility: she is not about to let one of her girls talk to some man on the street without keeping an eye open. The reason the girl went out – the coffee, the malfunctioning machine – hardly matters, Camille brushes it aside with a wave. Though not entirely.

Because at the moment Anne stumbled out into the street, the hairdresser was rushing back with five cups of coffee balanced on a tray. Clients in this neighbourhood are particularly annoying, being well heeled they feel entitled to be demanding, as though exercising some ancestral right.

"Serving lukewarm coffee would be a disaster," the manageress explains with a pained expression.

Hence the young hairdresser's haste.

Surprised and intrigued by the two gunshots she hears coming from the Galerie Monier, she is trotting along with her tray when she runs straight into a crazed woman, covered in blood, staggering out of the arcade. It is a shock. The two women collide, the tray goes flying and with it the cups, the saucers, the glasses of water, the coffee spills all over the blue trouser suit the hairdressers in the salon wear as a uniform. The gunshots, the coffee, the delay, she can deal with, but trouser suits are expensive. The voice of the manageress is shrill now, she wants to show Camille the damage. "It's fine," he waves away her concerns. She demands to know who is going to pay for the dry cleaning, the law must surely provide for such eventualities. "It'll be fine," Camille says again.

"And she didn't even stop," the woman insists, as though this were a prang with a moped.

By now, she is telling the story as though it happened to her. She imperiously takes over because, when all is said and done, this was one of "her girls", and having coffee spilled all over her uniform means she has rights. Customers are all alike. Camille grabs her arm, she looks down at him curiously, as though observing a piece of dog shit on the pavement.

"Madame," Camille says with a snarl, "stop pissing me about."

The woman cannot believe her ears. And a dwarf at that! Now she's seen it all. But Verhœven stares her down; it is unsettling. In the awkward silence, the young hairdresser tries to prove how anxious she is to keep her job.

"She was moaning . . ." the girl says, to distract Camille's attention.

He turns to her, wants to know more. "What do you mean, moaning?"

"She was making these little cries, it was like . . . I don't know how to explain it."

"Try," says the manageress, eager to redeem herself in the eyes of the policeman, you never know when it might be useful. She nudges the girl. Come on, tell the gentleman, what did they sound like, these cries? The girl stares at them, eyelashes fluttering, she is not sure what she is being asked to do and so, rather than describing Anne's cries, she tries to mimic them. She begins to mouth little moans and whimpers, trying to find the right tone – *aah, aah* or maybe *uhh, uhh*, yes, that's it, she says, concentrating now, *uhh, uhh*, and having found the right tone the moans grow louder, she closes her eyes then opens them wide and seconds later *uhh, uhh*, it sounds as though she is about to come.

They are standing in the street, a crowd begins to gather on the spot where street cleaners have carelessly hosed away Anne's blood, which is still trickling into the gutter, they step on the fading scarlet blotches leaving Camille distraught . . . The crowd sees a diminutive police officer and, opposite him, the young hairdresser with the sallow tan who is staring at him strangely and making shrill, orgasmic sounds under the approving gaze of a brothel madam. Good heavens, it's is hardly the sort of thing one expects to see in this neighbourhood. The other shopkeepers stand in their doorways, looking on appalled. The gunshots were bad enough – not the sort of publicity that's going to attract customers – but now the whole street seems to have descended into a grotesque farce.

Camille goes on taking witness statements, comparing one to the other, trying to piece together what finally happened.

Utterly disoriented, Anne emerges from Galerie Monier onto the rue Georges-Flandrin next to number 34, turns right and staggers up towards the junction. A few metres on, she bumps into the hairdresser, but she does not stop, she hobbles on, leaning on the parked cars for support. Her bloody handprint is found on the roof and doors of several vehicles. To those on the street who heard the gunshots from the Galerie, this woman covered from head to foot in blood seems like an apparition. She seems to float, swaying this way and that but never stopping, she no longer knows what she is doing, she simply staggers on, groaning like a drunk, but moving forward. People stand aside to let her pass. One man dares to venture a concerned "Madame?", but he is traumatised by so much blood.

"I can tell you, monsieur, I was truly terrified at the sight of the poor woman . . . I didn't know what to do."

He is clearly distraught, this elderly man with his calm face and his pitifully scrawny neck, his eyes are misted over. Cataracts, Camille thinks, his father suffered from cataracts before he died. After each phrase, the old man seems to slip into a dream. His eyes are fixed on Camille and there is a long pause before he picks up his story. He is overcome and he opens his frail arms wide; Camille swallows hard, assailed by conflicting emotions.

The old man calls out "Madame!", but he dares not touch her, she is like a sleepwalker; he lets her pass, Anne stumbles on.

At this point, she turns right again.

There is no point wondering why. No-one knows. Because in doing so she turns into the rue Damiani. And two or three seconds after Anne turns into the street, the robbers' car appears, driving at breakneck speed.

Heading straight towards her.

Seeing his victim within range, the tall man who smashed her head in and twice failed to shoot her cannot resist reaching for his shotgun. To finish the job. As the car comes alongside, the window winds down and the barrel of the gun is levelled at her. Everything happens quickly: Anne sees the gun, but is incapable of even the slightest movement.

"She stared at the car . . ." said the man, "I don't know how to put it . . . it was like she was expecting it."

He realises the enormity of what he is saying. Camille

understands. What the old man means is that he senses a terrible weariness in Anne. After everything she has been through, she is ready to die. On this point everyone seems to agree: Anne, the shooter, the old man, fate, everyone.

Even the young hairdresser: "I saw the barrel of the gun poking out the window. And the lady, she saw it too. Neither of us could look away, but this lady, she was right there, right in the firing line, you understand?"

Camille holds his breath. Everyone, then, is in agreement. Everyone except the driver of the car. According to Camille – who has given the matter long and careful thought – at the time, the driver did not know about the carnage in the Galerie. Sitting in the getaway car, he probably hears the gunshots, knows too that the robbery was taking longer than planned. Panicked and impatient, he drums nervously on the steering wheel, he may even be thinking about driving away but then he sees the two men appear, one of them pushing the other towards the car . . . "Was anyone killed?" he wonders. "How many?" Finally, the robbers climb into the car. Under pressure, the driver starts the car and drives away, but as they come to the corner of the street – they have travelled scarcely two hundred metres since the car had to slow down at the traffic lights – he sees a woman lurching along the pavement, covered in blood. At that moment, the shooter probably shouts at him to slow down, rolls down his window, maybe even gives a howl of victory: one last chance, he cannot pass it up, it is as though fate itself is calling, as though he had found his soul mate, just when he had given up all hope she appears. He grabs the shotgun, brings it to his shoulder and aims. In the split second that follows, the driver suddenly imagines himself being held as an accomplice to cold-blooded murder in front of at least a dozen witnesses, to say nothing of whatever may have happened in the Galerie in which he is already implicated. The robbery has gone horribly wrong. He had not expected things to turn out like this . . .

"The car screeched to a halt," says the hairdresser. "Just like that! The scream of the brakes . . ."

Traces of rubber on the street will make it possible to determine that the getaway car was a Porsche Cayenne.

Everyone in the vehicle pitches forward, including the gunman. His bullet shatters the doors and the side windows of the parked car next to which Anne stands, frozen, waiting to die. Everyone nearby drops to the ground, everyone except the elderly man who does not have time to move. Anne collapses just as the driver floors the accelerator, the car lurches forward and the tyres squeal. As the hairdresser gets to her feet she sees the old man, one hand leaning against a wall for support, the other clutching his heart.

Anne is lying on the pavement, one arm dangling in the gutter, one leg beneath a parked car.

"Glittering," according to the old man, which is not surprising since she is covered with shards of glass from the shattered windscreen.

"It looked like a fall of snow . . ."

10.40 a.m.

The Turks are not happy.

Not happy at all.

The big man with his dogged expression is driving carefully, but as he negotiates the roundabout at the place de l'Étoile and heads down the avenue de la Grande-Armée, his knuckles on the steering wheel are white. He is scowling. He is naturally demonstrative. Or perhaps it is part of his culture to readily show emotion.

The younger brother is excitable. Volatile. He is swarthy with a brutish face, he is obviously thin-skinned. He too is demonstrative, he jabs the air with his finger, it's exhausting. I don't understand a word he's saying – I'm Spanish – but it's not hard to guess: we were hired to pull off a quick, lucrative robbery, and find ourselves caught up in the Gunfight at the O.K. Corral. He flings his arms wide: what if I hadn't stopped you, what then? There is an awkward silence in the car. He spits the question, he's obviously demanding to know what would have happened if the girl had died. Then, suddenly, he snaps, he loses his rag: we were supposed to be raiding a jeweller's, not committing mass murder!

Like I said, it gets a bit wearing. Good thing I'm a peaceable man because if I'd got angry, things might have got out of hand.

Not that it really matters, but it's frustrating. The kid is wasting his breath dishing out the blame when he'd be better off saving his strength, he's going to need all his energy.

Things didn't go exactly as planned, but we got a result, that's all I care about. There are two big bags on the floor. Enough to be going on with for a while. And this is just the beginning, because I've got big plans, and there are more bags where those ones came from. The Turk is eyeing the bags too as he jabbers away to his brother, it sounds like they're planning something, the driver is nodding. They carry on like I'm not here, they're probably calculating the compensation they think they're entitled to. *Entitled* . . . that's a fucking laugh. From time to time, the little guy turns to me and yells something. I catch a couple of slang terms: "dosh", "divvy up". Where the fuck they learned them, I've no idea, they've hardly been in the country twenty-four hours. Who knows, maybe the Turks have a gift for languages. Not that I give a shit. Right now, the best thing I can do is look confused, play it cool, nod my head and give them an apologetic smile. We're coming in to Saint-Ouen, traffic is light, we're in the clear.

The *banlieue* flashes past. Jesus, the big Turk has got some pair of lungs on him. With all the shouting, by the time we get to the lock-up, the air in the car is unbreathable, it feels like he's just getting to his Unified Theory of Everything. The little guy yells at me, asking the same question over and over, he's demanding an answer, and to show he's serious he flashes an index finger and taps it against his closed fist. Maybe it's an offensive gesture back in Izmir, but here in Saint-Ouen it's a different matter. The gist is obvious enough, it's intended as a threat, the best course of action is to nod my head and agree. I don't feel I'm being dishonest, because things are going to be sorted out soon enough.

Meanwhile, the driver has got out of the car and he's struggling to open the padlock on the metal shutters of the garage. He twists the key this way and that, comes back to the car looking puzzled, he's obviously thinking back: when he locked up, the key was working fine. He turns back towards the car and stands there sweating while the engine runs. There's not much chance of us being spotted on this dead-end road in the middle of nowhere, but even so I don't fancy hanging around for ever.

As far as they're concerned, the padlock is just one more unexpected hitch. One too many. By now, the little guy is almost apoplectic. Nothing has gone according to plan, he feels conned, betrayed – "fucking French bastard" – the best thing I can do is look baffled, this whole thing about the lock not working is bizarre, we tried it yesterday and the garage door opened. I calmly step out of the car, looking surprised and confused.

The magazine of a Mossberg 500 holds seven rounds. Instead

of yelling and screaming like a pack of hyenas, these arseholes would have been better off counting the spent rounds. They're about to find out that if you don't know shit about locks, you'd better know a thing or two about arithmetic. Because once I'm out of the car, all I have to do is walk slowly as far as the door to the lock-up, gently push the driver to one side – "Here, let me give it a go" – and when I turn, I'm perfectly positioned. There are just enough bullets to quickly aim at the driver and put a 70mm shell in his chest that flings him back against the concrete wall. Now for the little guy. I turn slightly and feel a sense of relief as I blast his brains out through the windshield. See the blood spurting. The shattered windscreen, the side windows dripping blood, I can't see anything else. I step closer to inspect the damage: his head has been blown to pieces, all that's left is his scrawny neck and his body, which is twitching still. Chickens run around after they've had their heads chopped off. Turks are much the same.

The Mossberg makes a hell of a racket, but the silence afterwards!

There's no time to lose now. Unload the two bags, dig out the right key to open the lock-up, drag the big brother into the garage, roll the car in with the kid inside in two neat pieces – I have to roll it over the other guy, but it doesn't matter, he's not going to make a fuss now – pull down the metal shutters, lock it and it's done and dusted.

All I need to do now is pick up the bags, walk to the far end of the cul-de-sac and get into the rental car. Actually, we're not quite done yet. You might say this is just the beginning. Time to settle the scores. Take out the mobile phone, punch in the number that will set off the bomb. I can feel the shock wave from here. I'm a fair distance away, but even at forty metres I feel the rental car shake from the force of the blast. Now that's an explosion. For the Turks, it's a one-way ticket to the Gardens of Delight. They'll be able to feel up a few virgins. A plume of black smoke rises over the roofs of the workshops – most of them are boarded up, the local municipality has the land earmarked for redevelopment. I've just given them a helping hand with the demolition. It's possible to be an armed robber and still have a sense of civic duty. Within thirty seconds, the fire brigade will be on their way. There's no time to lose.

Stash the bags of jewellery in a left-luggage locker at the Gare du Nord. Drop the key into a letterbox on the boulevard Magenta.

My fence will send someone to pick up the haul.

Finally, assess the situation. They say killers always return to the scene of the crime. I like to respect tradition.

11.45 a.m.

Two hours before going to Armand's funeral, Camille receives a phone call asking whether he knows a certain Anne Forestier. His number is the first entry in the contacts list on her mobile and the last number that she dialled. The call sends a cold shiver down his spine: this is how you learn that someone is dead.

But Anne is not dead. "She has been the victim of an assault. She has been taken to hospital." From the tone of the woman's voice, Camille immediately knows that Anne is in a bad way.

In fact, Anne is in a *very* bad way. She is much too weak to be questioned. The officers in charge of the investigation have said they will call round as soon as possible. It took several minutes of heated negotiation with the ward sister – a thirty-year-old woman with bee-stung lips and a nervous tic affecting her right eye – for

Camille to get permission to go into Anne's room. And then only on condition that he not stay too long.

He pushes open the door and stands for a moment on the threshold. Seeing her like this is devastating.

At first he can only make out her bandaged head. She looks as though she might have been run over by a truck. The right side of her face is a single, blue-black bruise so swollen that her eyes, barely visible, seem to have withdrawn into her skull. The left side is marked by a gash at least ten centimetres long, the edges where the wound has been sutured are a sallow red. Her lips are split and inflamed, her eyelids blue and puffy. Her nose has been broken and has swollen up to three times its normal size. Anne keeps her mouth slightly open, her bottom gums are bleeding, and a thread of spittle trickles onto the pillow. She looks like an old woman. Her arms, bandaged from her shoulders to her splinted fingers, lie on top on the sheets. The dressing on the right hand is smaller and it is possible to make out a deep wound that has been stitched.

When she becomes aware of Camille's presence, she tries to reach out her hand, her eyes fill with tears, then her energy seems to drain away. She closes her eyes then opens them again. They are glassy and expressionless; even her beautiful green irises seem colourless.

Her head lolls to one side, her voice is hoarse. Her tongue seems heavy and clearly painful where unconsciously she bit into it; it is difficult to make out what she is saying, the labial consonants are inaudible.

"I feel sore . . ."

Camille cannot utter a word. Anne tries to speak, he lays a hand on the sheet to calm her, he does not dare to touch her. She suddenly seems nervous, agitated; he wants to do something to help, but what? Call a nurse? Anne's eyes are shining, there is something she urgently needs to say.

"... graaa' ... 'eet ... ard .."

She is still dazed by the suddenness of what has happened, as though it has just happened now.

Bending down, Camille listens carefully, he pretends to understand, he tries to smile. Anne sounds as though she is talking through a mouthful of scalding soup. Camille can hear only mangled syllables, but he concentrates and after a minute he begins to decipher words, to guess at meaning ... Mentally, he translates. It is amazing how quickly we can adapt. To anything. Amazing, and a little sad.

"Grabbed," he hears, "beat ... hard."

Anne's eyebrows, her eyes grow wide with terror as though the man were once more standing in front of her, about to club her with the rifle butt. Camille gently reaches out and rests a hand on her shoulder, Anne flinches and gives a strangled cry.

"Camille ..." she says.

She turns her head, it is difficult to make out what she says. The words are a sibilant hiss through three shattered teeth – the upper and lower incisors on the left hand side – that make her look like she is thirty years older, like Fantine in a crude production of "*Les Misérables*". Though she has begged the nurses, no-one has dared to give her a mirror.

In fact, though she can barely move, she tries to cover her mouth with the back of her hand when she speaks. More often than not she fails and her mouth looks like a gaping wound, the lips bruised and bluish.

"... going to operate ... ?"

This is what Camille thinks he hears. She starts to cry again; her tears seem to come independently of her words, with no apparent logic they suddenly well up and course down her cheeks. Anne's face is a mask of mute astonishment.

'"We don't know yet . . ." Camille says, his voice low. "Try to relax. Everything is going to be fine . . ."

But already Anne's mind is elsewhere. She turns her head away, as though she were ashamed. Her voice is barely audible now. Camille thinks he can make out the words "Not like this . . ." She does not want anyone to see her in this state. She manages to turn onto her stomach. Camille lays a hand on her shoulder, but Anne does not react, she stubbornly looks away, her body shaken by ragged sobs.

"Do you want me to stay?"

There is no answer. Not knowing what to do, Camille stays. After a long moment, Anne shakes her head at something though it is impossible to know what – at what is happening, at what has happened, at the grotesque farce that can engulf our lives without warning, at the injustice victims cannot help but see as personal. It is impossible to ask her. It is too soon. They are not in the same moment. There is nothing they can say.

It is impossible to tell whether she is asleep. Slowly, she turns onto her back, eyes closed. And does not move again.

There.

Camille gazes at her, listening intently, comparing her breathing to that when she is asleep, a sound he knows better than anyone in the world. He has spent hours watching her sleep. In the early days, he would get up in the middle of the night to sketch her features that looked like a swimmer's, because during the day he could never quite capture the subtle magic of her face. He has made hundreds of drawings, spent countless hours attempting to reproduce the purity of her lips, her eyelids. Or sketched her body silhouetted in the shower. His magnificent failures had taught him just how important she is: though he can draw an almost photographic likeness of anyone in a few scant minutes, there is something inexpressible, something indefinable about Anne that eludes his gaze, his senses, his powers of observation. The woman who lies swollen and bandaged before him now has nothing of the magic, all that remains is the outer shell, and ugly, terribly prosaic body.

It is this that, as the minutes pass, fuels Camille's anger.

From time to time, Anne wakes with a start, gives a little cry, glances round wildly and in those moments Camille sees a new and utterly unfamiliar expression, one he saw on Armand's face in the weeks before he died: the incredulous shock that things have come to this. Incomprehension. Injustice.

Hardly has he recovered from the upset than the nurse comes to tell him visiting hours are over. She is self-effacing, but she waits for him to leave. She wears a name-tag that reads "FLORENCE". She keeps her hands clasped behind her back, at once determined and respectful, her compassionate smile rendered utterly artificial by collagen or hyaluronic acid. Camille wants to stay until Anne can tell him everything, he is frantic to know what happened. But all he can do is wait. Leave. Anne needs to rest. Camille leaves.

It will be twenty-four hours before he begins to understand.

And twenty-four hours is much more time than a man like Camille might need to lay to waste the whole earth.

Emerging from the hospital, Camille knows only those few details given him over the telephone and later, here, at the hospital. In fact, aside from broad strokes, no-one knows anything; it has so far been impossible to retrace the precise sequence of events. Camille's only piece of evidence is Anne's disfigured face, a harrowing image that merely serves to fuel the anger of a man inclined to strong emotions.

By the time he has reached the exit, Camille is seething.

He wants to know everything, to know it now, to know it before everyone else, he wants . . .

Camille is not a vengeful man by nature, although, like anyone, there have been moments when he was tempted. But Philippe Buisson, the man who killed his first wife, is still very much alive, despite the fact that, given his contacts, it would have been a simple matter for Camille to have ordered a hit on him in prison.

And this time, seeing the attack on Anne, he is not motivated by a desire for revenge. It is as though what has happened threatens his own life. He needs to act, to do *something*, because he cannot grasp the magnitude of this incident that has almost destroyed his relationship with Anne, the only thing since Irène's death that has given it meaning.

What to others might seem like pompous platitudes sound very different to someone who already feels responsible for the death of a loved one. Such things change a man.

As he dashes down the steps of the hospital, he sees Anne's face again, the yellow rings around her eyes, the livid bruising, the swollen flesh.

He has just pictured her dead.

He does not yet know how or why, but someone has tried to kill her.

It is this sense of *déjà vu* that panics him. After Irène was murdered . . . The circumstances are completely different. Irène was personally targeted by her killer whereas Anne simply ran into the wrong man at the wrong time, but in the moment, Camille is incapable of untangling his emotions.

But he is also incapable of letting things take their course without doing something.

Without trying to do something.

In fact, though he does not realise it, he instinctively began to act from the moment he received the telephone call. Anne had "sustained injuries", he was told by the woman from the Préfecture de Police, having been involved in an "altercation" during an armed robbery in the 8th arrondissement. "Altercation" is one of Camille's favourite words. Everyone on the force loves it. Police officers are also fond of "perpetrator" and "stipulate", but "altercation" is particularly practical since in four syllables it covers everything from a heated argument to a vicious beating, leaving the other party to infer whatever they please.

"What kind of 'altercation'?"

The officer did not know, she was probably reading from a report, Camille could not help but wonder whether she even understood what she was saying.

"Armed robbery. Shots fired. Madame Forestier did not sustain gunshot wounds, but she was injured during an altercation. She has been taken to the nearest casualty department."

Shots fired? At Anne? During a hold-up? It is difficult to make sense of the words, impossible to imagine the scene. Anne and "armed robbery" are concepts that have nothing in common . . .

The woman on the telephone explained that, when she was found, Anne did not have a bag or any form of identification; officers had discovered her name and address from the mobile telephone lying nearby.

"We called her home number, but there was no reply."

So they had dialled the number Anne had called the most frequently – Camille's number.

The woman asked his surname for her report. She pronounced it "Verona". Camille corrected her: "Verhœven". There was a brief silence and then she asked him to spell it.

This triggered something in Camille's mind.

Verhœven is hardly a common surname, and in the police force it is very unusual. And, frankly, Camille is not the sort of policeman people forget. It is not simply the matter of his uncommonly small stature, every officer knows his history, his reputation, they know about Irène, about the Alex Prévost case. To most people, Camille might as well have a tattoo reading "As seen on T.V.". He has made a number of high-profile appearances on television; cameramen favour an angled shot of his hawk-like features, his balding pate. But the assistant had clearly never heard about Verhœven, the renowned *commandant de police*, the T.V. appearances: she asked him to spell his name.

In hindsight, Camille decides that this is the first piece of good news in a day that bodes no others.

"Ferroven, did you say?" the girl said.

"That's right," Camille replied, "Ferroven."

And he spelled it for her.

2.00 p.m.

Such is the nature of the human animal: give them an accident and people immediately hang out of their windows. As long as there's a flashing police light or a smear of blood, there will be a rubbernecker there to pry. And right now, there are lots of them. I mean, an armed robbery in the middle of Paris, shots fired . . . Disneyland has nothing on this.

In theory the street is cordoned off, but that doesn't stop pedestrians strolling past. The order has been given that only residents are allowed through the barrier, but it's a waste of time – everyone claims to be a resident because everyone wants to know what the hell is going on. Things have calmed down a little, but from what people are saying, it was chaos this morning. With all the police cars, police vans, forensics teams and motorcycles clogging up the Champs-Élysées, the city was gridlocked from Place de la Concorde to l'Étoile and from the boulevard Malesherbes to the Palais de Tokyo. I have to say that just knowing I'm responsible for all that chaos is kind of exhilarating.

When you've fired a shotgun at a woman covered in blood and made off, tyres shrieking, in a four-by-four with fifty grand's worth of jewels, coming back to the crime scene gives you a little thrill, like Proust and his madeleine. It's quite pleasant, actually. It's not hard to be cheerful when your plans work out. There's a little café on Georges-Flandrin right next to the Monier. The perfect location. It's called Le Brasseur. The noise is deafening. Everyone babbling and arguing. It's very simple: everyone saw everything, heard everything, knows everything.

I stand at the far end of the bar, keeping a low profile, away from the people milling in the doorway, I blend in, I listen.

Fuckwits, the lot of them.

2.15 p.m.

The autumn sky looks as though it has been painted especially for this cemetery. There are lots of people. This is the advantage of serving officers, they turn up to funerals *en masse* so you are guaranteed a crowd.

From a distance, Camille spots Armand's family, his wife, his children, his brothers and sisters. Well groomed, ramrod straight, desolate, serious. He does not know what they are like in reality, but they look like a family of Quakers.

Armand's death four days earlier devastated Camille. It also liberated him. For weeks and weeks he had been visiting the hospital, holding Armand's hand, talking to him even when the doctors could no longer tell whether he could hear or understand. And so now he simply nods to Armand's widow from afar. After the longs months of agony, after all the words he has said to Armand's wife, his children, Camille has nothing left. He did not even need to come today: he has given everything he had to give.

Camille and Armand had a number of things in common. They had started out together at the police academy, a youthful connection made all the more precious by the fact that neither of them had ever truly been young.

Then there was Armand's pathological tight-fistedness. He waged a battle to the death against expense and, ultimately, against money. Camille cannot help but think of his death as a victory for capitalism. It was not this meanness that united them but the fact that, in their different ways, they were small men with an overwhelming need to compensate. It was a kind of solidarity for the differently abled.

Moreover his long, slow death had confirmed that Armand thought of Camille as his best friend.

What we mean to others can be a powerful bond.

Of the four original members of his team, Camille is the only one now standing in the cemetery, something he finds difficult to accept.

His assistant, Louis Mariani, has not yet arrived. Camille is not worried, Louis is a man with a strong sense of duty, he will be here – for someone of Louis' social class, missing a funeral, like farting at the dinner table, is unimaginable.

Cancer of the oesophagus gives Armand the perfect excuse for absence.

That leaves Maleval, whom Camille has not seen for several years. Maleval was a brilliant young officer before he was dismissed from the force. Despite their differences, he and Louis were good friends, they were roughly the same age and they complemented each other. Until it was discovered that Maleval had been feeding information to the man who murdered Irène. He had not done so deliberately, but he had done it all the same. At the time, Camille could happily have killed him with his bare hands, the *brigade criminelle* came very close to suffering a tragedy worthy of the House of Atreus. But after Irène's death, Camille was a broken man; he spent years ravaged by depression and afterwards his life seemed meaningless.

He misses Armand more than anyone. With his death, Verhœven's team has been wiped off the face of the earth. This funeral is the beginning of a new chapter in which Camille will try to rebuild his life. Nothing could be more fragile.

Armand's family are just going into the crematorium when Louis arrives. Pale cream Hugo Boss suit, very elegant. "Hi, Louis." Louis does not say "Hello, guv." Camille has forbidden the expression, they're not in some T.V. police series.

The question that sometimes nags Camille about himself is even more relevant to his assistant: what the hell is this guy doing on the force? He was born into a wealthy family and, as if that were not enough, is gifted with an intellect that saw him accepted into the finest schools a dilettante can attend. Then, inexplicably, he joined the police to work for a schoolteacher's salary. At heart, Louis is a romantic.

"You O.K.?"

Camille nods, he is fine, in fact he's not really here at all. Most of him is still back at the hospital where Anne, doped up on painkillers, is waiting to be taken for X-rays and a C.A.T. scan.

Louis stares at his boss for just a second too long, nods, then gives a low *hmm*. Louis is man of great tact for whom *hmm*, like the tic of pushing his hair back with the left or right hand, is a private language. This particular *hmm* clearly translates: that long face isn't just about the funeral, is there something else going on? And for that something else to intrude on Armand's funeral, it must be pretty serious . . .

"The team is going to be assigned to deal with an armed robbery up in the 8th this morning . . ."

Louis cannot help but wonder whether this is the answer to his question.

"Many casualties?"

Camille nods, shrugs, yes, no.

"A woman . . ."

"Dead?"

Yes, no, not really, Camille frowns, staring straight ahead as though through dense fog.

"No . . . Well, not yet . . ."

Louis is rather surprised. This is not the kind of case the team usually work on, Commandant Verhœven has no experience in armed robbery. Then again, why not? Louis thinks, but he has known Camille long enough to realise that something is wrong. He manifests his surprise by looking down at his shoes, a pair of impeccably polished Crockett & Joneses, and coughs briefly, almost inaudibly. For Louis, this is the height of expressible emotion.

Camille jerks his chin towards the cemetery, the crematorium.

"As soon as this is over, I'd like to fill you in. Unofficially . . . The team hasn't been called in yet . . . [Camille finally dares to look at his assistant.] I just want us to be ahead of the game."

He glances around for Le Guen and quickly spots him. It would be difficult to miss him, the man is a colossus.

"O.K., we should go . . ."

Back when Le Guen was *commissaire* and his direct superior, Camille had only to lift a finger to get whatever he wanted; these days, things are more complicated.

Next to Contrôleur Général Le Guen, Commissaire Michard waddles along like a goose.

2.20 p.m.

This is one of the greatest moments in the Café Le Brasseur's history. The regulars unanimously concur that an armed robbery on this scale happens just once a century. Even those who saw nothing are agreed. The witness statements are piling up. People variously saw a girl, or two girls, or a woman, with a gun, with no gun, empty-handed, screaming. This was the owner of the jeweller's? No, it was her daughter. Really? Do you remember her mentioning a daughter? There was a getaway car. Make and model? The answers cover pretty much the entire range of imported cars currently available in France.

I slowly sip my coffee, this is the first moment I've had to relax in what has already been rather a long day.

The *patron* – who has a face just begging to be slapped – has decided that the haul from the robbery was five million euros. Not a cent less. I've no idea where he came by the figure, but he sounds convincing. I feel like handing him a loaded Mossberg and steering him towards the nearest jeweller's. Let him rob the place, scuttle back to his little café and fence the loot – if the dumb fuck gets a third of the sort of figure he's expecting, he can retire, because he won't do any better.

And that car they fired into! What car? The one over there – it looks like it stopped a charging rhino. Did they launch a mortar at it? And so begin the ballistic speculations and, as with the make and model of the car, there are advocates for every possible calibre. Makes a man want to fire a warning shot to shut them up, or shoot into the crowd to get a bit of peace.

Strutting and swaggering, the *patron* peremptorily announces, ".22 long rifle."

He closes his eyes as he says the words as though to confirm his expertise.

I cheer myself up by imagining him headless, like the Turk, from a blast with the 12-bore. Whether it was a .22 Long Rifle rimfire or a blunderbuss, the crowd are impressed; these idiots don't know shit. With witnesses like this, the cops are in for a treat.

2.45 p.m.
"Wha . . . why would you want to do that?" asks the *commissaire divisionnaire*, wheeling around, making a sweeping revolution on her major axis: a titanic, positively Babylonian arse that is preposterously disproportionate. Commissaire Michard is a woman of between forty and fifty. Hers is a face that promised much and failed to deliver; she has a shock of jet-black hair, probably dyed, buck teeth and a pair of heavy, square-rimmed glasses that proclaim her as a woman of authority, a safe pair of hands. She is gifted with a personality usually described as "forceful" (she is a pain in the

neck), a keen intelligence (this exponentially increases her ability to infuriate) but, most of all, she is blessed with an arse with a capital A. It is incredible. It seems a wonder she can keep her balance. Curiously, Commissaire Michard has a rather placid face at odds with everything one knows about her: her undeniable competence, her exceptional strategic sense, her mastery of firearms; the sort of boss who works ten times harder than everyone else and is proud of her leadership skills. When she was promoted to *commissaire*, Camille resigned himself to the fact that in addition to dealing with an overbearing female at home (Doudouche, his beloved cat, is emotionally unstable and borderline hysterical), he would now have to deal with one at work.

Hence her question: "Why would you want to do that?"

There are some people with whom it is difficult to remain calm. Commissaire Michard comes over and stands very close to Camille. She always does this when she speaks to him. Between her well-upholstered physique and Camille's slight, scrawny frame, they look like characters from an American sit-com, but this woman has no sense of the ridiculous.

They stand facing each other, blocking the entrance to the crematorium; they are among the last to go in. Camille has carefully orchestrated things so that at the moment he makes his request, they are overtaken by Contrôleur Général Le Guen – Camille's old friend and Michard's predecessor as *commissaire divisionnaire*. Now, everyone knows that Camille and Le Guen are more than simply friends; Camille has been best man at Le Guen's weddings – a time-consuming responsibility given that Le Guen has just got hitched for the sixth time, remarrying his second wife.

Since she was only recently appointed, Commissaire Michard

still needs to "run with the hare and hunt with the hounds" (she loves such clichés, which she strives to inject with a certain freshness), she needs to "hit the ground running" before she can afford to "rock the boat". So when the best friend of her direct superior makes a request, she falters. Especially as they are the last members of the cortège. Though she would like time to mull it over, she has a reputation for thinking on her feet and prides herself on making quick decisions. The service is about to begin. The funeral director glances anxiously towards them. Wearing a double-breasted suit, with a shock of bleached blond hair, he looks like a footballer – clearly undertakers are not what they used to be.

This question – why would Verhœven want his team to take on the case? – is the only one to which Camille has prepared an answer, because it is the only pertinent question.

The robbery took place at 10.00 this morning, it is not yet 3.00 p.m. Back at the Galerie, the forensics officers are completing their examination of the crime scene, various officers are taking witness statements, but the case has not yet been assigned to a squad.

"I've got an informant," says Camille. "Someone on the inside..."

"You had information about the robbery before it happened?"

Michard's eyes widen dramatically, reminding Camille of the furious glares of samurai warriors in Japanese lithographs. This is the sort of stock expression Michard loves; the look means: you're either telling me too much or not enough.

"Of course I didn't," Camille snaps. (He plays this scene very convincingly; he sounds genuinely affronted.) "I knew nothing about it, though I'm not sure about my source . . . I'm telling you this guy's prepared to spill his guts, he's desperate to cut a deal. [Verhœven is convinced this is the sort of cliché that appeals to

Michard.] Right now, he's prepared to cooperate . . . it would be a pity to not use him."

A single glance is all it takes to shift the conversation from matters of protocol to simple tactics. Camille's brief glance towards the man at the far end of the cemetery is enough for the tutelary figure of the *contrôleur général* to loom over the conversation. Silence. The *commissaire* smiles to indicate that she understands: O.K.

"Besides, it's not just an armed robbery," Camille adds for the sake of form. "There's the attempted murder . . ."

The *commissaire* nods slowly and shoots Camille a quizzical look as though she has seen beyond the *commandant*'s somewhat heavy-handed ploy some faint glimmer, as though she is trying to understand. Or has just understood. Or is about to understand. Camille knows how perceptive the woman is: the slightest false step triggers her highly sensitive seismograph.

So he takes the initiative, speaking quickly, using his most persuasive tone: "Let me explain. This informant of mine is connected to another guy, a member of a gang involved in a different job – that was last year, and it's not directly connected to this case, but the thing is . . ."

Commissaire Michard cuts him short with a weary wave that says she has problems enough of her own. That she understands. That she realises she is too new to her post to intervene between her superior and her subordinate.

"It's fine, *commandant*. I'll talk to the examining magistrate, Juge Pereira."

This is exactly what Camille was hoping would happen, though he is careful not to show it.

Because had Michard not given up so quickly, he has not the first idea how he would have finished his sentence.

3.15 p.m.

Louis left quickly. Camille, given his rank, was forced to wait around until the bitter end. The service was long, very long, and everyone wanted a chance to speak. Camille slipped away as soon as was decently possible.

As he walks back to his car, he listens to the voicemail he has just received from Louis, who has already managed to put in several calls and has come up with a lead.

"I've been through the files and the only incidence of a Mossberg 500 being used in an armed robbery was on January 17 last. The similarity between the jobs is unquestionable. And the last case was pretty grim . . . Can you call me back?"

Camille calls him back.

"The incident last January was a lot more vicious," Louis explains. "The gang held up four separate outlets. One person was killed. The leader of the gang was identified. Vincent Hafner. There's been no sign of him since the January robberies, but today's comeback stunt was clearly designed to attract attention . . ."

3.20 p.m.

There's a sudden flurry of excitement at Le Brasseur.

The babble of conversation is interrupted by a wail of sirens and the customers hurry out onto the terrace to gawk as the sirens seem to rise in pitch. The *patron* peremptorily announces it is the *ministre de l'Intérieur*. People vainly rack their brains trying to remember the minister's name. They'd remember if it was a game-show host. The chattering starts up again. A few pundits decide there has been some new development, maybe they've found a body or something; the *patron* closes his eyes and adopts a self-important air. The customers' conflicting theories are a testament to his erudition.

"It's the *ministre de l'Intérieur*, I'm telling you."

With a little smile he calmly goes on polishing glasses, he does not even trouble to glance towards the terrace, thereby demonstrating his faith in his own prognostication.

The customers wait feverishly, holding their breath, as though expecting the arrival of the Tour de France.

3.30 p.m.

It feels as though her brain is filled with cotton wool surrounded by veins thick as arms that hammer and throb.

Anne opens her eyes. The room. The hospital.

She stiffly tries to move her legs, like an old woman plagued by rheumatism. It is agonising, but she succeeds in lifting one knee, then the other. Drawing up her legs gives her a brief moment of relief. Tentatively, she moves her head to see how it feels. Her head seems to weigh a ton, her bandaged fingers look like the claws of a crab. There comes a rush of blurred images: the toilets in Galerie Monier, a pool of blood, gunshots, the skull-splitting howl of the ambulance, the face of the radiologist and, from behind him, the faint voice of a nurse saying "What on God's earth did they do to her?" She feels a wave of emotion, she blinks back tears, takes a deep breath; she needs to keep her self-control, she cannot afford to give in, to give up.

She has to stand up if she is to stay alive.

She throws back the sheet – despite the excruciating pain in her hand – and manages to slide first one leg and then the other over the side. She feels a dizzying rush and waits for a moment, balanced precariously on the edge of the bed, then plants her feet firmly on the ground, hauls herself upright and is immediately forced to sit down again; only now does she truly feel pain rack her

56

body, savage, specific, shooting through her back, her shoulders, her collarbone, she feels crushed, she struggles to catch her breath, hauls herself up again and finally she manages to stand, though she is clutching the nightstand for support.

The toilet is directly opposite. Like a climber, she gropes for handholds – the headboard, the bedside table, the door handle, the washbasin – until finally she is staring into the mirror. Dear God, can this be her?

This time, she can do nothing to stop the sobs welling in her. The blue-black bruises, the broken teeth, the gash along her left cheek where the bone has been shattered, the trail of sutures . . .

What on God's earth did they do to her?

Anne grips the sink to stop herself from falling.

"What are you doing out of bed?"

As she turns, Anne suddenly faints, the nurse only just has time to catch her as she falls and lay her carefully on the floor. The nurse gets to her feet and pops her head out into the corridor.

"Florence, could you give me a hand?"

3.40 p.m.

Camille strides along fretfully. Louis walks beside him, half a pace behind; the precise distance he maintains from his boss is a calculated mixture of respect and familiarity. Only Louis would come up with such nuanced permutations.

Though Camille is anxious and harried, he nonetheless glances up at the buildings that line the rue Georges-Flandrin – typical exponents of Hausmann architecture blackened by years of grime and soot, buildings so commonplace in this part of the city that one hardly notices them. His eye is caught by a line of balconies supported at either end by twin Atlases with loincloths distended by large bulges, each balcony is supported by a caryatid with preposterously large breasts that stare into the heavens. It is the breasts that point heavenward; the caryatids' eyes are demurely lowered in that coy expression of supremely confident women. Camille gives an admiring nod and strides on.

"René Parrain would be my guess," he says.

Silence. Camille closes his eyes and waits to be corrected.

"More likely to be Chassavieux, don't you think?"

It was ever thus. Louis may be twenty years younger, but he knows twenty thousand times more than Camille. What is most irritating is that he is never wrong. Almost never. Camille has tried to trap him, has tried and tried but to no avail; the guy is a walking Wikipedia.

"Yeah," he mutters grudgingly, "maybe."

As they come to the Galerie Monier, Camille stumbles past the wreckage of the car blasted by the 12-bore just as a tow truck is hoisting it onto the flatbed.

Later, he will find out that Anne was standing on the other side of the car when the shots were aimed directly at her.

The little guy is the one in charge. Police officers these days are like politicians, their rank is inversely proportional to their size. Everyone recognises the little one, obviously, given his height. Once seen, never forgotten. But his name is another matter. The café customers come up with a range of suggestions. They know it's a foreign surname, but what? German, Danish, Flemish? One of the regulars thinks it might be Russian, then another triumphantly shouts "Verhœven." "That's it." Everyone laughs. "You see? I told you it was something foreign."

He appears at the corner of the passage. He does not flash his warrant card – when you're less than five foot shit, you get special dispensation. The people peer through the café windows, waiting with bated breath, when they are distracted by something even more miraculous: a tanned, dark-haired girl has just walked into the bar. The *patron* greets her loudly and everyone turns to look. It is the hairdresser from the salon next door. She orders four espressos – the coffee machine in the salon is not working.

She knows everything, she smiles modestly as she waits to be served. To be quizzed. She pretends that she does not have time for questions, but her blushes speak volumes.

They want to know everything.

3.50 p.m.

Louis shakes hands with the officers already on the scene. Camille demands to see the C.C.T.V. footage. Right now. Louis is shocked. He knows only too well that Camille has little respect for etiquette and protocol, but such a gross disregard for procedure is shocking in a man of his rank and experience. Louis delicately pushes his fringe back with his left hand, then follows his boss into the shop's back room which has been temporarily requisitioned as an incident room. Camille absently shakes hands with the owner, a woman decked out like a Christmas tree who is smoking a Gauloise set in a long, ivory cigarette-holder of the sort that went out of fashion a century ago. Camille does nothing to stop her. The first officers on the scene have already tracked down the footage from the two C.C.T.V. cameras.

As soon as the laptop computer is set up in front of him, Camille turns to Louis.

"Right. I'll go through the videos. You go and find out what we've got so far."

He jerks his chin towards the front of the shop, which amounts to showing Louis the door. Without waiting for a reply, he sits at the desk and stares at everyone. He looks for all the world as though he wants to be alone to watch a porn film.

Louis acts as though his boss's behaviour is perfectly logical. There is something of the gentleman's gentleman about him.

"Go on," he says, ushering everyone out, "we'll set up the incident room in here."

The footage Camille is interested in is from the camera position just outside the jeweller's.

Twenty minutes later, while Louis is watching the video, comparing details of the footage with the first witness statements, Camille goes out into the arcade and stands on the spot where the gunman stood.

The forensics team has finished collecting evidence, the shards of glass have all been picked up and collected, the crime scene has been taped off. Once the insurance assessors and structural surveyors arrive, the last officers will slink away and two months from now, the arcade will have been completely refurbished, new shops will open up ready for the next crazed gunman to turn up during opening hours and target their customers or their staff.

The scene is being guarded by a *gendarme*, a tall, thin officer with a jaded expression, a jutting chin, and bags under his eyes. Like a supporting actor whose name no-one can ever remember, Camille dimly recognises the man as someone he has seen at a hundred other crime scenes. They nod vaguely to each other.

Camille gazes at the looted shop, the smashed display cases. Though he knows little or nothing about jewellery, he cannot but wonder if this is the sort of place he himself would have chosen for a hold-up. But he also knows that appearances are deceptive.

A bank might not be much to look at, but steal everything inside one and you would have enough to come back and buy the place.

Camille does what he can to stay calm; his hands are stuffed into the pockets of his overcoat because ever since he watched the video – replaying the harrowing, horrifying images over and over – his hands have not stopped trembling.

He brusquely shakes his head as though he had water in his ears, as though were trying to dispel this excess of emotion, to regain a sense of composure. But it is impossible. The crimson halos on the tiled floor are Anne's blood; she lay exactly there, curled into a ball, while the man with the gun stood over there. Camille takes a step back and the tall *gendarme* watches him uneasily. Suddenly, Camille turns, holding an imaginary shotgun by his side; the *gendarme* makes to reach for his police radio. Camille takes three more steps, glances from where the shooter was standing towards the exit and then suddenly, without warning, he starts to run. This time, the *gendarme* grabs his radio but seeing Camille stop abruptly he does not press the button. Camille anxiously touches a finger to his lips and retraces his steps, he looks up at the *gendarme* and they smile warily at one another like two men with no common language eager to be friends.

What exactly happened here?

Camille glances to left and right, he looks up towards the shattered fanlight blasted by the shotgun, he walks forward again and comes to the exit that leads onto the rue Georges-Flandrin. He is not sure what he is looking for, some clue, some detail, some pointer – his near eidetic memory for places and people stores information differently.

Inexplicably, he somehow knows he is on the wrong track.

That there is nothing to see here. That he is approaching the case from the wrong angle.

And so he leaves the arcade and goes back to questioning the bystanders. He tells the first officers on the scene who have already taken witness statements that he wants "his own sense of things"; he interviews the bookseller, the antiques dealer, out on the pavement he questions the hairdresser. The woman who owns the jeweller's has already been taken to hospital. Her assistant saw nothing, having spent the raid with her face pressed to the floor and her arms over her head. He cannot help feeling sorry for this shy, insignificant girl, hardly more than a child. Camille tells her to go home, asks whether she would like someone to drive her, she tells him she is waiting for a friend at Le Brasseur, nodding towards the far side of the road where the café terrace is thronged with rubberneckers staring back at them. "Go on," Camille says, "get out of here."

He has listened to the witnesses, studied the C.C.T.V. footage.

As the raid began to unravel, the unbearable tension might account for Anne's attempted murder as events spiralled out of control.

But there is something about the gunman's fury, his relentless determination to slaughter her . . .

The examining magistrate has been appointed, he is expected to arrive any minute now. In the meantime, Camille goes over everything that has been said. Every detail of this robbery matches a hold-up that took place in January.

"That's what you said, right?"

"Absolutely," Louis says. "The difference is one of scale. The raid today targeted a single jeweller's, whereas in January there were four separate incidents. Four jeweller's held up in the space of six hours . . ."

Camille gives a low whistle.

"The M.O. is identical. A team of three men, one breaking open the display cases and taking the jewellery, one standing guard with a sawn-off shotgun, and the third waiting in the getaway car."

"You said someone died during the January robberies?"

Louis flicks through his notes.

"The first target was in the 15th. They stormed the place first thing in the morning, right after it opened, and they were in and out in less than ten minutes. This was the only raid that went to plan. At 10.30, they burst into a jeweller's on the rue de Rennes, and this time they clubbed one of the staff who had been slow to open the safe. They left him unconscious – blunt force trauma to the head – and the guy spent four days in a coma. He pulled through, but he has suffered serious after-effects and he's suing the company for a disability pension."

Camille is listening anxiously. Anne clearly had a narrow escape. Camille's nerves are frayed, he forces himself to breathe deeply, to relax his muscles – what was it again? – the sterno-claudio . . . fuck.

"Just after lunch, at about 2.00, the gang turn up in a jeweller's in the Louvre des Antiquaires. By now, they're using brute force, they're in and out within minutes again, leaving a customer lying on the pavement . . . He's not as badly injured as the guy on the rue de Rennes, but his condition is considered critical."

"Things are escalating," Camille says, reading between the lines.

"Yes and no," Louis says. "The gang are not out of control, they're savagely, single-mindedly doing their job . . ."

"Still, it's already a great deal to do in one day . . ."

"True."

Even for an experienced gang with the means and the motivation, four hold-ups in the space of six hours requires extraordinary efficiency and discipline. After a while, fatigue is bound to take over. A hold-up is like skiing; accidents always happen at the end of the day, it is the last effort that causes the greatest damage.

"The manager of the jeweller's on the rue de Sèvres fights back," Louis picks up the story again. "Just as the gang are about to leave he tries to stall them, he grabs the sleeve of the man who has been rifling the display cases and tries to shove him to the ground. Before the lookout has time to aim his Mossberg, the other guy has pulled a 9mm and put two bullets in the manager's chest."

There is no knowing whether this was the last raid they had planned or whether the manager's death forced them to get the hell away.

"Aside from the number of heists they pulled off, the M.O. for the robberies is classic. Most kids who pull this sort of heist bark orders, wave their guns around, fire warning shots, jump over the counter; they carry the sort of massive weaponry they've seen in video games, you can tell that they're scared witless. But these guys are organised, they're single-minded, they don't put a foot wrong. If they hadn't happened on some have-a-go hero, they would have left only minor collateral damage."

"So what was the haul?" Camille asks.

"Six hundred and eighty thousand euros," Louis says. "That's what was declared."

Camille raises a quizzical eyebrow, not because he is surprised that the jeweller's would minimise the value of what was stolen – they would have undeclared valuables in stock – he simply wants to know the true amount.

"The probable value is significantly upwards of a million. Resale, probably six hundred, six hundred and fifty thousand. A good day's work."

"Any idea where they might have offloaded the stuff?"

Given the nature of the haul – high-end, one-off pieces – resale would bring in a fraction of the real value, and few fences in Paris would be prepared to take it.

"We're assuming it was trafficked through Neuilly, but who knows . . ."

Obvious. It would be the ideal solution. Rumour has it the fence in Neuilly is a defrocked priest. Camille has never bothered to check, but he does not find the idea so strange: to him, the two professions have much in common.

"Send someone out to nose around."

Louis makes a note. In most of their cases, it is he who assigns tasks to the team.

At this point Juge Pereira, the examining magistrate, arrives. His eyes are a dazzling blue, his nose a little too long for his face, his ears droop like a spaniel's. Nervous and harried, he shakes Camille's hand – *bonjour, commandant* – as he passes. Strutting behind him comes the court clerk, a stunning woman with a plunging neckline that reveals too much cleavage and with preposterously high heels that click-clack across the tiled floor; someone should have a quiet word with her about appropriate work attire. The magistrate is well aware that she is causing a stir, but despite her revealing dress it's clear that she wears the trousers. If she felt so inclined, she could parade around chewing gum and blowing bubbles. Camille cannot help but think that, at thirty or so, the Lolita look is rather sluttish.

Everyone gathers around: Camille, Louis and the two other members of the squad who have just arrived. Louis takes charge. Analytical, precise, methodical and intelligent (in his day, he was awarded a scholarship to the elite *École nationale d'administration* but chose to study at Sciences Po). The *juge* listens thoughtfully. There is talk of the fact that witnesses identified Eastern European accents, the possibility that they are dealing with a gang of violent Serbs or Bosnians; much is made of the fact that they fired shots when they could have avoided doing so. Someone mentions Vincent Hafner and his string of convictions for gun-related offences. The magistrate nods. Hafner teaming up with a Bosnian gang would be a dangerous combination; it's surprising there were not more casualties. Those guys are animals, the *juge* says, and he is right.

Juge Pereira moves on to enquire about the witnesses. Usually, there are three members of staff in the jeweller's to open up: the manageress, her assistant, and another girl, but she was late this morning. She showed up just in time to hear the last gunshot. When staff in a shop or a bank are miraculously absent during a hold-up, the police are immediately suspicious.

"We've taken her in for questioning," says one of the officers (though he does not seem altogether sure). "We'll look into it, but right now she seems clean."

The court clerk is plainly bored. She squirms on her high heels, shifting her weight from one foot to the other, staring pointedly towards the exit. Her nails are painted blood red, the top two buttons on her figure-hugging blouse have popped open to reveal the pale, cavernously deep furrow of her cleavage while all eyes are drawn to the third button, precariously held in place by straining fabric drawn out like a predatory smile. Camille glances at her, mentally sketching a portrait. She is certainly striking, but only taken as a whole. Because the details tell a different story: her feet are too big, her nose too short, her features are a little crude, her buttocks are amply proportioned but too high. An arse worthy of an alpine climber. And the perfume exudes . . . salt water and sea air. She could be a fishwife.

"Right," the *juge* whispers, taking Camille to one side. "*Madame la commissaire* tells me you have an informant . . . ?" The phrase "*madame la commissaire*" is said in the obsequious tone of someone preparing for the day when he gets to say "*monsieur le ministre*". The clerk is vexed by their *tête-à-tête*. She heaves a long, loud sigh.

"I do," Camille confirms. "I'll know more tomorrow."

"So in theory we should be able to wrap the case up quickly?"

"In theory . . ."

The magistrate seems satisfied. He may not be a *commissaire*, but he appreciates favourable statistics. He decides it is time to leave. He shoots an angry glance at the clerk.

"Mademoiselle?"

His tone is curt, imperious.

From the look on Lolita's face, it is clear he will pay a heavy price.

4.00 p.m.

The little hairdresser proves to be an effective witness. She runs through the statement she gave to the police earlier, eyes coyly lowered like a blushing bride. It's by far the most accurate account I've heard. The girl's got a keen eye. With witnesses like her, it's a good job we were wearing balaclavas. Given the hustle and bustle outside, I stay next to the bar, as far as possible from the terrace. I order another coffee.

The woman involved in the incident is not dead. The parked car took most of the force of the blast. She was taken away in an ambulance.

Time to head for the hospital. The casualty department. Before she's discharged or transferred to another ward.

But first, I need to reload. Seven cartridges in the Mossberg.

The fireworks display is only just beginning.

I'm planning to paint the walls red.

6.00 p.m.

Despite his agitation, Camille cannot drum his fingers on the steering wheel. He drives a specially adapted car with centrally located controls – he has no alternative given that his arms are short and his feet dangle off the ground. And in a vehicle designed or adapted for handicapped persons, you have to be careful where you place your fingers on the steering wheel; one wrong move and the car could go off the road. To make matters worse, Camille is not particularly good with his hands; aside from artistic ability, he is downright clumsy.

He pulls up outside the hospital and walks across the car park, mentally rehearsing what he plans to say to the doctor – the sort of pithy phrases you spend hours polishing only to forget as soon as the moment arrives. When he came here this morning, reception had been crowded so he had immediately gone up to Anne's room. This time he stops. The desk is at eye level (about one metre forty, Camille estimates). He goes around and, without a second thought, pushes open the door marked "AUTHORISED PERSONNEL ONLY. NO ENTRY".

"What the hell?" the receptionist yells. "Can't you read?"

"Can't *you*?" Camille retorts, holding out his warrant card.

The woman bursts out laughing and give him a thumbs-up.

"Good one!"

She is a slim black woman of about forty, sharp-eyed, with a flat chest and bony shoulders. From the Antilles. Her name-tag reads "OPHÉLIA". She is wearing an ugly frilly blouse, a pair of huge, white movie-star glasses shaped like butterfly wings and she stinks of cigarettes. She holds up a fleshy hand telling Camille to wait a moment while she answers the phone, patches the call through, hangs up, then turns and looks at him admiringly.

"Well, ain't you a little thing? For a policeman, I mean . . . Don't they have some kind of height requirement?"

Though Camille is in no mood to deal with this, the woman makes him smile.

"I got a special dispensation," he says.

"You got someone to pull some strings, is what you did!"

Within five minutes, their banter has become a friendly conversation. She seems unfazed by the fact that he is a police officer. Camille cuts it short and asks to speak to the consultant dealing with Anne Forestier.

"At this time of night, you'd need to talk to the on-call doctor up on the ward."

Camille nods and heads towards the lifts, only to come back again.

"Were there any phone calls for her?"

"Not that I know . . ."

"You sure?"

"Take my word for it. It's not like the patients in that wing are up to taking calls."

Camille walks away again.

"Hey, hey!"

The woman is fluttering a sheet of yellow paper, as though fanning someone taller than her. Camille traipses back to the desk. Ophélia gives him a smouldering look.

"A little love letter from me to you . . ."

It is a bureaucratic form. Camille stuffs it into his pocket, takes the lift up to the intensive care unit and asks to see the registrar. He will have to wait.

The car park outside A. & E. is full to bursting. It's the perfect place to hide in plain sight: as long as you don't park here for too long, no-one is going to notice one more car. All you have to do is be alert, discreet. Ready to act.

It helps if you have a loaded Mossberg under a newspaper on the passenger seat. Just in case.

Now all I need to do is think; plan for the future.

One option is just to wait until the woman is being transferred from the hospital. Probably the simplest solution. Shooting up an ambulance is a breach of the Geneva Convention – unless, that is, you don't give a flying fuck. The C.C.T.V. cameras over the entrance are useless: they're there to deter any prospective criminals, but there's nothing to stop someone from shooting them out before getting down to serious business. Morally, it's a no-brainer. Technically, it's not exactly rocket science.

No, the only snag with his option is logistical: the security barrier at the ambulance bay creates a bottleneck. Obviously it would be possible to put a bullet in the security guard, break through the security barrier – there's no mention of security guards in the Geneva Convention – but it's hardly an elegant solution.

The second possibility is to wait until the ambulance clears the security area. There's a brief window of opportunity here, since it will be forced to turn right and wait for the traffic light on the filter lane to turn green. Though it might arrive with sirens blaring and tyres squealing – after all, it has urgent deliveries to make – the ambulance will be a little less pressurised when it leaves. While it's waiting at the lights, a determined shooter could step up behind, and in three seconds – one second to open the tailgate, one to aim and one to fire – leave the paramedic and any bystanders shitting themselves so much he'd have more than enough time to jump back in his car, floor the accelerator, drive forty metres against one-way traffic before reaching the dual carriageway and the Périphérique. Piece of piss. Job done. Everything back on track. I can almost smell the money.

Both options mean waiting for her to leave, either to be discharged or transferred to another hospital. If that window of opportunity doesn't open up, I'd need to look at other possibilities.

There's always the option of making a home delivery. Like a postman. Like a florist. Just go up to the room, knock politely, enter, deliver my bouquet and leave. It would mean a precisely timed operation. Or alternatively, going in with all guns blazing. Each strategy has its advantages. Option one, the clean kill, would require more skill and be more satisfying, but it smacks of narcissism, it's more about the killer than the victim, it shows a lack of generosity. Firing at random on the other hand is much more generous, more magnanimous, it's almost philanthropic.

In the end, events usually make the decision for us. Hence the need to assess the situation. To plan ahead. That was the Turks' big mistake – they were well organised, but when it came to planning for all eventualities, they screwed up. When you leave some god-forsaken country to go and commit a crime in a major European capital, you plan ahead. Not them. They just showed up at Rois-sy airport, scowling and knitting their bushy eyebrows so I would think I was dealing with big-time gangsters. Jesus Christ! They were cousins of some whore at Porte de la Chapelle, the biggest heists they'd been involved in were robbing some shop in Ankara and knocking over a petrol station in Keskin . . . Given what I need-ed them to do, it's not like I had to recruit top-flight specialists, but even so, hiring dumb fucks like them was almost humiliating.

Forget about them. At least they got to see Paris before they died. They could have said thanks.

It seems good things come to those who wait. I've just spotted the little policeman scuttling through the car park on his way into the hospital. I'm three steps ahead of him, and I plan to keep it that way. I can see him standing at the reception desk. Whoever is behind the desk probably only sees his bald patch looming over the surface, like the shark in "Jaws". He's tapping his foot, he's clearly on edge. He's gone around the back of the desk.

Short but sure of himself.

It doesn't matter, I'll take him on his home turf.

I get out of the car and go for a scout around. The key thing is to act fast, get it over and done with.

6.15 p.m.

Anne is asleep. The bandages around her head are stained a dirty yellow by haemostatic agents, giving her skin a milky whiteness, her eyelids are swollen shut and her lips . . . Camille is committing every detail to memory, every line he would need to sketch this ruined face, when he is interrupted by someone popping their head around the door and asking to speak to him. Camille steps out into the corridor.

The on-call doctor is a solemn-faced young Indian with small, round glasses and a name-tag bearing an impossibly long surname. Camille flashes his warrant card again and the young man studies it carefully, probably trying to work out how to react. Although it is not unusual to have cops in A. & E., it's rare to get a visit from the *brigade criminelle*.

"I need to know the extent of Madame Forestier's injuries," Camille explains, nodding towards Anne's room. "The examining magistrate will want to question her . . ."

The on-call doctor tells him this is a matter for the consultant, only he can decide when she will be fit to be questioned.

"I see . . ." Camille nods. "But, will she . . . How is she?"

The doctor is carrying a file containing Anne's X-rays and her notes, but does not need to consult it, he knows it by heart: her nose is broken ("a clean break that will not require surgery," he stresses), a fractured collarbone, two broken ribs, sprains to her left wrist and ankle, two broken fingers (also clean breaks) and numerous cuts and contusions to her arms, her legs and her stomach, her right hand suffered a deep cut and although there is no nerve damage, she may need physiotherapy; the long gash down her face is a little more problematic and may leave a permanent scar, she has also sustained serious bruising. Even so, the results of the preliminary scan are encouraging.

"It's amazing, but there's no sign of any damage to the neurophysiological or autonomic systems. There are no fractures to the skull, though she will require dental surgery. She may need a plaster cast . . . but we can't be sure. We'll know more tomorrow when we do the M.R.I. scan."

"Is she in pain?" Camille says and quickly adds, "The reason I'm asking is because if the magistrate needs to question her . . ."

"She's suffering as little as is possible. We have a lot of experience with pain relief."

Camille manages to smile, stammers his thanks. The doctor gives him a curious look, his eyes are piercing. "He seems unusually emotional for a policeman," he seems to be thinking. He seems about to question Camille's professionalism, to ask to see his warrant card again. In the end, he draws on his reserve of compassion.

"It will take time for her to heal," he says, "the bruises will fade, she may have a couple of minor scars, but Madame . . . [he glances down at his file] Madame Forestier is out of danger and she has suffered no permanent damage. I'd say the main problem now is not dealing with her physical injuries, but dealing with the trauma she will have suffered. We'll keep her under observation for a day or two. After that . . . well, she may need some support."

Camille thanks the man again. He should go, there is nothing more for him to do here. But it is out of the question. He is physically incapable of leaving.

The right wing of the hospital offers no possible entry, but things are much better on the left-hand side. There is an emergency exit. This is familiar territory. It's a door like the one in the Monier, a fire-door with a horizontal crash bar that is easily jimmied with a length of flexible metal.

I stand and listen for a minute – which is pointless, since the door is too thick. Never mind. A quick glance around me, slide the metal between the door and the jamb, open it and find myself in a corridor. At the far end is another corridor. I take a few steps, walking boldly, deliberately making noise in case I should bump into someone and seconds later I come to the end of the hallway and emerge behind the reception desk. It's like hospitals are designed with killers in mind.

On the wall to my right is an emergency evacuation plan. The building is complicated, sections have been remodelled, new wings added – it must be a nightmare for security guards. Especially since people never bother to look at official signs. The hospital should organise an impromptu fire drill some day. To visitors, the sight of an evacuation plan, especially in a hospital, is reassuring . . . It gives the feeling that, however overworked the staff might be, you're in safe hands. But an intimate knowledge of the emergency evacuation plan is even more useful when you're faced with a single-minded killer carrying a sawn-off shotgun.

Who cares?

I take out my mobile and snap a picture. The floors are all laid out the same way, since they have to take into account the position of the lift shafts, the conduits and the outflow pipes.

Go back out to the car. Think carefully. Failing to assess the risks is precisely the sort of thing that can mean snatching defeat from the jaws of victory.

6.45 p.m.
Camille does not turn on the light in Anne's room, he sits in the half-light on one of the high hospital chairs trying to collect his thoughts. Everything seems to be moving so quickly.

Anne is snoring softly. She has always snored a little, depending on her position. Whenever she becomes aware of it, she feels embarrassed. Today, her face is a mass of bruises, but usually when she blushes, she looks even more beautiful. She has the complexion of a redhead, with tiny, pale freckles visible only when she is embarrassed.

"You don't snore, you just breathe heavily," Camille invariably reassures her. "It's not the same at all."

She flushes pink, fiddling with her hair to hide her self-consciousness.

"The day you finally recognise my faults as faults," she smiles, "it'll be time to call it a day."

She often casually refers to the time when they will break up. She talks of those moments when they are a couple and those that will occur after they separate as though any difference between them is inconsequential. Camille finds this reassuring. It is the reflexive reaction of a widower, a depressive. He does not know whether he is still a depressive, but he is still a widower. Everything seems less straightforward, less clear-cut since Anne came into his life. They move together towards a future in which time is unknowable, uncertain, endlessly renewed.

"Camille, I'm so sorry . . ."

Anne has just opened her eyes. She articulates each word very deliberately. Despite the leaden vowels, the sibilant consonants, the hand shielding her mouth, Camille understands every word.

"What on earth do you have to be sorry for, darling?"

She gestures towards her mutilated body, it is a gesture that encompasses the hospital bed, the room, Camille, their life together, the world entire.

"Everything . . ."

Her vacant eyes recall the thousand-yard stare of victims who survive a tragedy. Camille reaches for her hand, but he can feel only the splints on her fingers. "You need to get some rest.

You're safe now. I'm here." As though that means anything. Even overwhelmed by private anguish, he finds himself resorting to the platitudes of his profession. Still he cannot shake off the nagging question of why the man at the Galerie Monier was so intent on killing her. So determined that he has made four separate attempts. There would have been the terrible pressure of the hold-up, things spiralled out of control, but even so . . .

"At the jeweller's, during the raid . . . did you see or hear anything else?" Camille says.

"Anything else . . . what do you mean?"

No. Nothing. He attempts a smile, but it is less than convincing, he lays his hand on her arm. Let her sleep for now. But she needs to talk to him as soon as possible. Needs to tell him everything, every last detail; there may be something she does not realise she knows. The crucial thing is to find out what.

"Camille . . ."

He bends down towards her.

"I'm so sorry . . ."

"Come on now," he gently chides her, "that's enough of that."

In the half-light of the hospital room, swathed in bandages, her swollen face black with bruises, her ruined mouth, Anne looks terribly ugly. Already Camille can see time pass, see the black, swollen bruises fade to blue, to purplish yellow. He will have to leave, whether he wants to or not. What pains him most are Anne's tears. They course down her cheeks even when she is asleep.

Camille gets to his feet. This time, he is resolved to go. Besides, there is nothing he can do here. As he leaves, he very carefully closes the door, quietly, as he might the door to a child's bedroom.

6.50 p.m.

Most of the time, the receptionist is snowed under with casualties, but whenever the flood of new patients slows to a trickle, she pops out for a cigarette or two. It's hardly surprising: to hospital workers, cancer is like a colleague. She stands outside, arms folded, smoking miserably.

This is the perfect opportunity. I dash to the side of the building, open the emergency exit, check the switchboard operator hasn't come back from her break. I can see her standing outside the glass doors. Three more steps, reach out and there it is, the admissions file. Ask and it shall be given to you.

They keep all medications in the cabinet under lock and key, but patient files are right there for the taking. It's logical: as a nurse, you assume that danger lies in infection and intoxicants; you're not expecting an armed robber.

Pickup: Galerie Monier, 8th arrondissement, Paris
Ambulance Crew: LR-453
Time of arrival: 10.44 a.m.
Full Name: Forestier, Anne
Room: 244
D.O.B.: unknown
Address: 26, rue de la Fontaine-au-Roi
Discharge/Transfer: decision pending
Ongoing Treatment: X-Rays, C.T. Scan
Consultant: T.B.A.

Back out to the car park. The receptionist is lighting another cigarette – I could have taken my time and photocopied the whole patient file.

Room 224. Second floor.

Back in the car, I lay the Mossberg across my lap and stroke it like a pet. I had hoped to find out if and when the patient was being discharged or transferred to a different unit, but no. It's been a waste of time.

There's a lot at stake here, a hell of a lot. And given all the planning I've had to do to get this far, I'm not about to blow this deal by taking my eye off the ball.

I take out my mobile, study the picture of the floor plan and realise no-one really knows the warren of passageways and corridors in the hospital. It's like one of those "Magic Eye" pictures – turn it one way and it looks a little like a folded star, turn it around again and it's a polygon, turn it again and it's a skull. Not exactly subtle for a hospital.

It doesn't matter. I reckon I should be able to take the emergency stairs to the second floor and from there, room 224 is only about ten metres away. I'll need to be a bit more creative about my getaway – up one floor, down the hall, take the stairs to the fourth floor, past neurosurgery, through three sets of double doors, take the lift down to the reception desk, twenty paces from the emergency exit, then a long route through the car park to the car. I don't mind making a big entrance, but when I leave, I like to make a discreet exit.

There's still the possibility that she'll be transferred. If so I'd be better off sitting tight. Now I know her name, I can just call for any news.

I look up the number for the hospital and dial.

Press 1, press 2, it's all so laborious. The Mossberg is altogether more efficient.

Having not set foot in the office all day, Camille calls Louis for an update. Right now, the team are dealing with a transvestite who has been strangled, a dead German tourist, probably a suicide, a driver stabbed in a road-rage incident, a homeless man who bled to death in the basement of a gym, a teenage junkie fished out of the sewer in the 13th and a crime of passion to which a suspect has confessed – the suspect is seventy-one. Camille listens, he gives instructions, authorises tactics, but he is not really there. Thankfully, Louis can take care of the day-to-day running of the squad.

By the time he hangs up, Camille can barely remember a word that was said. The only thing that seems clear is the terrible damage inflicted.

Pausing to take stock, he assesses his own situation. He has put himself in a difficult position: he has lied to the *commissaire* about a non-existent informant, lied to his superior officers, even given a false name at the Préfecture de Police, all so that this case would be assigned to him.

To make matters worse, he is involved in a relationship with the primary victim, who also happens to be the key witness in an armed robbery which is directly linked to an earlier heist in which a man was murdered.

Coldly considering the sequence of events, this series of rash decisions unworthy of an officer of his experience, he is appalled. He feels like a prisoner of his choices, his impulses. He has been a complete idiot: he is behaving as though he has no faith in his colleagues, a dangerous thing for a man with precious little faith in himself. He is incapable of outstripping himself and so is forced to do what he can do. In this case he has allowed his intuition, usually his greatest asset, to turn to emotion, to recklessness, to blind anger.

His behaviour seems all the more ludicrous given that the case is not all that complicated. A gang of thugs about to commit an armed robbery bump into Anne, she sees their faces, they beat her senseless and drag her with them to the jeweller's in case she gets any silly ideas about making a run for it – which, in the end, is precisely what she tries to do. The man acting as lookout fires his shotgun, misses, and when he tries to fire again his accomplice intervenes. They decide to take their haul and get out. Driving along the rue Georges-Flandrin, the man with the shotgun has one last unexpected opportunity, but there is an argument between him and his accomplices and it is this which saves Anne's life.

The man's savage determination seems terrifying, but he was caught up in the fury of the moment, he targeted Anne simply because she was there.

Now, the die is cast.

The robbers will be far away by now – they are hardly likely to hang around. With the haul they took, they can go anywhere they like, they are spoiled for choice.

The only chance of their being caught depends on Anne being able to identify at least one of her attackers. Given the meagre resources of the *brigade criminelle* and the number of cases they are currently working on – a number that steadily increases every day – there is only a one-in-thirty chance that they will be caught immediately, one in a hundred that they will be tracked down within a reasonable period and one in a thousand that – by pure chance or by a miracle – they will be tracked down one day in the future. However you look at it, it is already a cold case. So many robberies are committed daily that if the suspects are not arrested at the scene, if they are professionals, they have every chance of disappearing without trace.

So, the best thing he can do, Camille thinks, is to stop this charade before it involves someone more senior than Le Guen. Right now, his friend can make all this go away. One more white lie is not likely to faze him, after all he is the *contrôleur général*, but if it goes any further, it will be too late. If Camille comes clean now, Le Guen can have a quiet word with Commissaire Michard, who will be only too happy to have her superior officer owe her a favour – one she will doubtless need some day. She would probably see it as an investment of sorts. Camille has to put a stop to things before Juge Pereira sticks his nose in.

Camille can rationalise things, say that he was angry, that he was tempted, that he was blinded by emotion; no-one would have much trouble recognising such qualities in him.

He is relieved by his decision.

He will give up the case.

Let someone else look for the robbers, his fellow officers are more than capable. He should spend his time with Anne, taking care of her, that is what she will need most.

Besides, what can he do that his colleagues cannot?

"Excuse me . . ."

Camille walks over to the receptionist.

"A couple of things," she says. "The admissions form, you stuffed it in your pocket earlier. I know, I know, you don't give a tinker's damn, but the pen-pushers in this place, they're a little pernickety about these things."

Camille digs out the form. With no social security number, it has been impossible to process Anne's admission. The woman behind the desk points to a faded, tatty poster Sellotaped to the glass partition and recites the slogan in a sing-song voice.

"*In hospital, there is no social contract without social security.* They even make us take courses in this bullcrap, that should tell you how important it is . . . They lose millions every year, that's what they tell us."

Camille shrugs, he will have to go to Anne's apartment. He nods to the woman behind the desk. He hates this sort of red tape.

"One more thing." The receptionist gives him what she hopes is a seductive smile that fails miserably. "I don't suppose you can do anything about parking tickets – or is that too much to ask?"

He hates this fucking job.

Camille wearily holds out his hand. In a split second, the woman has opened the top desk of her drawer. There are at least forty parking fines. She gives a broad smile, as though handing him a trophy. Her teeth are crooked.

"Thing is," she says in a wheedling tone, "today I'm working the night shift, but not every day . . ."

"I get it," Camille says.

He hates this fucking job.

There are too many parking tickets to fit in one pocket and so he has to divide them up between left and right. Every time the automatic glass doors open, a blast of icy air whips at his face but does little to wake him up.

He is exhausted.

No plans to transfer or discharge her. Nothing is likely to happen for at least a couple of days, according to the girl on the phone. And I have no intention of hanging around this car park for two days. I've waited long enough already.

It's nearly eight. He seems to keep odd hours, this cop. He was about to leave and then he suddenly stopped, absorbed in thought, staring out through the glass doors as though he doesn't see them. Give it a minute or two and he will leave.

And then it's show time!

I turn the key in the ignition, drive to the far side of the car park, a deserted area, being so far from the entrance, next to the perimeter wall and the emergency exit I plan to use as my getaway, God willing. And He better be willing, because I'm in no mood to be crossed . . .

I slide out of the car, head back the way I came, keeping in the shadow of the parked cars and come to the fire-door.

Inside. No-one around.

As I pad down the hallway I spot the little cop, standing with his back to me, brooding.

He'll have a fuck of a lot more to brood about soon enough, I plan to launch him into the stratosphere.

7.45 p.m.

As he pushes the glass door leading into the car park, Camille remembers the call he got this morning at the police station and suddenly he realises that providence has anointed him Anne's next of kin. Obviously he is not, but even so he was the first person contacted by the hospital, it is his responsibility to contact everyone else.

Everyone else? he thinks. Though he has racked his brain, he does not know anyone else in Anne's life. He has met one or two of her colleagues, he recalls seeing a woman in her forties with thinning hair and huge, tired eyes walking down the street, she seemed to be shivering. "One of my colleagues . . ." Anne told him. Camille tries to remember her name. Charras? Charron? Charroi, that's it. They were crossing a boulevard, she

84

was wearing a blue coat, she and Anne nodded to each other, exchanged a conspiratorial smile. Camille found it touching. Anne turned back to him. "A complete bitch . . ." she whispered, still smiling.

He always calls Anne on her mobile. Before leaving the hospital, he tracks down her office number. It is eight o'clock, but you never know, there might still be someone.

"Hello, you've reached Wertig and Schwindel. Our offices . . ."

Camille feels a rush of adrenaline. For a second, he could have sworn it was Anne's voice. He feels suddenly distraught because precisely the same thing happened with Irène. One month after she died, he accidentally called his home number to be greeted by Irène's voice: "Hello, you've reached Camille and Irène Verhœven. We're not able to take your call . . ." Dumbfounded, he had burst into tears.

Leave a message. He stammers: "Hi, I'm calling about Anne Forestier. She is in hospital and she won't be able to . . . [what?] to come back to work . . . I mean not straight away, she's been in an accident . . . it's not serious, well, actually it is [how to put this?], she'll call you as soon as she can . . . if she can." A rambling, incoherent message. He hangs up.

He feels self-loathing rising in him like a raging tide.

He turns round, the receptionist is staring at him, she looks as if she is laughing.

8.00 p.m.

Up to the second floor.

To the right, the stairs. Everyone takes the lift, no-one takes the stairs. Especially not in hospitals; people don't need the hassle.

The barrel of the Mossberg is just over forty-five centimetres long. It has a pistol grip and fits easily into the large, inside pocket of a raincoat. You have to walk a little stiffly, a little stilted, lumbering like a robot, trying to keep the barrel pressed against your thigh, but it's the only way. At any moment, you have to be ready to fire or fuck off. Or both. Whatever you do, you need to be accurate. And driven.

The little cop has gone downstairs, she's alone in her room. If he hasn't left the building yet, he'll hear the blast, at which point he'd better get his arse in gear or he'll be charged with professional misconduct. I wouldn't bet much on his future in the force.

I come to the first floor. A long corridor. I go all the way across the building and take the opposite stairwell. Up to the second.

The great thing about the public sector is everyone is so overworked, no-one gives you a second look. The corridors are full of distraught families or anxious friends tiptoeing in and out of rooms as though they're in church, while harried nurses scurry past.

The second-floor corridor is deserted. Wide as a boulevard.

Room 224 is right at the other end, ideally situated for those who need a long rest. And speaking of a long rest, I think I can make it permanent.

I take a few steps towards the room.

I need to be careful as I open the door, a sawn-off shotgun clattering on the floor of a hospital is likely to panic people, they just aren't very understanding. The handle turns as quietly as an angel, I take a step across the threshold, shift the Mossberg from one hand to the other, opening the raincoat wide. She is lying on the bed, from the doorway I can see her feet, lifeless, unresponsive, like the feet of a dead woman. I lean a little to the side and now I can see her whole body . . .

Jesus, the face on her!

I did a bang-up job.

She's lying on her side, asleep, a trickle of drool hanging from her lips, her eyelids swollen shut – she's no oil painting. Instinctively I remember the expression "to rearrange someone's face". It seems appropriate. She looks like a mid-period Picasso. The bandages probably help, but even the mottled colours of her skin. Her skin looks like parchment. Or canvas. Her head is grotesquely bloated. If she was planning a night on the town, she'll need to take a rain check.

Stand in the doorway. Make sure the shotgun is visible.

Let her know I didn't come empty-handed.

The door is now wide open to the corridor, but she doesn't wake up. I go to all this trouble and this is the kind of welcome I get? Usually wounded people are like animals, they sense things. She's bound to wake up; just give her a couple of seconds. Survival instinct. She'll see the gun – she and the Mossberg know each other well, they're practically friends.

When she sees me with the shotgun, she'll be terrified. Obviously. She'll toss and turn, try to sit up against the pillows, her head thrashing about.

And she'll howl.

Given the serious damage I did to her jaw, she won't be up to much in the way of intelligible conversation. The best she'll probably manage is "Heeeeehhh" or "Heeeeeppp", something like that, but to compensate for her lack of clarity she'll go for volume, a full-throated scream to bring everyone running. If this happens, then before we get down to business, I'll signal for her to be quiet – *shhhh* – bring my finger to my lips. *Shhh.* She will carry on screaming the place down. *Shhhh,* this is a hospital for fuck's sake!

"Monsieur?"

In the corridor, just behind me.

A distant voice.

Don't turn round, stand stock-still.

"Are you looking for someone . . . ?"

Usually it's impossible to get anyone's attention in a hospital, but show up with a sawn-off shotgun and suddenly you've got some nurse eager to help you.

Glance up at the number on the door like someone who has just realised their mistake. The nurse is closer now. Without turning, stammer awkwardly:

"Sorry, got the wrong room . . ."

Keep a cool head, that's the most important thing. Whether you're pulling off a heist or paying a visit to a friend in hospital, a cool head is crucial. Mentally, I picture the evacuation plan. Go to the stairwell, up one floor, turn left. Better get a move on, because if I'm forced to turn round now, I'll have to pull out the Mossberg and open fire, thereby depriving a public hospital of a fine nurse when they're short-staffed already. I lengthen my stride. But first, lock and load. You never know.

Loading a round into the chamber takes both hands. And the pump action makes a distinct metallic click. Which echoes ominously down hospital corridors.

"The lifts aren't that way . . ."

A dry clack and the voice suddenly breaks off, giving way to a nervous silence. A young voice, at once pure and troubled, shot down in mid-flight.

"Monsieur!"

With the shotgun loaded, all I need to do is take my time and be meticulous. Keep my back to her at all times. The rigid line of the barrel is visible through the fabric of my trench coat; it looks as though I have a wooden leg. I take three steps. The flap of the coat flicks open for a fraction of a second revealing the end of the barrel. A brief glimmer like a beam of light, like the sun glinting on a shard of glass. Barely noticeable, barely recognisable, and if you've only seen guns in the movies you're unlikely to realise what it is. Still, you know that you've seen something, you hesitate, thinking it might be . . . No, it's too preposterous . . .

In the time it takes for the penny to drop . . . the man turns, head bowed, apologises for his mistake, closes the flap of his coat and goes into the stairwell. But he does not go down, he goes up. He's not running away, otherwise surely he would have gone downstairs. But that stilted way he was walking . . . Very weird. What was that thing under his coat? From a distance, it looked just like a gun. Here? In a hospital? No – she can't bring herself to believe it. Just time to run up the stairs . . .

"Monsieur . . . monsieur?"

8.10 p.m.

Time to leave. As a police officer, Camille cannot afford the luxury of behaving like some star-crossed lover. Detectives don't spend the night at the victim's bedside. He has already made enough blunders for one day.

And at precisely that moment his mobile vibrates, he checks the screen: Commissaire Michard. He stuffs the phone back into his pocket, turns back to the receptionist and waves goodbye. She winks and crooks her finger, gesturing to him. Camille hesitates, pretends he does not understand, but too weary to resist he trudges back. He already has the parking tickets, what more can she want?

"You finally off, then? Don't get much sleep on the force, do you?"

This is meant as an innuendo, because she smiles, showing off her crooked teeth. To think he wasted his time for this. He sighs heavily, gives a half-hearted smile. He desperately needs to sleep. He has taken three steps when she calls after him.

"Oh, there was a phone call, I thought you'd like to know."

"When was this?"

"A while ago . . . around seven o'clock."

And before Camille has time to ask . . .

"Her brother."

Nathan. Camille has never met Anne's brother, but he has heard him on her voicemail. Nervous, excitable and young. He is fifteen years younger than his sister, a researcher in some incomprehensible subject – photons, nanotechnology, some field whose very name is meaningless to Camille.

"And for a brother, he's not exactly polite. Listening to him, I'm glad I'm an only child."

A sudden realisation explodes inside Camille's head: how would Nathan have known Anne was in hospital?

Suddenly wide awake, he races round to the other side of the desk. The receptionist does not even wait for him to formulate the question.

"A man's voice, he was . . . [Ophélia rolls her eyes] well, he was ignorant and rude. 'Forestier . . . Yeah, with an F, how else would you spell it, with two Fs? [She mimics his curt, arrogant tone.] What exactly is wrong with her? And what did the doctors say? [Her imitation is beginning to verge on caricature.] What do you mean, they don't know?' [Her tone now is shocked, outraged.] . . ."

Did he have an accent?

The receptionist shakes her head. Camille glances around. The conclusion will come to him, he knows that, he is simply waiting for the neural pathways to connect, it is only a matter of seconds.

"Did he sound young?"

"Not *young*-young. Forty-something, I'd guess. Personally, I thought he . . ."

Camille is no longer listening, he is running, jostling anyone in his way. He wrenches open the door to the stairs which slams behind him. Already, he is taking the stairs as fast as his dumpy legs can manage.

8:15 p.m.

As soon as he heard my footsteps, he went upstairs, the nurse is thinking. About twenty-two, she has her hair in a skinhead crop and a ring through her bottom lip. On the outside she is all provocation, but inside is a different matter; if anything, she is too soft, too sensitive. She heard the stairwell door bang, but during those few seconds she spent hesitating the man could have gone anywhere – up to the fourth floor, down to reception, through the neurosurgical ward – there is no way of knowing where he went after that.

What was she supposed to do? She wasn't sure what she had seen and you don't go setting off the alarm in a hospital when you're not sure . . . She heads back to the nurses' station. The whole idea is ridiculous. Who would bring a shotgun into a hospital? But if it wasn't a gun, what was it? Some sort of prosthesis? There are visitors who bring giant bunches of gladioli – are gladioli in season now? He got the wrong room, that's what he said.

Still, she has her doubts. She did a course on battered women at nursing college, she knows how brutal men can be, she knows they're quite capable of attacking their wives even in a hospital. She retraces her steps and pops her head around the door of room 224. The woman in the room cries all the time; every time the nurse comes in she is in tears, running her fingers over her face, following the line of her lips. She covers her mouth when she speaks. Twice, the nurse found her in front of the bathroom mirror, though she barely has the strength to stand.

But still, she thinks as she leaves the room, worried now, what could the man have had under his raincoat? It looked like a broom handle, in the split second when his coat fell open, there was a glint of metal, of cold steel. She tries to think of something else, something that might be mistaken for a shotgun barrel. A crutch?

This is what she is thinking as the policeman bursts through the doors at the far end of the corridor, the little officer who spent all afternoon sitting with the patient – no more than five feet tall, his handsome face is grave, unsmiling. He rushes past like a lunatic, almost knocking her over, jerks open the door to room 224 and dashes inside. He looks as though he is about to throw himself on the bed.

"Anne, Anne . . ." he yells.

The way he's acting makes no sense, thinks the nurse, he's a policeman, but you'd think he was her husband. The patient seems very agitated. She shakes her head wildly, raises her hand to ward off the torrent of questions: stop yelling.

"Are you O.K. ?" the policeman whispers over and over. "Are you O.K. ?"

I talk to him, try to keep him calm. The patient lets her arm fall limply by her side, she looks at me. "I'm fine . . ."

"Did you see anyone?" the policeman turns back to me. "Did someone come into this room? Did you see him?"

His voice is grim, anxious.

"Did someone come into the room?"

Yes, I mean not really, I mean no . . .

"There was a man . . . he said he'd got the wrong floor, he opened the door . . ."

The policeman doesn't even wait for me to finish. He turns back to the patient, looks at her intently, she shakes her head, she seems confused, bewildered. She doesn't say anything, she simply shakes her head. She didn't see anyone. She slumps back on the bed, pulls the sheets up to her chin and starts to sob quietly. All these questions are frightening her. The little cop is hopping around like a flea. I need to say something.

"Monsieur, I'll thank you to remember that this is a hospital!"

He nods, but you can tell he's thinking about something else.

"And besides, visiting hours are over."

He turns back to me.

"Which way did he go?"

I pause for a split second and before I can answer he's shouting.

"This guy you saw, the one who said he'd got the wrong room, which way did he go?"

I reach down, take the patient's wrist and take her pulse. This is none of my business, what matters is the patient's welfare. I'm not in the business of reassuring jealous lovers.

"He took the stairs, over by . . ."

Before I've even finished the sentence, he's off like a shot, racing towards the emergency door, I hear his feet on the stairs, but it's impossible to tell whether he is going up or down.

But the shotgun . . . Did I just imagine it?

The concrete stairwell echoes like a cathedral. Camille grabs the banister, hurtles down the first few steps. Then stops.

No. If he were the killer, he would go up.

He does a U-turn. The treads are not standard size, the steps are about half a centimetre taller than expected; ten steps and you're tired, twenty and you're exhausted. Especially Camille with his short legs.

Panting, he arrives on the third floor, where he hesitates, racking his brain, trying to decide what he would do. Keep going up? No – he would go back into the maze of corridors. Bursting through the doors, Camille crashes into a doctor.

"What the . . . ? Look where you're going, can't you!"

A quick glance reveals a man of indeterminate age, his white coat freshly ironed (the pleats are still visible), his hair quite grey, he is standing frozen, hands in his pockets, flustered by Camille's frantic appearance . . .

"Did you see a man go past just now?"

The doctor takes a deep breath, struggles to recover his dignity and is about to stalk off.

"Are you fucking deaf?" Camille roars. "Did you see a man go past or didn't you?"

"No . . . I, um . . ."

This is answer enough for Camille, he turns on his heel, jerks the door as though trying to rip it off its hinges, tears back downstairs and into the corridor, he goes right, then left, gasping for breath, there is no-one. He retraces his steps, breaks into a run when he suddenly has a nagging hunch (doubtless fuelled by exhaustion) that tells him he is going the wrong way: the moment such doubts creep in, your pace begins to slacken, in fact it becomes impossible to run faster. As he reaches the end of the corridor where it turns at a right angle, Camille crashes into an electrical cupboard. The door is seven feet high and plastered with lightning bolts and other symbols, all of which mean "Danger of Death". Thanks for the tip.

The true art of a job like this is to leave as unobtrusively as you arrived.

This is no easy feat, it requires determination, concentration, vigilance and a cool head – qualities rarely found in one man. It's like a hold-up: when things go wrong, it's usually at the end. You show up with non-violent intentions, encounter a little resistance and unless you can keep calm, you find yourself spraying bullets and leaving carnage in your wake, all for want of a little self-control.

This time, I had a clear run. I didn't encounter anyone, apart from some doctor loitering inexplicably in the stairwell, and I managed to dodge him.

I get to the ground floor, I walk quickly towards the exit. In hospitals, everyone is always in a hurry, but no-one ever runs, so when you walk quickly it attracts attention, but I'm gone before anyone has time to react. Besides, what is there to react to?

On my right, the car park. The cold air feels good. Under my coat, I keep the Mossberg clamped against my leg; no point scaring the patients now – if they're in A. & E., they're already in a bad way. Down here, everything seems calm, but I'm guessing that things are kicking off upstairs. That pipsqueak fucking cop is probably sniffing around like a prairie dog, trying to work out what happened. The little nurse isn't really sure what she saw. And, O.K., maybe she talks to the other nurses. A gun? Are you kidding? You sure it wasn't a heat-seeking missile? Maybe they tease her. You know you shouldn't be drinking on the job! You been smoking crack again, girl? But then one of them says: all the same, you should maybe say something to the ward sister . . .

But by then, I've had more than enough time to get back to the car, start her up and join the queue of other vehicles leaving the hospital; three minutes later, I reach the street, I turn right and stop at the traffic light.

Now, this is a spot that might offer a window of opportunity.

And if not here, then somewhere close by.

All it takes is a little determination . . .

Camille feels beaten, but he forces himself to run faster. He takes the lift, tries to catch his breath. If there were no-one else in it, he would pound in the walls, instead he simply takes a deep breath. Arriving back in reception, he calmly assesses the situation. The casualty department is teeming with patients and nurses, para-medics are constantly coming and going, a corridor on the right leads to an emergency exit and another on the left leads out to the car park.

There must be at least half a dozen routes by which a man could leave the hospital without being noticed.

Protocol would suggest questioning witnesses, taking state-ments. But who would he question? Who is there to give a statement? By the time his team arrived at the scene, two-thirds of these people would have been discharged and their places taken by others.

He could kick himself.

Calmly, he goes back up to the second floor and over to the nurses' station. Florence, the girl with the bee-stung lips, is poring over patient files. Her colleague? She doesn't know, she says without looking up. Camille is insistent.

"We're overworked here on the ward," she says.

"In that case, she can't have gone very far . . ."

She is about to say something, but Camille is already gone. He paces up and down the corridor, popping his head around every door that opens, he is about to check the women's toilets – in the mood he is in, nothing would stop him – when the nurse finally reappears.

She seems annoyed, she runs a hand over her skinhead crop. Mentally, Camille sketches her, her features are regular and the cropped hair makes her look fragile. She looks intimidated, but in fact she is sensible and pragmatic. Her immediate reaction confirms this. She does not break her step and Camille is forced to run to keep up with her.

"The guy got the wrong room. It happens. He apologised."

"You heard his voice?"

"Not really . . . I heard him say sorry, that's about it."

Hurrying along a hospital corridor, trying to wheedle information out of this woman, information he needs if he is to save the life of the woman he loves. He grabs the nurse's arm, forcing her to stop, to look down; she is struck by the single-mindedness she can read in his face, by the determination in his calm, measured growl as he says, "I need to you to pay attention . . ."

Camille glances at her name-tag: Cynthia. Her parents clearly watched too many soap operas.

"I need you to tell me everything, 'CYNTHIA'. I need every last detail . . ."

She tells him, the man standing in the open doorway, the way he kept his head down when he turned around – embarrassed probably – the raincoat he was wearing, O.K., so he had a rather stiff way of walking . . . He headed straight for the stairs and a man who is running away would go down, not up, it's only logical, isn't it?

Camille sighs and nods; of course, it's only logical.

9.30 p.m.
"It'll be here any minute . . ."

The head of hospital security is not best pleased. It is late, he had to get dressed and come back to work when he could be at home watching the match. A former *gendarme*, self-important, big-bellied, no-necked, red-faced, the product of a staple diet of beef and red wine. To watch the C.C.T.V. footage, he needs a warrant. Signed by the examining magistrate. In triplicate.

"On the phone, you told me you had a warrant . . ."

"No," Camille states categorically, "I told you I was *getting* one."

"Well, I wasn't aware of that."

Pig-headed. As a rule, Camille favours negotiation, but on this occasion he has neither the time nor the inclination.

"And what exactly are you aware of?" he barks.

"I don't know . . . that you had a sear—"

"No," Camille cuts him off, "I'm not talking about a search warrant. Are you *aware* that a man with a sawn-off shotgun gained access to this hospital? Are you aware that he went up to the second floor intending to kill one of the patients it is your job to protect? And that if anyone got in his way, he would have happily shot them too? Are you aware that if he comes back and butchers people, you're going to be in the dock?"

The conversation is academic since the cameras only cover the front entrance and there is little chance that this man – if he exists – came in that way. He is no fool. If he exists. And indeed, there is nothing on the footage during the period when he would have been in the hospital. Camille checks and double-checks. The head of security is hopping from one foot to the other, puffing and panting to signal his frustration. Camille peers at the screen, staring at the steady stream of ambulances, emergency vehicles and private cars, the people trudging in and out, the injured, the healthy, walking, running. Nothing of any relevance strikes him.

He gets up and leaves the security room, then comes back, presses the EJECT button on the machine, takes the D.V.D. and leaves.

"Do you take me for an idiot?" the security guard roars. "Where's my warrant?"

Camille gives a shrug that says: We'll deal with that later.

Back out in the car park, Camille surveys the area. If it were me, he thinks, I'd go around the side, use the emergency exit. He studies the fire-door closely. He takes out his glasses. There is no sign of forced entry.

When you go outside for a cigarette, who takes over?

It is the obvious question. Camille goes back into the reception area and, at the far end, he discovers the narrow corridor behind the desk that leads to the emergency exit.

Ophélia smiles, showing her yellow teeth.

"Listen, honey, they don't provide maternity cover in this place, so they're hardly likely to cover for cigarette breaks!"

Was he here?

As he walks back to the car, Camille listens to his voicemail messages.

"Commissaire Michard! [Her voice is grating.] Call me back. Doesn't matter what time it is. I need to know where things stand. And I'll have that report on my desk first thing tomorrow morning, yes?"

Camille feels alone. Terribly alone.

Night time in a hospital is unlike anywhere else. Silence itself seems suspended. Stretchers and trolleys continue to rattle along the corridors, there are distant cries, intermittent voices, the sound of running footsteps, the bleeping of alarms.

Anne manages to drift off, but her sleep is fitful, filled with pain and blood, she feels the tiled floor of the Galerie Monier beneath her hands, feels with eerie exactness the glass rain down on her; she sees herself crashing into the shop window, hears the gunshots behind her. Her breath now comes in halting gasps. The little nurse with the ring through her bottom lip is reluctant to wake her. But there is no need, since every time this loop of dream plays out, Anne wakes with a scream, jolting upright in bed. She can see the man, towering over her, pulling a balaclava over his face and then a close-up of the shotgun butt about to shatter her cheekbone.

In her sleep, Anne brings her fingers up to touch her face, she strokes the sutures, then her lips, feels for her teeth and finds bare gums and jagged stumps.

He wanted to kill her.

He will come back. He wants to kill her.

DAY 2

6.00 a.m.

Not a wink of sleep. When it comes to Camille's emotions, Doudouche has a sixth sense.

Last night, Camille went back to the station to sort out all the things he had not had the chance to deal with during the day; when he came home exhausted and dossed down fully dressed on the sofa, Doudouche crept up beside him and there they lay, motionless, all night. Camille did not feed her, but she did not mewl, she knows when he is anxious. She purrs. Camille knows by heart every nuanced register of her purring.

Not long ago, nights such as this – sleepless, tense, anxious, desolate – were spent for Irène. With Irène. Camille would think about their life together, go over every painful image. He could think of nothing more important than the death of Irène.

Camille is not sure whether what has pained him most today has been his fears for Anne, the sight of her ravaged face, her terrible suffering or the realisation that gradually, over the days and weeks, she has come to occupy his every thought. There is a sort of crassness about moving on from one woman to another, he feels like the victim of a cliché. He had never even thought about making a new life for himself, and yet a new life has appeared almost in spite of him. Yet for all that, the harrowing images of Irène still continue to haunt him and probably always will. They are immune to everything, to passing time, to encounters with other women. Or rather, encounter; there has only been one woman.

Camille was able to accept Anne since she insisted that she was only passing through. Like him, she has her dead to mourn; she is not looking to plan a future. And yet, without intending to, she has become a permanent part of his life. And in the age-old distinction between the one who loves and the one who is loved, Camille does not know which he is.

They met in spring. Early March. It had been four years since he lost Irène, two years since he re-emerged from grief, insensible but alive. An existence stripped of all risk, all desire that is the lot of men condemned to solitude. It is not easy for a man like Camille to meet women, but he no longer cared, he did not miss it.

To meet anybody is something of a miracle.

Anne is not given to anger, once and only once in her life did she throw a tantrum in a restaurant (she swore as much to him, hand on heart). It so happened that Camille was having dinner two tables away at Chez Fernand when a heated argument turned into a row. Insults are hurled, plates smashed, dishes overturned, cutlery is strewn across the floor, customers get to their feet and demand their coats, the police are called and all the while the owner, Fernand, is shouting at the top of his voice, calculating the damage in astronomical figures. Anne suddenly stops screaming and, surveying the destruction, she bursts out laughing.

She glances over at Camille.

He closes his eyes for a split second, takes a breath, slowly gets to his feet and shows his warrant card.

He introduces himself. Commandant Verhœven, *brigade criminelle*.

He seems to have appeared from nowhere. Anne stops laughing and looks at him worriedly.

"Lucky you were here!" roars the owner, then hesitates. "*Brigade criminelle*, you said?"

Camille nods wearily. He grabs the *patron* by the arm and takes him aside.

Two minutes later, he leaves the restaurant accompanied by

Anne, who is unsure whether to be amused, relieved, grateful or worried. She is free and, like most people, does not know what to do with her freedom. Camille is aware that, like any woman, at this moment she is wondering about the nature of the debt she has taken on. And how she might repay it.

"What did you say to him?" she says.

"I told him I was arresting you."

This is a lie. In fact, Camille threatened to have the place raided every week until the restaurant was left with no customers. A blatant abuse of authority. He feels a little ashamed, but then again a restaurant should be able to serve decent profiteroles!

Anne knows it is a lie, but she finds it funny.

As they reach the corner of the street and a police car screeches past on its way to Chez Fernand, she gives Camille her most devastating smile – her cheeks dimple, there are delicate laughter lines around her green eyes . . . Suddenly, the thought that she feels she owes him something begins to weigh on Camille.

"Are you taking the *métro*?" he says as they reach the station.

Anne thinks for a moment.

"I'll probably take a taxi."

This sounds good to Camille, although regardless of what she chose he would have taken the alternative. He gives her a little wave and trips down the stairs with affected composure, though actually he goes as fast as he can. He disappears.

They slept together the following night.

When Camille left the *brigade* at the end of his shift, Anne was waiting outside on the pavement. He pretended not to notice her and walked on towards the *métro*, but when he turned, she was still serenely standing there. The ploy made him smile. He was cornered.

They had dinner. An utterly routine evening. Indeed it would have been disappointing, but the lingering uncertainty about the debt she owes makes for a charged and gloomy atmosphere. As for the rest, what do a middle-aged man and a woman say when they first meet? They try to play down their failures without suppressing them altogether, allude to their wounds without revealing them, saying more than is necessary. Camille told Anne the essential in a few short words, about his mother, Maud . . .

"I thought as much . . ." Anne said, and seeing Camille's quizzical gaze she added, "I've seen some of her paintings." She hesitated. "Montreal?"

Camille was surprised she knew his mother's work.

Anne talked about her life in Lyons, about her divorce, about how she had left everything behind and it was clear just from looking at her that it was far from over. Camille would have liked to know more about this man, this husband, this relationship. The boundless curiosity men have for the innermost lives of women.

He asked if she would like to slap the restaurant manager now, or wait until after he had paid. Anne's bright, girlish laugh changed everything.

Camille, who had not been with a woman for longer than he could remember, did not have to do anything. Anne lay on top of him and after that it all followed naturally, not a word was said. It was both infinitely sad and extraordinarily happy. It was love.

They made no plans to see each other again. And yet from time to time, they did. As though touching only with their fingertips. Anne is a financial consultant, she spends most of her time visiting travel agencies, overseeing management structures, accounts, all those things of which Camille understands nothing. She is rarely in Paris more than two days a week. Her regular absences and her comings and goings lent a chaotic confusion to their encounters, as though they were constantly meeting by chance. From the beginning they did not understand the nature of their relationship. They met, they went out, they had dinner, they went to bed together, and steadily it grew.

Camille racks his brain, trying to recall the moment he first realised how much it took over in his life. He cannot remember.

All he knows is that with Anne's arrival, the white-hot memory of Irène's death has receded. He wonders whether some new being capable of living without Irène has finally appeared within him. Forgetting is inexorable. But to forget is not to heal.

Today he is devastated by what has happened to Anne. He feels responsible. Not for what has happened – there is nothing he can do about that – but for what is yet to happen, since that will depend on him, on his strength, his determination, his skill. It is overwhelming.

Doudouche has stopped purring, she is finally asleep. Camille slips off the sofa and the cat whimpers resentfully and turns onto her side. He pads over to the desk and picks up one of the Irène sketchpads. There once were countless notebooks, but this is all that remains. The others he destroyed one night when anger and despair got the better of him. The pad is filled with sketches of Irène: sitting at a table raising her glass and smiling, drawings of Irène here and there, sleeping, pensive. Camille puts the book down again. The past four years without her have been the most gruelling, the most miserable of his life and yet he cannot help but think they have been the most interesting, the most emotional. He has not left his past behind. It is the past that has become more . . . he struggles for a word. Subdued? More bearable? More muted? Like the remainder in a Euclidean division he never did, Anne is utterly unlike Irène, they are different galaxies light-years apart, converging on a single point. What distinguishes them is that Anne is still here while Irène has left.

Camille remembers Anne almost leaving him, but she came back. It is August. Standing by the window with her arms folded, naked, thoughtful, she says, "It's over, Camille," without turning to look at him. Then she dresses without a word. In a novel, this would take a minute; in real life it takes an age for a naked woman to get dressed. Camille sits, motionless; he looks like a man suddenly overtaken by a storm, resigned to his fate.

And she leaves.

Camille does nothing to stop her; he understands. Her leaving is not a tragedy, it is a fathomless gulf, a dull, gnawing pain. He is sorry that she is leaving, but he accepts it because he always felt it was inevitable. He is long accustomed to feeling unworthy. For a long time he sits there, frozen, then finally he lies back on the sofa. It is close to midnight.

He will never know what happens in that moment.

It has been more than an hour since Anne left, but suddenly he gets to his feet, goes to the door and, driven by some inexplicable conviction, he opens it. Anne is sitting at the top of the stairs, her back to him, her arms wrapped around her knees.

After a few seconds, she gets up, steps around him and goes into the apartment, lies down on the bed fully dressed and turns her face to the wall.

She is crying. It is something Camille remembers from his time with Irène.

6.45 a.m.

From the outside, the building does not look too bad, but inside the extent of the dilapidation is clear. A bank of battered

108

aluminium letterboxes has been half corroded by neglect. On the last box in the row, the label reads "6th Floor: Anne Forestier" in her spidery scrawl; at the right-hand edge where she ran out of space, the E and R are so close together they are all but illegible.

Camille ignores the tiny lift.

It is not yet seven o'clock when he taps lightly on the door to the apartment opposite Anne's.

The door immediately opens, as though the neighbour were expecting him. Madame Roman, who owns Anne's apartment, recognises Camille. It is one of the advantages of his height; people do not forget him. He delivers the lie.

"Anne has been called away urgently . . . [He feigns the benevolent smile of a patient, long-suffering friend in search of an ally.] She had to leave quickly and she forgot half the things she needed, obviously."

The macho, casually sexist "obviously" appeals to Madame Roman. She is a single woman, close to retirement age; her chubby, doll-like face makes her look like a child who has aged prematurely. She has a slight limp; some problem with her hip. From what little Camille has seen, she is terrifyingly methodical, with every last detail arranged and classified.

She screws up her eyes and gives Camille a knowing look, turns and hands him the spare key . . .

"Nothing serious, I hope?"

"No, no. [Camille gives her a broad smile.] Nothing serious. [He nods towards the key.] I'll keep this until she gets back . . ."

It is impossible to say whether this is a statement, a question or a request; Madame Roman hesitates. Camille makes the most of this brief pause to give her a grateful smile.

The kitchenette is immaculate. Everything in the little apartment is carefully arranged. Women and their obsession with neatness, thinks Camille. The large living room is partitioned and one half serves as a bedroom. The sofa converts into a double bed with a huge dip in the middle, a yawning chasm that draws them in so they end up sleeping on top of each other. It has its advantages. And a bookcase is lined with a hundred paperbacks – a selection that defies logic – and a few knick-knacks that, when he first visited, struck Camille as rather tawdry. He told her he found the place a little sad.

"I had very little money," Anne had said, suddenly tight-lipped. "Besides, I can't really complain."

Camille tries to apologise, but Anne cuts him dead.

"This is the price of divorce."

When she has something serious to say, Anne stares at you defiantly, as though prepared for a confrontation.

"When I left Lyons, I left behind everything I owned. This furniture, these ornaments, I bought second-hand here in Paris. I didn't want things anymore. I don't want things anymore. Maybe one day, but right now this place suits me."

This place is provisional – this is Anne's word. The apartment is provisional, their relationship is provisional. This is clearly why they go so well together.

"The thing that really takes time after a divorce is the clear-out," she says.

That nagging obsession with neatness.

Her blue hospital gown looks like a straitjacket, so Camille has decided to bring her some clothes. He thinks it might cheer her up. He even thinks that, if all goes well, she might go for short walks along the corridor, or downstairs to the little shop on the ground floor.

He made a mental list, but now that he is here, he cannot remember a single thing. Oh, yes: the dark-purple tracksuit. By association of ideas, he suddenly remembers a pair of trainers, the ones she uses for jogging, well worn, the soles still caked with sand. After that it's more difficult. What else?

Camille opens the small wardrobe. For a woman, Anne has very few clothes. A pair of jeans, he thinks, but which? He takes a pair. A T-shirt, a thick jumper. After that it all seems too complicated. He gives up and stuffs what he has into a sports bag with a random assortment of underwear.

He remembers her papers.

Camille goes over to the bureau. Above it a tarnished mirror that probably dates from when the apartment was built. Into one corner of the frame, Anne has slipped a picture of Nathan, her brother. He looks about twenty-five in the photo, an unprepossessing boy, smiling and withdrawn. Perhaps because he knows a little about him, Camille finds that there is something otherworldly about the face. Nathan is a scientist. From what Camille knows, he is pretty disorganised and tends to run up debts. Anne is forever bailing him out. Like a mother. "Actually, that's what I've always been to him," she says. She has always been there for him. She smiles, as though amused, but in fact it is worry. The studio flat, the university fees, the holidays, Anne has financed everything; it is hard to tell whether she is proud or dismayed. In the photograph, Nathan is standing in a little square that could be in Italy, the sun is shining, everyone is in shirtsleeves.

Camille goes through the bureau. The right-hand drawer is empty, in the one on the left are a number of creased envelopes, a couple of receipts from clothes shops, restaurants and a pile of brochures bearing the logo of her travel agency, but there is no sign of what he is looking for: her *carte vitale*, and her mutual insurance policy. They must have been in her handbag. Under the travel brochures he finds her sports clothes. He goes through the pile again. He expected to find pay slips, bank statements, utility bills for the water, the electricity, the telephone. Nothing. He turns around. His eyes are drawn to the small statue, a copy of an Egyptian cosmetic spoon in the Louvre, the dark wooden handle carved into the naked figure of a young woman swimming, with hair and eyes outlined in black paint. And a perfect arse. Camille gave it to Anne as a present. He bought it in the Louvre. They had been to see the Leonardo exhibition, Camille had spent the whole time explaining the paintings, his knowledge of the subject is encyclopaedic, he could talk for ever about them. In the gift shop, they had seen the carved copy of this girl from the late Eighteenth Dynasty, with her perfectly curved *derrière*.

"I swear, Anne, it's just like yours."

Anne had smiled as though to say "I wish! But thank you for saying so . . ." Camille was adamant. She wondered whether he was being serious. He leaned towards her and whispered insistently.

"Honest to God."

Before she had time to say anything, he had bought it, and that night he had undertaken a professional comparison of the two arses. At first, Anne had laughed a lot, then she moaned and gradually one thing led to another. Afterwards, she had cried; she sometimes cries after they make love. Camille thinks this probably has something to do with clearing out.

Just now, the carved figure looks lonely on the shelf; there is a broad space between it and the collection of D.V.D.s at the other end. Camille spins around, surveying the room. His talent as an artist comes from his unerring sense of observation and he quickly arrives at a conclusion.

Someone has been in the apartment.

He goes back and peers into the right-hand drawer of the bureau: it is empty because her personal papers have been taken. Camille goes back to the front door and examines the lock. Nothing. So it can only have been one of the gang who found Anne's address and her keys in the handbag he picked up as he left the Galerie Monier.

Is this the same man who was in the hospital last night, or have they divided up the work?

Their determination to hunt her down seems absurd and out of all proportion to the situation. We're missing something, Camille thinks, not for the first time; there is something about the case we don't understand.

From the sheaf of personal documents they have, the gang probably know everything about Anne, they know where they are going to find her in Paris and in Lyons, they know where she works, they know every place she might go to hide.

With all this information, tracking her, finding her, becomes child's play.

Killing her becomes an exercise in style.

The moment Anne sets foot outside the hospital, she is dead.

He cannot tell the *commissaire* that the apartment was searched without admitting that he knows Anne intimately and that he has lied to her from the start. Yesterday, it was no more than a slight misgiving. Today, no more than a suspicion. To his superiors, it would be indefensible. A forensics team could be sent in, but given the sort of men they are dealing with, they would find nothing. Not a trace.

There is more: Camille entered the apartment without authorisation, without a search warrant, he gained admittance because he lied to get the key, because Anne sent him to pick up her social security documents, Madame Roman would be able to testify that he has regularly been in the apartment . . .

The catalogue of his lies is becoming dangerously long. But it is not this that terrifies Camille. It is knowing that Anne's life is hanging by a thread. And he is utterly powerless.

7.20 a.m.

"No, it's not a bad time."

If a co-worker says this when you phone at 7.00 a.m., ask no questions. Especially when that co-worker is the *commissaire*.

Camille starts to fill her in on what has been happening.

"Where's your report . . ." the *commissaire* interrupts.

"I'm working on it."

"And . . . ?"

Camille starts again from the beginning, groping for words, trying to remain professional. The witness was hospitalised and, from the available evidence, it would appear that one of the armed gang infiltrated the premises, made his way to her private room and attempted to kill her.

"Hold on a minute, *commandant*, I'm not sure I follow you. [She enunciates each word as though her formidable intellect were banging against a brick wall.] The witness in question, Madame Foresti, she . . ."

"Madame Forestier."

"If you prefer. The witness maintains she saw no-one come into her room, am I right? [She does not give him time to answer.] And the nurse claims that she saw someone, but in the end she's not sure, is that it? So, first off, who is this 'someone'? And even if it is one of the gang, did he go into the room or didn't he?"

There is no point wishing Le Guen were still in charge. If he were still *commissaire*, he would be asking the same questions. Ever since Camille requested that this case be assigned to him, everything has gone wrong.

"I'm telling you he was there!" Camille is insistent. "The nurse glimpsed the barrel of a shotgun . . ."

"Oh, well that's just perfect!" the *commissaire* says admiringly. "She 'glimpsed', did she . . . ? So, enlighten me, has the hospital filed a report?"

From the moment the conversation began, Camille knew how it would end. He tries his best, but he does not want to cross swords with his superior officer. She earned her promotion. And if Camille's friendship with Le Guen made it possible for him to be assigned the case, it will not protect him for long – in fact, it will probably work against him.

Camille feels a prickling in his temples, a wave of heat.

"No, there's no official police report. [Don't let yourself get riled, be patient and calm, polite and persuasive.] But I am telling you the guy was there. He didn't think twice about going into a hospital carrying a loaded weapon. From the nurse's description, it could possibly be the pump-action shotgun used in the armed robbery."

"'It could possibly be' . . ."

"Why won't you believe me?"

"Because in the absence of an official complaint, a witness, a shred of proof or a single scrap of tangible evidence, I'm having a little trouble imagining a common-or-garden robber going into a hospital to murder a witness, that's why!"

"A 'common-or-garden robber'?" Camille chokes on the words.

"O.K., I'll grant you the raid was pretty violent, but . . ."

"'Pretty' violent?"

"*Commandant*, are you going to repeat everything I say with quote marks? You are requesting police protection for this witness as though she were a supergrass in a mafia trial!"

Camille opens his mouth. Too late.

"I'll let you have one uniformed officer. Two days."

It is a despicable response. If she had refused to assign anyone, she would have been held responsible if anything happened. Assigning a single unarmed *gendarme* to stop a determined killer is like offering someone a beach windbreak to stop a tsunami.

"What possible threat can Madame Forestier be to these men, Monsieur Verhœven? From what I've heard, she witnessed an armed robbery, not a mass murder! By now they'll know that, although she was injured, they didn't kill her – I'm inclined to think they're relieved."

This seemed logical at the beginning. But there is something not quite right about the case.

"So, this informant of yours, what does he have to say?"

Precisely how we make our decisions is one of life's mysteries. At what point do we become aware that we have decided? It is impossible to know what role the subconscious plays in Camille's response, but it comes without a flicker of hesitation.

"Mouloud Faraoui."

Even Camille flinches when he hears himself say the name.

He feels a sickening lurch, the almost physical sensation of a moving rollercoaster, knowing the trajectory he has put himself on by mentioning this name is a blazing arc headed straight for a brick wall.

"So Faraoui is out on parole?"

And before Camille has time to respond:

"And while we're at it, what the hell has he got to do with this thing?"

Good question. Like doctors, criminals tend to specialise: armed robbers, fences, burglars, forgers, con men, racketeers, they all live in their separate worlds. Mouloud Faraoui is a pimp, so it would be astonishing for his name to crop up in an armed robbery.

Camille knows him vaguely, their paths have crossed once or twice, and Mouloud is a little too high-profile to be a snitch. Mouloud Faraoui is a sadistic thug, he controls his turf with brute violence and has been implicated in several murders. He is cunning, vicious and for a long time it proved impossible to make any charges stick. Until he found himself on a trumped-up charge for something he did not do: thirty kilos of ecstasy in a holdall in the boot of his car with his prints all over the bag. A textbook stitch-up. Though he swore blind that the holdall was one he used at the gym, he found himself banged up in a cell nursing a frenzied rage.

"Sorry?"

"Faraoui! What the hell has he got to do with this case of yours? And you said he's your cousin? Well, that's news to me . . ."

"No, he's not my cousin . . . Look, it's complicated, it's a six-degrees-of-separation thing, if you know what I mean . . ."

"No, I'm afraid I don't know."

"Look, I'll deal with it and I'll get back to you."

"You . . . you'll 'deal with it'?"

"Are you going to repeat everything I say with quote marks?"

"Don't fuck with me, *commandant*!" Michard roars, then quickly puts her hand over the receiver. Camille hears a faint, stammered "Excuse my language, darling" that plunges him into confusion. Does this woman have children? How old would they be? A daughter maybe, though from her tone it does not sound as though she is talking to a child. When the *commissaire* comes back on the line, her voice is calm but her fury is still palpable. From the sound of her breathing, Camille can tell she is going into another room. Up until this moment, she has treated Camille as a minor irritation, but now, though given the circumstances she is forced to whisper, her long-suppressed hostility boils over in seething rage.

"What the hell is your problem, *commandant*?"

"Well, first, it's not 'my' problem. And secondly, it's seven in the morning, so while I'd be happy to try and explain, I need time to . . ."

"*Commandant* . . . [Silence.] I don't know what you're doing. I don't understand what you're doing. [All the anger has drained from her voice, as though she has changed the subject. Which, in a sense, she has.] But I want your report on my desk by the end of the day, is that clear?"

"No problem."

The day is mild, but Camille is dripping with perspiration. A slick, cold sweat he recognises as it trickles down his back, the sort of sweat he has not felt since his race to find Irène the day she died. He had been blinkered that day, he had thought he could go it alone . . . No: he hadn't been thinking at all. He had behaved as though he were the only person who could do what needed to be done and he had been wrong: by the time he found her, Irène was dead.

And what about Anne now?

They say men who lose women always lose them in the same way; this is what terrifies him.

8.00 a.m.

They don't know what they're missing, the Turks. Two fat holdalls full of bling. If it was half the weight, it would still be a good haul, even allowing for the fence's cut. Everything's going according to plan. And, with a bit of luck, I plan to make a killing from this stuff.

If all goes well.

And if it doesn't, then there'll be some real killing.

To be sure, to be clear, you have to be methodical. You have to be determined.

In the meantime, bring up the lights, it's show time!

Le Parisien. Page 3.

Fire in Saint-Ouen.

Perfect! Cross the road. Le Balto. A dingy little café. Cigarette. Coffee and cigarettes, that's what it's all about. The coffee in this place is like dishwater, but it's eight o'clock in the morning, so . . .

Open the newspaper. Drum-roll, please.

SAINT-OUEN
TWO DEAD IN MYSTERY BLAZE

The emergency services were called to a major incident in Chartriers shortly after noon yesterday when a serious fire broke out following a fierce explosion. Fire officers quickly contained the blaze which destroyed a number of workshops and lock-up garages. The fire is all the more mysterious since the area, which is scheduled for urban redevelopment, is currently derelict.

In the rubble of one of the lock-ups destroyed by the blaze, police officers discovered the burned-out wreck of a Porsche Cayenne and the charred bodies of two individuals. This has been determined as the locus of the blast, and forensic evidence indicates the presence of Semtex. From fragments of electronic equipment found at the scene, forensics officers have suggested the explosion could have been triggered remotely.

Given the intensity of the blaze, it may prove difficult to identify the bodies of the victims. All available evidence points to a carefully premeditated killing intended to make such identification impossible. Investigators are hoping to determine whether the victims were alive or dead at the time of the explosion . . .

Done and dusted.

"Investigators are hoping to determine . . ." Don't make me laugh! I'm happy to take bets. And if the cops somehow manage to trace this back to a couple of Turkish brothers with no record, I'll donate their half to the Police Orphan Fund.

Nearly there. I'm on the Périphérique, I take the exit ramp at Porte Maillot and into Neuilly-sur-Seine.

It's nice to see how the other half lives. If they weren't so fucking dumb, you'd almost want to join them. I park outside a school where thirteen-year-old girls are trooping out wearing clothes that cost thirteen times the minimum wage. Almost makes me sorry that the Mossberg is not an acceptable social leveller.

I walk past the school and turn right. The house is smaller

than those on either side, the grounds are not as extensive despite the fact that every year enough loot from burglaries and armed robberies passes through to build a new skyscraper at La Défense. The fence is wary, a smooth operator, constantly changing the protocol. By now, he'll have had one of his delivery boys pick up the holdalls from the locker at the Gare du Nord.

One location for the pickup, a second to evaluate the merchandise, a third to deal with negotiations.

He takes a hefty cut to ensure the deal is secure.

9.30 a.m.

Camille would like to be able to question her. What exactly did she see in the Galerie? But letting her see how worried he is would mean letting her know that her life is in danger, it would terrify her and only add anguish to her suffering.

And yet, he has no choice but to ask again.

"What?" Anne howls. "See what? What do you want me to say?"

The night has done her no good, she woke more exhausted than she had been yesterday. She is fretful, constantly on the verge of tears, Camille can hear it in the quaver in her voice, but she is a little more articulate today, she is managing to enunciate more clearly.

"I don't know," Camille says. "It could be anything."

"What?"

Camille spreads his hands helplessly.

"I just need to be sure, don't you see?"

Anne does not see. But she struggles to rack her memory, tilts her head and stares at Camille. He closes his eyes: try to keep calm, try to help me.

"Did you overhear them talking?"

Anne does not move, it is impossible to know whether she understood the question. Then she makes an evasive gesture that is difficult to interpret.

"Serbian, maybe . . ."

Camille jolts upright.

"What do you mean, Serbian? Do you know any words of Serbian?"

He is sceptical. These days, he has more dealings with Slovenians, Serbians, Bosnians, Croats, Kosovars, waves of them are arriving in Paris, but despite all the time he has spent with them he still cannot tell the languages apart.

"No, I'm not sure . . ."

Anne gives up and slumps back on the pillow.

"Wait, wait," Camille says. "This is important."

Anne opens her eyes again and struggles to speak.

"*Kpaj* . . . I think."

Camille cannot believe it, it is like suddenly discovering that Juge Pereira's clerk speaks fluent Japanese.

"*Kpaj*? Is that Serbian?"

Anne nods, though she does not seem completely sure.

"It means 'stop.'"

"How . . . how do you know this?"

Anne closes her eyes again as though she is exhausted by having to tell him the same things over and over.

"I spent three years organising tours in Eastern Europe . . ."

It's unforgivable. She has told him a thousand times. She has been in the travel industry for fifteen years, and before moving into management, spent a long time organising trips all over the world. She dealt with all of the Eastern Bloc countries except Russia. From Poland all the way south to Albania.

"Did all of them speak Serbian?"

Anne simply shakes her head, but she needs to explain; with Camille, everything has to be explained.

"I only heard one of them . . . In the toilets. The other guy, I'm not sure . . . [Her speech is a garbled, but completely intelligible.] I'm not sure . . ."

But to Camille, this confirms his suspicions: the guy doing the shouting, rifling the display cases, jostling his accomplice, he is Serbian. The man acting as lookout is Vincent Hafner.

He is the one who beat Anne, he is the one who sneaked into the hospital and went up to her room, he is probably the one who broke into Anne's apartment. And he does not have an accent.

The receptionist was categorical.

Vincent Hafner.

When the time comes for her to go for the M.R.I. scan, Anne asks for a pair of crutches. It can be difficult to understand what she wants. Camille translates. She insists on walking. The nurses roll their eyes and are about to manhandle her into a wheelchair and cart her off, but she screams, pulls away from them, sits on the bed with her arms folded. No.

This time, there can be no doubt. Florence, the charge nurse with the bee-stung lips is called, she is peremptory – "This is ridiculous, Madame Forestier, we'll take you upstairs for your scan, it won't take long." She turns on her heel without waiting for a response, her brusque manner clearly signalling that she is up to her eyes this morning and is in no mood to deal with petulant demands . . . But before she can reach the door, she hears Anne's voice ring out clearly, her pronunciation is a little indistinct but the meaning is crystal clear: Absolutely not: either I go on foot, or I'm going nowhere.

Florence comes back, Camille tries to plead Anne's case, but the nurse looks daggers at him – who the hell is this guy, anyway? He steps aside, leans against a wall, he suspects that the charge nurse has just blown her only chance of finding a peaceful solution. Time will tell.

The whole floor of the hospital starts to shake, heads appear in the hallway, the nurses try to restore order – Go back to your rooms, there's nothing to see! Inevitably, the house doctor shows up, the Indian with the interminable name, who seems to be here from morning to night, working shifts as long as his name, and he is probably paid no better than the cleaners. He comes over, and while he bends down to listen to what Anne is saying, he surveys the cuts and contusions; she looks terrible, but it is nothing compared to how she will look in a few days as the bruises develop. Gently, he tries to reason with her. Then, he listens to her chest. The nursing staff are confused, they do not understand what he is doing, M.R.I. appointments are set in stone, they cannot afford to be late. But the doctor takes his time . . .

The charge nurse becomes impatient, the porters are champing at the bit. The doctor calmly concludes his examination, he smiles at Anne and requests a pair of crutches. His colleagues glare at him, they feel betrayed.

Camille looks at the frail figure slumped over the crutches, two porters walk on either side of Anne, supporting her.

She shuffles slowly, but she is moving. She is on her feet.

10.00 a.m.
"This is not an extension of the commissariat . . ."

The office is an indescribable mess. The man is a surgeon, one can only hope things are more organised inside his head.

124

Hubert Dainville, head of the Trauma Unit. They met in the stairwell the previous night while Camille was chasing a ghost. In that fleeting glance, he looked ageless. Today he looks fifty. He is obviously proud of his shock of curly grey hair, it is the symbol of his ageing masculinity, this is not a hairstyle, it is a world view. His hands are carefully manicured. He is the sort of man who wears blue shirts with white collars and a handkerchief in the breast pocket of his suits. An ageing beau. He has probably tried to screw half of his staff and doubtless attributes to his charm the few successes that are simply statistical anomalies. His white coat is still immaculately ironed, but he no longer has the befuddled air he had in the stairwell. On the contrary, he is brusque and overbearing. He carries on working while he talks to Camille, as though the matter were already settled and he does not have time to waste.

"Nor do I," Camille says.

"Pardon?"

Dr Dainville looks up, frowning. It pains him when he does not understand. He is unaccustomed to the feeling. He pauses in his rummage through the pile of papers.

"I said, nor do I . . . I don't have time to waste," Camille says. "I can see that you're busy, but as it happens I'm rather busy myself. You have your responsibilities; I have mine."

Dainville pulls a face, unconvinced by this line of reasoning, and returns to his paperwork. But still the officer hovers in the doorway, clearly unaware that the interview is at an end.

"The patient needs rest," Dainville mutters finally. "She has suffered severe trauma." He glares at Camille. "Her present condition is little short of a miracle, she could have been left in a coma. She could be dead."

"She could also be at home. Or at work. She could even have finished her little shopping trip. The problem is that she ran into a man with no time to waste. A man like you. A man who thinks that his concerns are more important than those of other people."

The doctor looks up and glowers at Verhœven. To a man like Dainville, the most innocuous conversation involves a confrontation, he is a shock of snowy locks atop a fighting cock. Tiresome. And pugnacious. He looks Camille up and down.

"I realise that the police consider themselves entitled to go anywhere, but a hospital room is not an interrogation suite, *commandant*. This is a hospital, not an assault course. I will not have you tearing around the corridors, upsetting my staff . . ."

"You think I'm running up and down the corridors to keep in shape?"

Dainville brushes the comment aside.

"If this patient does indeed represent a danger to herself or to this institution, then have her transferred to a secure unit. If not, leave us in peace to get on with our work."

"Do you have much free space in the mortuary?"

A startled Dainville gives a little jerk of his head. The cock.

"I only ask," Camille goes on, "because until we can question the witness, the examining magistrate will not authorise a transfer. You would not operate unless you were certain of your facts; the police likewise. And we have very similar problems, you and I. The later we intervene, the greater the potential damage."

"I'm afraid I don't understand your metaphors, *commandant*."

"Then let me be clearer. It is possible that a killer is targeting this witness. If you prevent me from doing my job and he wreaks havoc in your hospital, you will have two problems. You will not have space enough in your mortuary and, given that the patient is fit to answer questions, you will be charged with obstructing a police investigation."

Dainville is a curious man; he seems to operate like a light switch – there is either a current or there is none. Nothing in between. Now, suddenly, there is a current. He looks at Camille, amused, and gives him a genuine smile, revealing a mouthful of perfect, straight teeth. Dr Dainville thrives on confrontation, he may be surly, arrogant and boorish, but he likes complications. He is aggressive and argumentative, but deep down he likes to be beaten. Camille has met his fair share of such men. They beat you to a pulp and then give you a Band-Aid.

There is something feminine about him, which may explain why he is a doctor.

The two men look at each other. Dainville is an intelligent man, he is sensitive.

"O.K.," Camille says calmly. "Now let's talk about how we make this work in practice."

10.45 a.m.
"They don't need to operate."

It takes a second or two for Camille to absorb what Anne has said. He would like to whoop with joy, but instead he decides to be circumspect.

"That's good . . ." he says encouragingly.

The X-rays and the M.R.I. scan have confirmed what the young house doctor told him. Anne will need reconstructive dental surgery, but her other injuries will heal with time. She may be left with some scarring around her lips and on her left cheek. What does he mean, "some scarring"? Will there be several scars, will they be conspicuous? Anne has studied her face in the mirror; her lips are so badly split that it is too early to tell what will permanently scar and what will fade. As for the gash on her cheek, until the stitches are removed, it is impossible to assess the long-term damage.

"We need to give it time," the house doctor said.

From Anne's face, it is clear she does not believe this. And time is precisely what Camille does not have.

He has come this morning to deliver a message. The two of them are alone. He pauses for a second and then says:

"I'm hoping you'll be able to recognise the men . . ."

Anne gives a vague shrug that could mean many things.

"The man who fired the shots, you said he was tall . . . What did he look like?"

It is ridiculous to try to get her to answer questions. The investigating officers will have to start again from scratch; for Camille to persist now may even be counter-productive.

"Handsome." She enunciates carefully.

"What . . . ? What do you mean, 'handsome'?" Camille splutters.

Anne looks around. Camille cannot believe his eyes as she gives what can only be called a faint smile, her lips curling back to reveal three broken teeth.

"Handsome . . . like you . . ."

In the long months while he watched Armand dying, Camille experienced something like this many times: the least flicker of improvement turned the dial to unbridled optimism. Anne has made a joke. Camille almost feels like rushing down to reception to insist that she be discharged. Hope is a dirty trick.

He would like to laugh too, but she has caught him unawares. He stammers. Anne has already let her eyes close again. At least he knows that she is lucid, that she understands what he is saying. He is about to try again when he is interrupted by Anne's mobile phone vibrating on the nightstand. Camille passes it to her. It is Nathan.

"I don't want you to worry . . ." she tells her brother, squeezing her eyes shut. She immediately takes on the role of the long-suffering elder sister, weary yet forbearing. Camille can just make out Nathan's voice, panicked and insistent.

"I said all there was to say in my message . . ." Anne is making a much greater effort to speak normally than she has with Camille. She needs to make herself understood, but mostly she needs to calm her brother, to reassure him.

"No, there's no news," she says, her tone almost cheerful. "And I'm not on my own, so you don't need to worry."

She rolls her eyes and looks at Camille. Nathan sounds a little tiresome.

"No, of course not! Listen, I have to go for an X-ray, I'll call you. Yes, love you too . . ."

With a sigh, she turns her mobile off and hands it back to Camille. He makes the most of this moment of intimacy, he does not have long. He has one thing he needs to say.

"Anne . . . I shouldn't be involved with your case, you understand what I'm saying?"

She understands. She nods and gives a soft "Uh-huh".

"You sure you understand?"

Uh-huh. Uh-huh. Camille lets out a breath, releases the pressure, for himself, for her, for them both.

"I got a bit ahead of myself. And then . . ."

He holds her hand, strokes her fingers. His hand, though smaller, is manly and with pronounced veins. Camille has always had warm hands. He fumbles frantically for words, any words that will not leave her terrified.

Avoid saying: the scumbag who beat you is a vicious thug called Vincent Hafner, he tried to kill you and I'm sure he'll try again.

Say rather: I'm here, you'll be safe now.

Don't say: my superior officers don't believe me, but I know I'm right, the guy's a madman, he's utterly fearless.

Better to say: we'll have this guy in custody soon and this will all be over. But we need you to help us identify him. If you can.

Don't say: they're putting a uniformed officer outside the door for the day, but I can tell you now it's a waste of time because as long as this guy is on the loose, you're in danger. He'll stop at nothing.

Make no mention of the guys who broke into her apartment, the stolen papers, the determined efforts they have made to track her down. Or the fact that the resources at Camille's disposal are almost non-existent. Which, in large part, is his fault.

Say: everything will be fine, don't worry.

"I know . . ."

"You will help me, won't you, Anne? You will help?"

She nods.

"And don't tell anyone we know each other, alright?"

Anne agrees, and yet there is a wary look in her eyes. An uneasy silence hangs over them.

"The *gendarme* outside my room, why is he here?"

She spotted him in the corridor as Camille came in. He raises his eyebrows. Camille either lies with consummate ease or he babbles shamefacedly like an eight-year-old. He can shift from best to worst in a breath.

"I . . ."

A single syllable is enough. For someone like Anne, even this syllable is superfluous. From the flicker of hesitation in his eyes, she knows.

"You think he'll come here?"

Camille has no time to react.

"Are you hiding something from me?"

Camille hesitates for a second and by the time he is ready to answer, Anne knows that she is right. She stares intently at him. In this moment when they should be supporting one another, he feels utterly helpless. Anne shakes her head, she seems to be wondering what will happen to her.

"He's already been here?"

"Honestly, I don't know."

This is not the response of a man who honestly does not know. Anne's shoulders begin to shake, and then her arms, blood drains from her face, she looks towards the door, glances around the room as though she has been told that this is the last place she will ever see. Imagine being shown your own death bed. Ham-fisted as ever, Camille adds to the confusion.

"You're safe here."

The words are like an insult.

She turns towards the window and starts to cry.

The most important thing now is that she gets some rest, builds up her strength, it is on this that Camille focuses all of his energy. If she does not recognise anyone in the photographs, the investigation will go off a cliff. But if she can give them a thread, a single thread, Camille feels confident he can find his way through the maze.

And deal with this. Quickly.

He feels dizzy, as though he had been drinking, he feels a crackling in his skin, the world seems to be reeling.

What has he got himself into?

How will it end?

12.00 noon

The officer from *identité judiciaire* is Polish; some call him Krystoviak, others Kristowiak; Camille is the only one who can correctly pronounce it: Krysztofiak. He has bushy sideburns and looks like an ageing rockstar. He carries his equipment in an aluminium flight case.

Dr Dainville has given them one hour, assuming it might stretch to two. Camille knows it will take four. Krysztofiak, who has conducted thousands of photo line-ups as a forensic officer, knows it could take six hours. Spread over two days.

In his folder are thousands of mugshots from which he has to make a careful selection. The objective is not to show the witness too many since, after a while, faces begin to merge and the whole process becomes pointless. Buried among hundreds of pictures is Vincent Hafner and three of his known accomplices together with photographs of everyone in the police database of Serbian origin.

He leans over Anne.

"*Bonjour, madame . . .*"

He has a nice voice. Gentle. His movements are slow, precise, reassuring. Her face still swollen, Anne is sitting up in bed, propped up on pillows. She has had one hour's sleep. To show willing, she gives a faint smile, careful not to part her lips and show her shattered teeth. As he opens his aluminium flight case and lays out various files, Krysztofiak reels off the usual pat phrases. He has had lots of time to polish this routine.

"It could be all over quickly. You never know, sometimes we get lucky."

He flashes a broad, encouraging smile. He always tries to bring a light touch to the procedure because when he is called on to present a photo array it is usually because someone has been beaten or has witnessed a sudden, savage attack, the woman may have been raped or may have seen someone being murdered, so the atmosphere, unsurprisingly, is rarely relaxed.

"But sometimes . . ." he goes on, his tone serious and measured, ". . . sometimes it takes time. So if you start to feel tired, just tell me, O.K. ? We're in no rush . . ."

Anne nods. Her troubled eyes seek out Camille; she understands. She nods again.

This is the signal.

"O.K.," Krysztofiak says, "let me explain how this works."

12.15 p.m.

Suddenly, though he is no mood for such things, Camille tries to think of a joke, of one of Commissaire Michard's idiocies, anything but the serious matter at hand. The *gendarme* sent to stand guard is the same one Camille met yesterday at the Galerie Monier, the tall, raw-boned man, his eyes ringed with blue circles like something that has just crawled from the grave. If he were superstitious, Camille would see this as a bad omen. And he is superstitious, he knocks on wood, throws salt over his shoulder, he is petrified by signs and omens and when he sees this hulking zombie standing guard at Anne's door, he finds it hard to remain calm.

The *gendarme* makes to salute, but Camille stops him.

"Verhœven," he introduces himself.

"*Commandant!*" the officer replies, proffering a cold, skeletal hand.

About six foot one, Camille reckons. And organised. He has already commandeered the most comfortable chair from the waiting room and brought it out into the hall. Next to him, against the wall, is a small blue knapsack. His wife probably gives him sandwiches and a flask of coffee. But what Camille notices is the smell of cigarette smoke. If this were 8.00 p.m. rather than noon, Camille would send him packing on the spot. Because the first time he pops downstairs for a crafty cigarette, someone will be watching, timing this little ritual; the second time, the killer will confirm his schedule, the third time he has only to wait until the *gendarme* emerges before he can sneak into Anne's room and blast her. Michard has sent the biggest officer, but he may also be the dumbest. Right now, it is not much of a problem since even Camille cannot imagine the killer coming back so soon, and certainly not in broad daylight.

The night shift will be critical and he will deal with that when the time comes. Even so, Camille issues a warning.

"You don't move from that spot, is that understood?"

"No problem, *commandant!*" the *gendarme* says cheerfully.

The sort of response that makes your blood run cold.

12.45 p.m.

At the far end of the corridor is a small waiting room which is permanently deserted. It is in an impractical location and Camille cannot help but wonder why it is there at all. Florence, the charge nurse who wants to kiss life full on the lips, explains that there were plans to turn it into an office, but they were vetoed. There are regulations, apparently, so the waiting room is still there, useless. Those are the rules. It's something to do with Europe. And so, since there is a shortage of space, the staff use it to store supplies. Whenever there is a security inspection, everything is piled onto trolleys and taken down to the basement only to be brought up again afterwards. The security inspectors are happy and duly rubber-stamp the form.

Camille pushes piles of boxes back against the wall, pulls two chairs up next to the coffee table. Here, he sits down with Louis (charcoal grey suit by Cifonelli, white shirt by Swann & Oscar, shoes by Massaro, everything made to measure. Louis is the only officer at the *brigade criminelle* who wears his annual salary to work). Louis brings Verhœven up to speed on their current cases: the German tourist's death was suicide; the driver in the road-rage incident has been identified, he is on the run, but they will track him down within a day or two; the 71-year-old killer who has confessed, he was jealous. Having dealt with this, Camille comes back to what is really worrying him.

"If Madame Forestier identifies Hafner as—" Louis begins.

"Even if she doesn't identify him," Camille interrupts, "that doesn't mean it's not him."

Louis takes a breath. His boss is not quick-tempered by nature. There is something not right about this case. And it will not be easy to tell him that everyone has worked out what it is . . .

"Of course," Louis agrees, "even if she can't pick him out of the line-up, it could still be Hafner. The fact remains that he has disappeared off the face of the earth. I've been in touch with the officers who dealt with the raid last January – who, by the way, would like to know why this case wasn't assigned to them . . ."

Camille makes a sweeping gesture, he could not give a damn.

"No-one knows where Hafner has been since January. Oh, there are rumours – that he skipped the country or that he's on the Riviera. With a murder charge hanging over him, and given his age, it's hardly surprising that he would go to ground, but even those closest to him don't seem to know anything . . ."

". . . don't seem to know?"

"Yes. That was my first thought. Someone must know something. People don't just disappear overnight. What is really surprising is him doing a job now. You would have thought he'd want to stay in hiding."

"Any potential leaks?"

The question of information is wide open. Small-time crooks holding up shops are two a penny, but genuine professionals only do a job when they have solid information, when the expected haul is worth the effort if things go wrong. And the source of that information provides the first line of inquiry for the police. In the case of the Galerie Monier, the girl who turned up late for work has been eliminated as a suspect. And therefore it stands to reason . . .

"We will have to ask Madame Forestier what she was doing at the Galerie Monier," Camille says.

The question will be asked as a matter of form, knowing he is unlikely to get an answer. Camille will ask the question because he has to, because under normal circumstances, this would be his next question. He knows very little about Anne's timetable, he does not know which days she spends in Paris, he barely registers her trips, her meetings, he is happy just to know that he will see her tonight, or tomorrow night – the day after tomorrow is anybody's guess.

But Louis Mariani is a first-rate officer. Meticulous, intelligent, more cultured than he needs to be, intuitive and . . . and suspicious. Bravo. One of the cardinal virtues of a good officer.

For example, when Commissaire Michard questions whether Hafner was in Anne's hospital room, she is simply sceptical, but when she asks Camille what the hell he is playing at and demands his daily report, she is suspicious. And when Camille wonders whether Anne might have seen something important apart from the faces of the robbers, he is suspicious.

And when Louis is dealing with a case in which a woman was attacked during the course of a robbery, he asks himself why she was in that particular place at that particular time. On a day when she should have been at work. Just as the shops were opening up. When there would have been few passers-by and no customers except her. He could have asked the question himself, but for some unexplained reason Verhœven is the only officer who has questioned the woman. As though she were spoken for.

And so Louis did not question her directly. He found an indirect approach.

Camille has raised the issue, protocol has been respected and he is about to move on to the next point when he is distracted by Louis bending down and rummaging for something in his briefcase. He takes out a piece of paper. For a little while now, Louis has taken to wearing reading glasses. Presbyopia usually doesn't develop until later, Camille thinks. But then again, how old is Louis? It is a little like having a son, he can never quite remember his age, he asks the question at least three times a year.

Louis holds up a photocopy bearing the letterhead of Desfossés Jewellers. Camille puts on his own glasses and reads "Anne Forestier". It is a copy of an order for a luxury watch, eight hundred euros.

"Madame Forestier was there to pick up something she ordered ten days ago."

The jeweller asked for ten days to complete the engraving. The text to be engraved has been noted down in block capitals to avoid making a mistake on such an expensive gift . . . Just imagine the customer's face if a name were misspelled. In fact, Madame Forestier was asked to write it out herself so there could be no arguments if there was a problem later. Camille recognises Anne's large, graceful hand.

The name to be engraved on the watch: *Camille*.

Silence.

Both men take off their glasses and the synchronicity serves only to heighten their embarrassment. Camille does not look up, he gently pushes the photocopy across the table to Louis.

"She . . . she's a friend."

Louis nods. A friend. Fine.

"A close friend."

A close friend. Fine. Louis realises that he is playing catch-up. That he has missed several episodes in Camille Verhœven's life. As quickly as he can, he reviews the extent of his lacuna.

He thinks back to four years ago: he knew Irène, they got along, Irène called him "*mon petit Loulou*" and made him blush by asking questions about his sex life. After Irène's death came the psychiatric clinic, where Louis visited regularly until Camille said he would rather be alone. For a time, they saw each other only from a distance. It took Le Guen's most Machiavellian machinations to force Camille, two years later, to rejoin the serious crime squad investigating murders, kidnappings . . . and Camille asked that Louis be reassigned to his team. Louis has no idea what had been going on in Verhœven's private life since his time in the clinic.

But in the life of a man as punctilious as Camille, the sudden appearance of a woman should be obvious from countless little details, differences in behaviour, changes in routine, precisely the sort of things Louis generally notices. And yet he saw nothing, sensed nothing. Until today, he would have dismissed the notion of there being a woman in Verhœven's life as idle speculation, because in the life of a widower who is by nature a depressive, a serious romantic relationship would be a seismic event. And yet this feverishness, this exaltation today . . . There is something contradictory about it that Louis cannot quite grasp.

Louis stares at his glasses on the coffee table as though somehow they might help him see the situation more clearly: so, Camille has a "close friend", her name is Anne Forestier. Camille clears his throat.

"I'm not asking you to get involved, Louis. I'm up to my neck right now and I don't need anyone to remind me that what I'm doing is against regulations, that's my business and nobody else's. And I wouldn't ask you to take that kind of risk, Louis. [He looks at his assistant.] All I'm asking for is a little time. [Silence.] I need to close this thing down, and fast. Before Michard finds out that I lied in order to have a case involving someone very close to me assigned to my team. If we can arrest these guys quickly, none of that will matter. Or at least it can be dealt with. But if we don't, if the case drags on and this thing comes out . . . well, you know what Michard's like, there'll be hell to pay. And there's no reason for you to have to pay it too."

Louis is lost in thought, he does not seem to be here, he glances around him as though expecting a waiter to come and take his order. Finally, he gives a sad smile and nods towards the photocopy.

"Well, this isn't going to help the investigation much, is it?" he says. His tone is that of a man who thought he had discovered treasure only to be deeply disappointed. "I mean, Camille is a pretty common name. There's no way of even knowing if it refers to a man or a woman . . ."

And when Camille does not respond:

"What do you want us to do with it?"

He fiddles with the knot on his tie.

Pushes his hair back with his left hand.

He gets to his feet, leaving the piece of paper on the table. Camille picks it up, crumples it into a ball and stuffs it into his pocket.

1.15 p.m.

The officer from *identité judiciaire* has just packed away his things and left.

"Thank you, Madame Forestier, I think we did some good work," he said as he went. It is what he always says, regardless of the result.

Despite the fact that it makes her dizzy, Anne got out of bed and went into the bathroom. She cannot resist the temptation to look, to survey the extent of the damage. Now that the bandages around her head have been removed, she can see only her short, lank hair and the twin shaved patches where she needed stitches. Like holes in her head. There are more stitches along her jawline. Her face seems even more swollen today. It's normal, they tell her over and over, the swelling is always worse in the first few days, she knows, she's been told, but no-one told her what it would actually look like. She has swollen up like a balloon, her face has the flushed complexion of an alcoholic. A battered woman looks a little like a bag lady. Anne feels a fierce sense of injustice.

She brings her fingertips to her cheeks, feels a dull, diffuse, insidious pain that seems rooted there for ever.

And her teeth, my God, it gives her a pitiful air, she does not know why; it is like having a mastectomy, she thinks, she feels utterly violated. She is no longer herself, no longer whole, she will have to have dental implants, she will never recover from this ordeal.

Now, here she is. She has just spent hours reviewing dozens of photographs. She did as she was asked, she was meek, obedient, unemotional, when she recognised the man, she pointed with her index finger.

Him.

How will it end?

By himself, Camille cannot protect her. Who else can she count on, given that this man is determined to kill her?

He probably wants this ordeal to be over. Just as she does. They both, in their different ways, want it to end.

Anne wipes away her tears. She looks around for some tissues. Blowing your nose is a delicate affair when it is broken.

1.20 p.m.

Given my experience, I almost always end up getting what I want. Right now, I've had to resort to drastic measures, partly because I'm in a hurry, but partly because it's in my nature. That's just how I am: impatient, impetuous.

I need money, and I don't fancy losing all the loot I've sweated blood to earn. I like to think of it as a pension fund, but a little more secure. And I'm not about to let anyone siphon off my future prospects.

So, I redouble my efforts.

Having reconnoitred every inch of the area on foot, then in the car, then a second time on foot, I spend twenty minutes watching. Not a living soul. I take another ten minutes and survey the area using binoculars. I send a text message confirming my arrival, then walk quickly past the disused factory towards the van, open the rear door, climb in and slam it behind me.

The van is parked in an industrial wasteland. I don't know how the guy always manages to find places like this – he should be a location scout for the movies rather than an arms dealer.

The inside of the van is as well ordered as the mind of a computer analyst: everything is in its place.

My fence subbed me a small advance, pretty much the most he could give under the circumstances. At the sort of interest rate that should earn him a bullet between the eyes, but I don't have a choice, I need this thing settled right now. I have temporarily set aside the Mossberg in favour of .308 calibre M40 semi-automatic sniper rifle that takes six rounds. Everything is in the case: silencer, Schmidt & Bender telescopic sights, two boxes of ammunition for a clean, accurate, long-range kill. As a handgun, I opt for a 10-shot Walther P99 compact equipped with an astonishingly effective silencer. Lastly, I get a 6" Buck Special hunting knife, which is always useful.

That bitch has already had a sneak preview of my talents.

Now, I'm going to shift things up a gear; she could do with a thrill.

1.30 p.m.

It is Vincent Hafner.

"The witness positively identified him." Krysztofiak has joined

Louis and Camille in the waiting room. "She has an excellent memory."

"Though there was only a short period when she could see their faces . . ." ventures Louis.

"It can be enough, it depends on the circumstances. Some witnesses can stare at a suspect for minutes at a time and be unable to identify them an hour later. Other people, for reasons we don't understand, can accurately recall every detail of a person's features after one glance."

Camille does not react; it is as if they were talking about him. He can glimpse someone in the *métro* and, a month or two months later, make a detailed sketch of every line, every wrinkle.

"Sometimes, witnesses block out memories," Krysztofiak goes on, "but a guy who savagely beats you and fires at you from a car at point-blank range, that's a face people tend to remember."

Neither Camille nor Louis can tell whether this is somehow intended to be funny.

"We narrowed the selection down by age, physical characteristics and so on. She's absolutely certain that it's Hafner."

On his laptop screen, he pulls up a photograph, a tall man of about sixty, a full-length shot taken during a previous arrest. Five foot eleven, Camille calculates.

"Six foot, actually," Louis says, leafing through the police record. He who knows Camille's every thought, even when he is saying nothing.

Mentally, Camille merges the man in this photograph with the armed robber at the Galerie, picturing him in a balaclava, raising the shotgun, aiming, firing; he pictures him moments earlier, lashing out with the rifle butt at Anne's head, her belly . . . He swallows hard.

The man in the photograph is broad-shouldered, his angular face framed by salt-and-pepper hair, his thin, grey eyebrows accentuate his vacant, staring eyes. An old-school gangster. A thug. Louis notices that his boss' hands are trembling.

"What about the other two?" Louis asks, ever willing to create a diversion.

On the screen, Krysztofiak brings up another mugshot, a bearded guy with bushy eyebrows and dark eyes.

"Madame Forestier hesitated a little on this one. It's understandable, after a while these people all look the same. She looked through several photographs and came back to this one, asked to see some others, but kept coming back to this one. I'd classify it as a strong possibility. Name's Dušan Ravic. He's a Serb."

Camille looks up. They crowd around Louis' laptop as he keys the search into the police database.

"Moved to France in 1997." He quickly scrolls through the document. "A clever guy." He reads at the speed of sound and still manages to synthesise the data. "Arrested twice and released, the charges didn't stick. It's not impossible to imagine him working with Hafner. There are lots of thugs out there, but real professionals are rare and it's a small world."

"So where is this guy?"

Louis makes a vague gesture. There have been no sightings since January, he has completely disappeared, he is facing a felony murder charge for his part in the quadruple robbery and he has the means and the motive to hide out for a long time. It's astonishing that the same gang should show up again so soon. They already have one murder charge on file and they're upping the ante. It's bizarre.

They come back to the subject of Anne.

"How reliable is her testimony?" Louis asks.

"As always, it's a sliding scale. The first hit I'd say is extremely reliable, the second is fairly reliable, if there'd been a third, it would probably have ranked lower still."

Camille can hardly stand still. Louis is deliberately dragging out the conversation, hoping that his boss will regain his composure, but when the forensics officer finally leaves, he realises it was a waste of time.

"I have to find these guys," Camille says, calmly placing his hands flat on the table. "I have to find them now."

It is an emotional reflex. Louis nods automatically, but he wonders what is fuelling the blind rage.

Camille stares at the two mugshots.

"This guy" – he nods to the picture of Hafner – "we need to track him down first. He's the real danger. I'll take care of it."

He says these words with such single-mindedness that Louis, who knows him all too well, can sense the looming catastrophe.

"Listen . . ." he begins.

"You," Camille cuts him off, "you take care of the Serb. I'll go and see Michard and get the warrants. In the meantime, round up every officer on duty. Put a call in to Jourdan, tell him I'd like him to second the men in his unit. Talk to Hanol too, talk to everyone, I'm going to need a lot of bodies."

Faced with an avalanche of decisions, each more nebulous than the last, Louis pushes back his fringe with his left hand. Camille notices the gesture.

"Just do what I tell you," he says in a low voice. "If there's any flak, I'll take it. You don't have to worry about getti—"

"I'm not worried. It's just that it's easier to carry out orders when you understand them."

"You understand exactly what I'm saying, Louis. What else do you want to know?"

Camille's voice has dropped so low that Louis has to strain to hear. He lays a warm hand on that of his assistant. "I can't fuck this up . . . do you understand?" He is upset, but remains composed. "So we need to shake the tree."

Louis gives a nod that means: O.K., I'm not sure I completely understand, but I'll do what you've asked.

"The informers, the pimps, the whores, everyone – but I want you to start with the illegals."

The "illegals" refers to the undocumented workers on file to whom the police turn a blind eye because they are the best possible source of information about anything and everything. Talk or take a plane home is a particularly productive threat. If the Serb still has any ties to the community – and he would not last long without them – then tracking him down will take a matter of hours, not days. He was involved in a spectacular raid less than forty-eight hours ago . . . If he did not leave France with a murder charge and four robberies hanging over him, he must have very good reasons to be here.

Louis pushes back his fringe – right hand.

"I need you to get the team sorted as a matter of urgency," Camille says. "As soon as I get the green light, I'll call. I'll join you as soon as I can, but in the meantime, you can get me on my mobile."

2.00 p.m.
Camille is sitting in front of his computer screen.

Police file: Vincent Hafner.

Sixty years old. Almost fourteen years behind bars on various charges. As a young man, he dabbles in all sorts of things (burglary, extortion, pimping), but in 1972, at the age of twenty-five, he finds his true vocation. An armed raid on an armoured van in Puteaux. The raid gets a little messy, the police show up, one man is wounded. He is sentenced to eight years, he serves five, and learns from his experience: he has found a profession he really likes. His only mistake was carelessness, he is determined not to be caught again. Things do not quite work out as planned, he is arrested on a number of occasions, but the sentences are minor, two years here, three years there. Overall, a pretty successful career.

Since 1985, there have been no arrests. In his mature years, Hafner is at the peak of his powers. He is a suspect in eleven separate hold-ups, but is never arrested, never even questioned, there is no evidence, in every single case he has a cast-iron alibi and reliable witnesses. An artist.

Hafner is a major crime boss, and as his record confirms, he is not to be trifled with. He is intelligent and informed, his jobs are meticulously planned, but when his team go in, they go in hard. Bystanders are assaulted, beaten, battered, often with lasting consequences. No deaths, but no shortage of walking wounded. Hafner leaves a trail of victims hobbling, shambling, limping, to say nothing of scarred faces and years of physiotherapy. It is a simple technique: you earn respect by beating the shit out of the first person on the scene, the others get the message and after that everything runs like clockwork.

The first person on the scene yesterday was Anne Forestier.

The Galerie Monier raid fits neatly with Hafner's profile. Camille doodles the man's face in the margin of his notebook as he scrolls through the interviews from previous offences.

147

For several years, Hafner drew his accomplices from a small pool of about a dozen men, choosing on the basis of their talents and their availability. Camille quickly calculates that at any given point, on average three of them will be in jail, on remand or on parole. Hafner, for his part, manages to emerge unscathed. Crime is like any business: reliable, proficient workers are difficult to come by. But turnover is even higher in the armed robbery business since these are skilled craftsmen. In the space of a few years, at least six former members of Hafner's gang are put out of commission. Two get life sentences for murder, two are shot dead (twins, they stuck with each other to the end), the fifth is in a wheelchair after a motorcycle accident and the sixth is reported missing after a Cessna goes down off the Corsican coast. It is a serious blow for Hafner. For some time afterwards, he is implicated in no new cases. People begin to draw the logical conclusion: Hafner, who must surely have put a lot of money aside, has finally retired and the staff and customers of jeweller's all over France can light a candle to their patron saint.

Consequently, the quadruple raid in January came as a shock. Especially since, in Hafner's career, the size and scale of those raids were an anomaly. Armed robbers rarely indulge in assembly-line work. The physical force and nervous energy required for even a single raid is difficult to imagine, especially given the brutal, strong-arm methods employed by Hafner. Every last detail is planned to allow for all eventualities, so in order to rob four jeweller's in a single day one would have to be certain that each target was primed, that the distances between them were feasible, that . . . So many things needed to go without a hitch that it is hardly surprising that it went as badly wrong as it did.

Camille scrolls through the photographs of the victims.

First, the woman at the second raid in January. The assistant at the jeweller's on the rue de Rennes is a girl of about twenty-five. Her face after her encounter with these consummate professionals is so badly disfigured that . . . Next to her, Anne looks like a blushing bride. The girl spent four days in a coma.

The man injured during the third robbery. A customer. Though it hardly seems so from the photograph. He looks more like a victim of trench warfare than a customer of the Louvre des Antiquaires. His medical file indicates "critical condition". Anyone seeing his mutilated face (like Anne, he was beaten with a rifle butt) would be forced to agree: his condition is critical.

The last victim. He is lying in a pool of blood on the floor of the jeweller's on the rue de Sèvres. Neater, in a way: two bullets in the chest.

This is another anomaly in Hafner's career. Up until now, not one of his victims had died. The difference this time is that he cannot rely on his old gang, he has to put together a team from whoever is available. He went with the Serbs. Not an inspired choice. Serbs are fearless, but they're volatile.

Camille looks down at his notepad. In the middle, Vincent Hafner, a portrait drawn from one of his mugshots and around it, deft sketches of the victims. The most striking is the sketch, drawn from memory, of Anne's face as he saw it when he first came into her hospital room.

Camille tears out the page, crumples it into a ball and tosses it into the wastebasket. He jots down a single word that summarises his analysis of the situation.

"Critical."

Because Hafner does not come out of retirement in January and cobble together a makeshift team unless there is an overwhelming motive. Aside from the need for money, it is difficult to guess what that might be.

Critical, because Hafner does not simply slip back into his old ways. To maximise his profits, he takes the risk of staging a quadruple robbery with uncertain results.

Critical, because despite a huge haul in January – his share would have amounted to €200,000–€300,000 – six months later, he is back at work. The Hafner Comeback Tour. And if the haul this time was less than he expected, he will come back for another encore. There are innocent people out there living on borrowed time. Better to catch him first.

Anybody would realise there is something fishy about this whole affair. Though he cannot put his finger on it, Camille knows there is something amiss, something not quite right. He is hard-headed enough to know that a man like Hafner will be difficult to catch and that, right now, the most sensible approach is to track down his accomplice, Ravic, in the hope that they can flip him and get a lead on Hafner.

And if Anne is to survive, they need it to be a good lead.

2.15 p.m.

"And you feel this is . . . relevant?" Juge Pereira's voice on the other end of the line sounds suspicious. "It sounds to me like you want permission to conduct a mass round-up."

"Absolutely not, *monsieur le juge*, there will be no mass round-up."

Camille is tempted to laugh, but he stops himself: the examining magistrate is too shrewd to fall for such a ruse. But he is also too busy to question the methods of an experienced police officer who claims to have a solution.

"On the contrary," Camille argues, "it will be a carefully targeted operation, *monsieur le juge*. We have identified three or four known associates that Ravic might have approached for help while he was on the run after the January raid, we just need permission to shake the tree, that's all."

"What does Commissaire Michard have to say?"

"She agrees with me," Camille says with an air of finality.

He has not yet spoken to the *commissaire divisionnaire*, but he can predict how she will react. It is the oldest bureaucratic trick in the book: tell X that Y has already approved a course of action and vice versa. Like so many hackneyed ploys, it is very effective. In fact, when carefully executed, it is almost unassailable.

"Very well then, *commandant*, do as you see fit."

2.40 p.m.

The fat *gendarme* is staring at his mobile, engrossed in his game of solitaire, when he realises the person who just walked past is the woman he is supposed to be guarding. He scrabbles to his feet and runs after her shouting "Madame!" – he has forgotten her name – "Madame!" She does not turn, but pauses as she walks past the nurses' station.

"I'm going now."

It sounds casual, like saying "Bye, see you tomorrow". The big *gendarme* quickens his pace, raises his voice.

"Madame . . . !"

The young nurse with the ring through her lip is on duty. The nurse who thought she might have seen a shotgun but in the end decided that she hadn't, but then again . . . She rushes from behind the desk, past the *gendarme*, determined to take charge. She was taught to be firm in nursing school, but six months working in a hospital and she has learned to cope with anything.

As she draws level with Anne, she gently takes her arm. Anne, who has been expecting something of the sort, turns to face her. For the nurse, it is the patient's single-minded determination that makes this a delicate situation. For Anne, it is the young nurse's calm persuasiveness that complicates matters. She looks at the lip ring, the shaven head, there is a gentleness, a fragility to the girl, her face is utterly ordinary, but her big puppy-dog eyes could melt the hardest heart, and she knows how to use them.

There is no direct refusal, no warning, no lecture; the nurse takes a different tack.

"If you want to discharge yourself, I need to take out your stitches."

Anne brings her hand up to her cheek.

"No," the nurse says, "not those, it's too soon. I meant these two here."

She reaches up and gently runs her fingers over the shaved patch on Anne's head, her expression is professional, but she smiles and, assuming that this is now agreed, she leads Anne back towards her room. The *gendarme* stands aside, wondering whether or not to tell his superiors about this development, then follows the two women.

Just opposite the nurses' station, they step into a small treatment room used for outpatients.

"Take a seat . . ." As she looks around for her instruments, the nurse is gently insistent. "Please, take a seat."

Standing outside in the corridor, the *gendarme* discreetly looks away as though the two women were in the toilets.

"Shhhh . . ."

Anne flinched, though the young nurse's fingertips have barely grazed the wound.

"Is it painful?" She sounds concerned. "That's a little unusual. What if I press here? And here? I think it might be best to wait before removing the stitches, consult the doctor, he might want to get another X-ray. Are you running a temperature?"

She presses a hand to Anne's forehead.

"No headache?"

Anne realises that she is now precisely where the nurse wanted her to be: sitting meekly in a treatment room, ready to be taken back to her room. And so she bridles.

"No, no doctors, no X-rays, I'm leaving," she says, getting to her feet.

The *gendarme* outside reaches for his police radio; however this plays out, he needs to call in to ask for instructions. If the killer suddenly appeared at the far end of the hallway, armed to the teeth, he would do the same thing.

"That really wouldn't be wise," the nurse is saying, sounding concerned. "If there's an infection . . ."

Anne does not know what to think, whether there genuinely is a problem or whether the nurse is simply saying this to alarm her.

"Oh, that reminds me . . . [The nurse abruptly changes the subject.] We never did get your admission form filled in, did we? You asked someone to bring in your medical papers? I'll make sure a doctor sees you right now, and that the X-ray is done immediately so you can leave as soon as possible."

Her tone is honest, conciliatory, what she is proposing sounds like the best, the most reasonable solution.

Anne, by now exhausted, agrees and slowly trudges back towards her room, feeling as though she is about to faint, she tires so quickly. But she is thinking about something else, something she has just remembered. She stops, turns.

"You're the nurse who saw the man with the gun?"

"I saw a man," the girl snaps back, "not a gun."

She has been expecting this question. The answer is a formality. From the moment negotiations began, she could tell that the patient was scared witless. She is not trying to leave, she is trying to escape.

"If I'd seen a gun, I would have said so. And if I had, I'm guessing you wouldn't be here, right?"

Though young, she is extremely professional. Anne does not believe a word.

"No," she says, staring intently at the nurse as though she can read her mind, "you're just not sure what you saw, that's all."

Even so, she goes back to her room, her head is spinning, she overestimated her strength, she is completely drained, she needs to lie down. To sleep.

The nurse closes the door. Pensive. What could it have been, that long, bulky thing the guy had under his coat?

2.45 p.m.

Commissaire Michard spends most of her time in meetings. Camille has consulted her diary, an uninterrupted series of appointments back-to-back: it is the perfect opportunity. In the space of an hour, he leaves seven messages on her voicemail. Important. Serious. Urgent. Critical. In the messages, he all but exhausts the glossary of emergency-related clichés, piles on as much pressure as he can, when she calls back he is expecting her to be belligerent. Instead, the *commissaire*'s tone is patient and considered. She is even more shrewd than she appears. On the telephone, she whispers, she has clearly stepped into a hallway for a moment. "And the magistrate has signed off on this police round-up?"

"Absolutely," Camille insists, "precisely because it's not a 'round-up' in the strictest sense, we're look—"

"Precisely how many targets *are* you looking at, *commandant*?"

"Three. But you know how it is, one target can lead to another. Strike while the iron is hot and so forth."

When Camille resorts to a proverb, it means he has run out of arguments.

"Ah yes, the 'iron' . . ." the *commissaire* says wistfully.

"I'm going to need a few bodies."

In the end, everything comes down to resources. Michard lets out a long sigh. What is most frequently requested is always what is not available.

"Not for long, three, four hours, max."

"To bring in three targets?"

"No, to . . ."

"Yeah, to strike the proverbial iron, I get it, *commandant*. But aren't you worried about the effects of going in mob-handed?"

Michard knows how these things work, the bigger the operation the greater the chance the target will get wind of it and do a runner, the longer the search goes on, the more the chances of apprehending the suspect diminish.

"That's why I need more men."

The exchange could go on for hours. In fact, the *commissaire* doesn't give a damn if Verhœven wants to stage a round-up. Her strategy is simply to stand her ground long enough so that if the operation goes pear-shaped she can say "I told you so".

"Well, if the *juge* has signed off on it . . ." she says at last. "Sort it out with your colleagues. If you can."

*

Being an armed robber is like being an actor; you spend most of your time hanging around on set and do a day's work in a few minutes.

So here I am, waiting. Scheming, anticipating, calling on all my experience.

If the witness is strong enough to face it, the police are bound to have her do a line-up. If not today, then tomorrow, it's only a matter of hours. They'll go through a raft of mugshots and if she's a solid citizen and has even the vaguest memory, they'll be on the warpath. Right now, their best option would be to hunt down Ravic. That's what I would do in their shoes. Since it's the easiest and often the most effective method, they'll set up traps in corridors, break down a few doors. You make a lot of noise, use a little intimidation – it's the oldest trick in the police handbook.

And the place to start would be Luka's Bistro on the rue de Tanger, the principal stomping ground of the Serbian criminal fraternity. The goons who hang out at Luka's are tacky, low-rent mobsters who spend their time playing cards, betting on horses, from the stifling clouds of Russian cigarette smoke you'd think a beekeeper was smoking a hive. They pride themselves on being informed. If anything serious goes down, word reaches Luka's Bistro.

3.15 p.m.
Verhœven has given orders to loose the dogs. To get all hands on deck. It seems a little excessive.

Camille capitalises on the *commissaire*'s support to commandeer officers from anywhere he can. As Louis anxiously watches, he puts in calls to other units, calls in favours from colleagues, they let him borrow one man, two men, it is all a little chaotic, but gradually the team begins to swell. None of his colleagues is entirely sure what he is up to, but they don't ask too many questions, Camille makes his case with an air of authority, and besides, this is fun, they get to put flashing lights on unmarked cars and drive through the city like boy racers, shaking down drug dealers, pickpockets, brothel-keepers, pimps – and, in the end, the opportunity to play cops and robbers was part of the reason they joined the force. Camille says the operation will only last a couple of hours. They'll go in hard and fast, then everyone can go home.

Some of his colleagues are undecided: Camille sounds nervous, he is quick to give justifications but offers little in the way of hard evidence. More worryingly, the operation is beginning to sound rather different from how it had appeared originally. They believed they were being asked to assign officers for a series of simultaneous raids to take down three specific targets. What Camille is describing is just as violent, but on a much larger scale.

"Listen," Camille says, "if we catch the guy we're looking for, everybody wins, the top brass will be chuffed, they'll hand out medals to every senior officer. And besides, it's only a couple of hours, if we work fast, you'll be back at your units before your bosses start wondering where you stopped off for a beer."

This is all it takes for his friends to concede and give him the manpower. The officers pile into squad cars, with Camille leading the convoy. Louis stays behind and mans the telephone.

Operation Verhœven is not exactly a model of discretion. But this is precisely the point. An hour later, there is not a single thug in Paris from Zagreb or from Mostar who does not know about the frantic search for Ravic. He has to be hiding out somewhere. They smoke out tunnels and corridors, intimidate the prostitutes, and round up everyone in sight – especially the undocumented immigrants.

This is shock treatment.

Sirens wail, police lights strobe the buildings, a whole street in the 18th arrondissement is cordoned off, three men make a run for it and are caught. Standing by his car, Camille watches the scene as he talks on his mobile to the team ransacking a fleabag hotel in the 20th.

If he thought about it, Camille might even feel nostalgic. There was a time – back in the days of the Serious Crime Squad, of the Brigade Verhœven – when Armand would hole up in his office with case files, filling page after page with hundreds of names from related cases, and emerge two days later with the only two names that could move the investigation forward. Meanwhile, as soon as Louis' back was turned, Maleval would be kicking the arse of anyone who moved, slapping whores and forcing them to strip, and just when you were about to put him on a disciplinary charge, he would plead exigent circumstances and hand over a crucial witness statement that saved three days' work.

But Camille is not thinking about this. He is focused on the job in hand.

In sleazy hotels, he takes the stairs two at a time, flanked by officers who burst into the rooms catching couples *in flagrante*, dragging sheepish husbands with their shrivelled cocks off the beds so they can question the prostitutes beneath them – Dušan Ravic, we're looking for him, for his family, anyone, a cousin will do – but no, the name doesn't ring a bell; they carry on barking questions while the panicked johns scrabble to pull on their trousers, hoping to get out before they're spotted. The girls – half naked, scrawny, their breasts tiny, their hip bones jutting through their skin – have never heard of Ravic. "Dušan?" one of them says as though she has never heard the name before. But they are obviously terrified. "Take them in," Camille says. He needs to create an atmosphere of fear and he does not have much time. A couple of hours. Three, if all goes well.

Several miles north, outside a house in the suburbs, four officers put in a call to Louis to check they have the right address, then kick the door down and go in, armed and ready, toss the place, and come up with 200 grams of cannabis. No-one here has heard of Dušan Ravic. They take the whole family into custody save for the elderly grandparents.

Riding in a screeching car piloted by a boy racer who never drops below fourth gear, Camille keeps his mobile glued to his ear, in constant contact with Louis. Backed up by a barrage of orders and the persistent pressure on the teams, Verhœven's fury is contagious.

In the 14th, three young Kosovars are hauled into the police station. Dušan Ravic? The three boys look blank. We'll see. Meanwhile, rough them up a little so when they're released they can preach the Good News: the police are looking for Ravic.

Camille gets word that two pick-pockets from Požarevac are being held at the commissariat in the 15th arrondissement; he consults Louis who checks his map of Serbia. Požarevac is in the north-east, Ravic is from Elemir in the far north, but you never know. Camille gives the word: bring them in. The object is to spread fear.

Back at the *brigade criminelle*, Louis, perfectly calm, fields the calls, he has a mental map of Paris, he has categorised the neighbourhoods, prioritised those areas with residents likely to provide information.

Someone asks a question, little more than an idle suggestion, Camille thinks for a moment and says yes, and so officers round up the buskers in the *métro* stations, kick them along the platforms and drag them into the waiting police vans while they keep a tight grip on their little cloth bags jingling with change. Dušan Ravic? Blank stares, an officer grabs one of them by the sleeve. Dušan Ravic. The man shakes his head, blinking rapidly. "I want a home delivery on this guy," says Camille who has just come up for air because there is no signal in that part of the *métro* and he needs to know what is happening. He glances anxiously at his watch but says nothing. He is wondering how long it will take before Commissaire Michard comes down on him like a ton of bricks.

About an hour ago, the force descended on Luka's and carted off one guy in three – who knows on what charge, I doubt they know themselves. The point of the exercise is obviously to spread panic. And this is just the beginning. My calculations were spot on: in less than an hour the whole Serbian community will be turned inside out, and the rats will be deserting the ship.

I'd be happy to settle for one rat. Dušan Ravic.

Now that the operation is in full swing, there's no time to lose. I'm there in the time it takes to drive across Paris.

A narrow street, almost an alleyway, between the rue Charpier and the rue Ferdinand-Conseil in the 13th. A building whose ground-floor windows have been bricked up, the original door was "salvaged" long ago, there's no lock, no handle now, no door, only a sheet of rotting plywood that bangs with every gust of wind until someone comes down and wedges it shut, only for it to start banging again as soon as the next person arrives. There's a steady stream of people in this place, junkies, dealers, illegals, whole families of immigrants. I've spent too many days (and quite a few nights) holed up here for one reason or another, I know this street like the back of my hand. I loathe this shithole, I could happily get a couple of kilos of gelignite and blow the street to kingdom come.

This is where I brought that big lunk Dušan Ravic one night last January, while we were preparing the Heist of the Century. When we got to the building, he smiled with those thick red lips of his.

"When I find chick, I take her here."

A "chick" . . . Jesus. No-one has used that word in decades, you'd have to be a Serb.

"A chick," I said. "What chick?"

As I asked the question, I looked around. It didn't take much imagination to work out the kind of girl you could bring back here, where you'd find her and what you could do with her. Ravic is a class act.

"Not *one* chick," Ravic said. He liked to sound like a player. He liked to give details. The actual story was much simpler: this moron bunked down on a flea-ridden mattress in this hovel so he could fuck whatever skanky whores he could afford.

His sex life has obviously taken a nose-dive lately, because Ravic hasn't been here in an age – I should know, I've hidden out here often enough – and I'm sure he wouldn't come back for choice. Chick or no chick, no-one comes here for fun, they come here when they have nowhere else to run. And right now, if I'm lucky and if the cops do their job properly, he'll have to come here.

With the police shaking down the whole Serbian community, Ravic will quickly realise that this shithole is the only place where no-one will come looking for him.

I've unscrewed the silencer and slipped the Walther P99 into the glove compartment, there's just enough time to pop into a café for a drink, but I need to be back here in half an hour, because if Ravic does show up, I want to be the one to welcome him.

It's the least I can do.

There is a big guy in an interrogation room at the commissariat. According to his papers, he is originally from Bujanovac; Louis checks, it's a small town in southern Serbia. Dušan Ravic, his brother, his sister? The cops don't care, any scrap of information is welcome. The big guy doesn't understand the question, someone smacks him across the face. Dušan Ravic? This time he understands, he shakes his head, he doesn't know anyone by that name, the cop smacks him across the head. "Let it go," Camille says, "he doesn't know anything." Fifteen minutes later, back on the street, three Serbs, two of them sisters. It's heartbreaking: they're barely seventeen, they have no papers, they turn tricks at Porte de la Chapelle – without a condom for twice the price – they're all skin and bone. Dušan Ravic? They shake their heads. It doesn't matter, Camille tells them, he will hold them for as long as the law allows; the girls purse their lips, they know the beating their pimp doles out will be proportional to the length of time they are in custody, he can't afford to lose money, the city never sleeps, they should be out walking the streets, the girls start to tremble. Dušan Ravic? They shake their heads again and stare towards the waiting police car. Standing behind them, Camille gives one of the officers a nod: Let them go.

In police stations across the capital there are raised voices in the corridors, those who speak a little French threaten to call the consulate, the embassy, as if that is likely to help them. They can call the Pope himself, maybe he's a Serb.

Louis, his phone still pressed to his ear, gives instructions, keeps Verhœven up to date, coordinates the teams. There are flashing dots on his mental map of the city, especially in the north and the north-east. Louis consolidates, updates, dispatches. Camille climbs back into his car. No sign of Ravic. Not yet.

Are all the women scrawny? No, not really. In the condemned building somewhere in the 11th arrondissement the woman is seriously overweight, thirty-something, at least eight kids bawling in the background, her husband is a stick insect in a string vest, he has a moustache – all the men have moustaches – and though not particularly tall, he stares down at Camille. He goes over to a dresser to get their papers, the family are from Prokuplje; on the other end of the telephone, Louis says it is a town in central Serbia. Dušan Ravic? The man says nothing, he racks his brain, no, honestly: they cart him off, the kids start tugging at his sleeves, tragedy is their stock in trade, an hour from now they'll be out begging somewhere between Saint-Martin church and the rue Blavière carrying a misspelled cardboard sign scrawled in marker pen.

Where information is concerned, the card players at Luka's are as good a source as it gets. They spend their days chewing the fat while their wives slave away, their older daughters are on the game and the others are minding the babies. Seeing Camille show up with three officers, they wearily toss their cards down onto the table – this is the fourth time in a month the police have interrupted their game, but this time, they've got the dwarf with them. Wrapped up in his coat, hat pulled down over his forehead, Camille looks each of them in the eye, the brute determination in his gaze drilling into their retinas, as though the search is somehow personal. Ravic? Sure, they know him, but only vaguely, they look at each other – "You seen him around?" "No, you?"

They give apologetic smiles, they'd like to be able to help, but . . .
"Yeah, right," Camille says, and takes the youngest of them aside, a
gangling figure so tall it looks like Camille chose him deliberately,
which he did since it means he has only to stretch out his hand
to grab the guy by the balls. He looks away as the guy falls to his
knees, howling up in pain. Ravic? If he is not saying anything now,
it's because he doesn't know anything. "Or because his balls have
stopped working," says one of the other officers. The others laugh.
Camille, stone-faced, stalks out of the café. "Bring them all in!"

An hour later, bent double, the officers race down a flight of
steps into a cellar as wide as an aircraft hangar with a ceiling
barely five feet high. Eighty-four sewing machines in serried
ranks, eighty-four illegals. It must be thirty degrees down there,
they are working stripped to the waist, not one of them older than
twenty. Cardboard boxes are stuffed with polo shirts branded
Lacoste, the owner tries to explain, but is cut short. Dušan Ravic?
This particular instance of local craftsmanship is tolerated, the
police turn a blind eye because the owner regularly feeds them
information; this time he screws up his eyes, racks his brain –
hang on a minute, hang on a minute – someone suggests they call
in Commandant Verhœven.

Before Camille arrives, the officers tip out the contents of the
boxes, seize the few identity papers they can find and call Louis,
spelling out surnames while the workers hug the walls as though
trying to disappear into the stone. Twenty minutes later, the heat
in the cellar has become intolerable and the officers have hauled
everyone outside; lined up in the street, the illegals look either
resigned or petrified.

Camille shows up a few minutes later. He is the only one who
does not need to crouch to go down the steps. The owner is from

Zrenjanin in northern Serbia not far from Ravic's village, Elemir. Ravic? "Never heard of him," the man says. "You sure?" Camille insists.

You can tell this is eating him up inside.

4.15 p.m.

I wasn't away very long, too worried I might miss my old friend's arrival. I've spent more than my fair share of time on stakeouts, so I'm not about to make the mistake of sparking up a cigarette or cracking a window to let some air into the car, but if Ravic is planning to show his face, he'd better get a move on, because I'm dead on my feet here.

The cops are moving heaven and earth to track him down, so he's bound to turn up any moment.

Speak of the devil and who do I see rounding the corner? If it isn't my old friend Dušan, I'd know him anywhere, no neck, built like a brick shithouse, feet turned out like a clown.

I'm parked about thirty metres from the doorway, about fifty from the corner where he just appeared. I get a good look at him as he shambles towards me, stopping slightly. I don't know whether he's got a chick back at the henhouse, but Ravic isn't looking too good.

Not exactly cock of the walk.

From the clothes (a shabby duffel coat at least ten years old), and the worn-out shoes, it's obvious he's flat broke.

And that's a bad sign.

Because, by rights, given his share of the haul last January, he should be dressed to kill. When he's got some cash, Ravic's the kind of guy who buys shiny suits, Hawaiian shirts and crocodile shoes. Seeing him dressed like a tramp is worrying.

On the run with a murder charge and four armed robberies on his back, he's been reduced to living by his wits. And if he's been holed up here, he must be on his uppers.

In all probability, he was double-crossed. Just like me. Probably should have seen it coming, but it's pretty demoralising. Just have to suck it up.

Ravic shoves open the plywood door and nearly takes it off its hinges. He was never subtle, in fact you might say he's reckless.

It's because he has a short fuse that we're in this mess, if he hadn't put a couple of 9mm slugs into that jeweller in January . . .

I slink out of the car and get to the door a few seconds behind him, I can hear his lumbering footsteps somewhere to my right. There's no bulb in the hall, so the only patches of light come from the open doors off the corridor. I tiptoe up the stairs after him, first floor, second, third, Jesus the stink in this place, stale piss, hamburgers, weed. I hear him knocking and I wait on the landing below. I suspected there would probably be other people here, which might make the job a little difficult, depending on how many of them there are.

Above me, I hear a door open and close, I creep upstairs, there is a lock, but it's an old model, easily picked. I carefully press my ear against the wood, I hear Ravic's hoarse croak – too many cigarettes. It's a strange feeling, hearing his voice again. It took a lot of effort to track him down, to flush him out.

Ravic doesn't sound happy. There's a lot of crashing and banging coming from the apartment. Eventually, I make out a woman's voice, young, soft-spoken, crying, though not very loudly, whimpering more like. I keep listening. Ravic's voice again. I want to be sure there are only two of them, so I stand there for several minutes listening to my heart pounding. O.K., I'm pretty sure there's just two of them. I pull on my cap, carefully tuck my hair under it, slip on a pair of rubber gloves, take out the Walther, rack the slide, shift the gun to my left hand while I pick the lock and shift it back as soon as I hear the last pin click and push the door open. I see the two of them, they have their backs to me, bent over something or other. Sensing someone behind them, they straighten up and turn; the girl is about twenty-five, dark-haired, ugly.

And dead. Because I put a bullet between her eyes, watch them grow wide in surprise as though someone has just offered to pay three times her usual fee, as if she's just seen Santa Claus show up in his underpants.

Ravic immediately reaches for his pocket, I put a bullet in his left ankle, he leaps into the air, hops from one foot to the other like he's on hot bricks, then crumples to the floor with a howl.

Now that we've dealt with the pleasantries, we can get down to more serious discussions.

The apartment is just one room, albeit a very large one, with a kitchenette, a bathroom, but everything about it is dilapidated and the place is filthy.

"Not much of a cleaner, that girl of yours."

At a glance I spotted the coffee table strewn with syringes, spoons, and tinfoil . . . I hope Ravic didn't squander all his cash on smack.

When the 9mm slug hit her, the girl collapsed onto a grubby mattress laid on the floor. The veins in her bony arms are riddled with track marks. I had only to lift her legs and she was laid out on her bier. The jumble of clothes and blankets beneath her was like a patchwork, it looked very original. Her eyes were still open, but her earlier shocked expression is more serene now, she seems to have come to terms with her fate.

Ravic, on the other hand, is still wailing. He is hunkered on the ground, balanced on one buttock, one leg stretched out, reaching towards the shattered ankle pissing blood, babbling "Oh fuck, oh fuck . . ." Nobody gives a shit about noise round here, you can hear T.V.s blaring, couples fighting and probably guys playing the drums at 3 a.m. when they're off their faces . . . But even so, I need my Serbian friend to concentrate, if only so we can talk in peace.

I pistol whip-him with the Walther, one smack straight to the face just to focus his attention on the conversation; he calms down a little, he's still hugging his leg, but he stops yowling and whimpers softly between clenched teeth. It's progress, I suppose, but I'm not sure I can count on him to stay quiet, he's not discreet by nature. I pick a T-shirt off the floor, roll it into a ball and stuff it into his mouth. And to make sure I get some peace, I tie one hand behind his back. With his other hand, he's still trying to staunch his bleeding ankle, but his arm is too short, he bends his leg under him, contorts himself, writhing in pain. Though you wouldn't think it to look at it, the ankle is a very sensitive part of the body, it's full of tiny, fragile bones – simply twisting your ankle on a step can leave you hobbling in pain, but when reduced by a 9mm slug to a bloody pulp of muscle and shattered bone and connected only by a few tendons, it is sheer agony. And seriously incapacitating. In fact, as I put a second bullet into the splintered remains of his ankle, I can tell he is not faking it, he really is in excruciating agony.

"Well, it's probably best that 'chick' of yours is dead, you wouldn't want her seeing you in this state."

Maybe it wasn't true love, but whatever the reason, Ravic doesn't seem bothered about the fate of the girl. He seems to care only about himself. The air in the place is unbreathable, what with the stench of blood and the smell of gunpowder, so I go over and crack open a window. I hope he got a good deal on the rent, the only view is a blank wall.

I come back and crouch over him, the guy is sweating buckets, he can't sit still, he's twisting and turning, clutching his leg with his free hand. His head is bleeding. Despite the gag in his mouth, he manages to drool. I grab him by the hair, it's the only way of getting his attention.

"Now listen up, big boy, I don't plan to spend the whole night here. So I'm going to give you a chance to talk and, for your sake, I hope you're planning to be cooperative because I'm not feeling especially patient right now. I haven't had a wink of sleep in two days, so if you care about me at all, you'll answer my questions and we can all get off to bed, me, you, your chick here, O.K. ?"

Ravic's French was never very good, his conversation is peppered with errors of syntax and vocabulary, so it's important to communicate in a way he understands. Simple words accompanied by persuasive gestures. So, as I carefully choose my words, I plant the hunting knife into the remnants of his ankle, the blade cuts clean through and embeds itself in the floorboard. Probably leaves a hole in the parquet floor, the sort of damage that will cost him when he tries to get his deposit back, but who cares? Ravic manages to scream through the gag, he struggles and squirms like a worm, his free hand fluttering like a butterfly.

I think he understands the seriousness of the situation now, but I give him a moment or two to think about it, to let the information sink in. Then I explain:

"The way I figure it, you and Hafner planned to double-cross me from the start. Like him, you thought that a three-way split was less attractive than sharing the loot between two. And it does make for a bigger share, I'll grant you that."

169

Ravic looks up at me, his eyes are filled with tears – of pain, rather than sorrow – but I can tell I've hit the nail on the head.

"Jesus, you're thick as pigshit, Dušan! You're a fucking moron. Why do you think Hafner picked you? Because you're a moron. Do you get it now?"

He grimaces, his ankle really is giving him grief.

"So, you help Hafner to double-cross me . . . and then he double-crosses you. Which confirms my initial analysis: you're as thick as two short planks."

Ravic does not seem to be overly preoccupied with his I.Q. right now. He is more worried about his health, about keeping count of his limbs. It's a sensible preoccupation because the more I talk the angrier I feel.

"My guess is you didn't go after Hafner – the guy's too dangerous, you weren't about to settle scores with him, you haven't got the balls and you know it. Besides, you had a murder charge hanging over you, so you decided to lie low. But the thing is, I need to find Hafner, so you're going to help me track him down, you're going to tell me everything you know: every detail of your little agreement and everything that happened afterwards, are we clear?"

It sounds like a reasonable proposition to me. I remove the gag, but Ravic's rather volatile temperament gets the better of him and he starts screaming something I can't understand. With his one good hand, he makes a grab for my collar. The guy has a powerful fist, but by some miracle I manage to dodge him. This is what I get for trusting people.

And he spits at me.

Under the circumstances, it's an understandable reaction, but even so, it's a little uncouth.

I realise that I have been going about things the wrong way. I have tried to behave in a civilised fashion, but Ravic is a peasant, such subtle nuances go right over his head. He is in too much pain to put up any serious resistance so I lay him out with a couple of kicks to the head and, while he struggles to remove the knife pinning his leg to the floor, I go to find what I need.

The girl is sprawled across the bed. Never mind. I grab one corner of the filthy duvet and tug hard, sending her rolling onto her stomach, her skirt rucked up, revealing her thin, pasty legs and needle marks on the backs of her knees. Even if I hadn't hurried things along, she was living on borrowed time.

I turn back just as Ravic manages to prise the knife out of his ankle. The guy is strong as an ox.

I put a bullet in his knee and his reaction, if you'll pardon the expression, is explosive. He literally launches his whole body into the air and howls, but before he has time to get his bearings, I manage to turn him over, throw the duvet over him and sit on it. I try to find the best position: I don't want him to suffocate, I need Ravic, but I need him to focus on my questions. And I need him to stop screaming.

I pull his arm towards me. It feels strange, sitting on him as he bucks and bridles like a fairground ride or a rodeo bull. I grab the hunting knife, force his hand flat on the floor, but he's strong. I'm pitching and reeling like a big-game fisherman reeling in a 200-lb marlin.

I start by cutting his little finger off at the second phalanx. Usually, I would take the trouble to make a clean cut at the joint, but such refinements are wasted on Ravic. I simply hack it off, which is irksome to an aesthete like me.

I'm prepared to bet that within fifteen minutes, Ravic will have told me everything I need to know. I continue to ask questions, but this is simply for form's sake: he is not concentrating yet and besides, what with the duvet and me on top of him, to say nothing of his ankle and his knee, he is having trouble stringing a coherent sentence together.

I continue my work, moving on to the index finger – it's incredible how much he struggles – and I think about my visit to the hospital.

Unless I'm very much mistaken, in a few minutes my Serbian friend is going to break the bad news to me. In which case, the only solution is to put pressure on the woman in the hospital. Logically, by now she should be prepared to be cooperative.

I hope so, for her sake.

5.00 p.m.
"Verhœven?"

Not even a courtesy "*commandant*". The *commissaire* is obviously livid. No pleasantries, no extraneous chit-chat. Commissaire Michard has so much to say she does not know where to begin.

"I'm going to need a detailed report . . ." is her first reflex.

Bureaucracy is the last refuge of the uninspired.

"You assured the judge that this was to be a 'targeted operation', you spin me some story about 'three known suspects', then you turn the whole city upside down. Are you deliberately trying to piss me off?"

On the other end of the telephone, Camille opens his mouth to speak, but Michard cuts him off.

"To tell the truth, I don't give a shit. But you're going to stand down your men right now, *commandant*, call off this little show of force, it's a waste of time."

A clusterfuck. Camille closes his eyes. He was on the final sprint, only to be overtaken a few yards from the finishing post. Next to him, thin-lipped, Louis looks away. Camille jerks his thumb to let him know the operation is dead in the water, and waves for him to round up all the officers. Louis immediately begins punching in the numbers on his telephone. From the look on Verhœven's face, he knows how things stand. All around, the other officers hang their heads, feigning disappointment, they will all be bawled out tomorrow, but at least they had some fun. As they head back to their cars, one or two flash a complicit smile, Camille responds with a fatalistic gesture.

The *commissaire divisionnaire* is giving him time to digest the information, but her pause is expressly melodramatic, insidious, pregnant with menace.

Anne is standing in front of the mirror again when one of the nurses appears. Florence, the older nurse. Though she is not exactly old . . . She is probably younger than Anne, but her desperate attempt to look ten years younger prematurely ages her.

"Everything alright?"

Their eyes meet in the mirror. As she records the time on the clipboard at the end of the bed, the nurse flashes her a broad smile. Even with those lips, I'll never be able to smile like that again, thinks Anne.

"Everything alright?"

What a question. Anne does not feel like talking, especially not to Florence. She should never have let herself be persuaded by the other nurse, the young one. She should have walked out of the hospital, she feels in danger. And yet she cannot quite make up her mind, there seem as many reasons to stay as to go.

And then, there is Camille.

The moment she thinks of him, her whole body starts to tremble, he is alone, helpless, he will never manage to do it. And even if he does, it will be too late.

45, rue Jambier. The *commissaire* is already on her way. Camille will meet her there in fifteen minutes.

The Operation Verhœven raids have produced results, though not the ones anticipated. Desperate to be left in peace – to prosper, to live or simply to survive – the whole Serbian community came together to track down Ravic. The search turned out to be child's play. An anonymous tip-off gives his location as 45, rue Jambier. Camille had hoped to find a live body; he is sorely disappointed.

At the first wail of a police siren, every adult in the building disappeared within seconds: there will be no witnesses, no-one to question, no-one who heard or saw anything. Only the children were left behind – there was nothing to fear and everything to gain, since the children will be able to tell them exactly what happened when they get back. Right now, uniformed officers have them corralled out on the pavement. The kids are eager and excited, laughing and catcalling. For children who do not go to school, a double murder constitutes playtime.

Upstairs, the *commissaire* is standing in the doorway of the apartment, hands clasped in front of her as though she were in church. Until the forensic technicians from *identité judiciaire* get here, she will allow only Verhœven inside, no-one else. It is a perfunctory and probably futile precaution, so many men have traipsed through this hovel that the forensics team will probably come up with at least fifty sets of fingerprints, stray hairs and sundry bodily fluids. The crime scene will be documented, but it is merely a question of protocol.

When Camille arrives, the *commissaire* does not turn, she does not even look at him, she simply takes a step into the room, her movements careful and deliberate. Camille follows her footsteps. Silently, each of them begins to detail the scene, to draw up a list of obvious facts. The girl – an addict and a prostitute – died first. Seeing her lying on her belly, turned towards the wall as though she is sulking, it is apparent that the duvet that discreetly covers Ravic's body was jerked out from under her, hurling her against the partition. Were there only her pallid corpse, stiffening now with rigor mortis, there would be little to be said. They have witnessed this scene a hundred times. So many prostitutes die in circumstances such as these: an overdose, a murder. But there is another body which tells a very different story.

The *commissaire* moves slowly, walking around the pool of blood seeping into the grimy floorboards. The ankle, a mass of splintered bone, is attached to the leg by ragged ribbons of skin. Hacked? Slashed? Camille takes out his glasses and hunkers down for a closer inspection, his eyes move over the floor until he finds the bullet hole, then back at the ankle; there is evidence of knife marks on the bone, a short blade, possibly a dagger. Camille crouches lower, like an Indian listening for an enemy approaching, and sees the deep groove where a blade was buried in the wood. As he gets to his feet, he mentally tries to reconstruct this part of the scene. The ankle first, then the fingers.

The *commissaire* makes an inventory. Five fingers. The right number, but the wrong order: the index is here, the middle finger there, the thumb a little further away, each cut off at the second phalanx. The anaemic stump of the hand lies on the bed, the sheet is saturated with black blood. Cautiously, using a ballpoint pen, the *commissaire* lifts the hand away to reveal Ravic's face. His contorted features speak volumes about the pain he suffered.

The *coup de grâce*: a bullet in the back of the neck.

"Come on then . . ." the *commissaire* says, her tone almost jubilant; she is expecting good news.

"The way I see it," Camille begins, "the guys came in . . ."

"Spare me the bedtime story, *commandant*, anyone can see what happened here. No, what I want to know is what the hell you're doing."

What is Camille doing? Anne wonders.

The nurse has left, they barely spoke. Anne was aggressive, Florence pretended not to notice.

"Can I get you anything?"

No, nothing. Anne gives a curt nod, but already her mind is elsewhere. As every other time, she finds looking in the mirror devastating and yet she cannot help herself. She comes back, goes back to bed, comes back again. Now that she has had the results of the X-rays and the M.R.I. scan, she cannot sit still, this hospital room troubles and depresses her.

She has to run away.

She summons the instincts she had as a little girl for running away and hiding. What she feels has something in common with rape: she feels ashamed. Ashamed of what she has become, this is what she saw when she looked into the mirror.

What is Camille doing? she wonders.

Commissaire Michard steps back and leaves the apartment, carefully setting her feet in precisely the same places as she did when she entered. As in a well-choreographed ballet, their exit coincides with the arrival of the forensics team. The *commissaire* is forced to move along the hall in a crab-like fashion, given the size of her posterior, then comes to a stop in the doorway. She turns back to Camille, folds her arms and gives him a smile that says: so, tell me everything.

"The four robberies in January were the work of a gang led by Vincent Hafner, a gang that Ravic was a member of." He jerks his thumb back towards the room, now lit by a blaze of forensics spotlights. The *commissaire* nods: we know all this, get on with it.

"The gang abruptly reappeared yesterday and robbed the jeweller's in the Galerie Monier. The raid went pretty smoothly, except for one small problem – the presence of a customer, Anne Forestier. I don't know exactly what she saw besides their faces, but something obviously happened. We're still questioning her, insofar as her injuries permit, but we haven't got to the bottom of it. Whatever it was, it was serious enough for Hafner to come after her and try to kill her. He even came to the hospital . . . [He raises a conciliatory hand.] I know, I know! We've got no hard evidence that it was him."

"Has the *juge* ordered a reconstruction of the robbery?"

Camille has not contacted the examining magistrate since his first visit to the Galerie. By now, he has a lot to say. He will have to choose his moment carefully.

"Not yet," Camille says confidently, "but given how fast things have developed, I'm sure that as soon as the witness is able . . ."

"So what happened here? Did he come to relieve Ravic of his share of the haul?"

"Whatever Hafner wanted, he needed to make Ravic talk. Maybe about the haul . . ."

"The case has thrown up a lot of questions, Commandant Verhœven, none of them more serious than the questions it raises about your own behaviour."

Camille tries to smile; he is prepared to try anything.

"Perhaps I have been a little overzealous . . ."

"Overzealous? You've broken every rule in the book, you tell your superiors you're mounting a targeted operation and then turn half the city upside down without so much as a by-your-leave!"

She is making the most of this.

"You clearly exceeded the authorisation given you by the *juge*."

This moment was bound to come, but it is too soon.

"And by your superior officers. I'm still waiting for that report I requested. You're behaving like a free radical. Who exactly do you think you are, Commandant Verhœven?"

"I'm doing my job."

"And what job would that be?"

"*To Protect and to Serve*, isn't that our motto? I'm pro-TEC-ting!"

Camille takes three steps, repressing the urge to grab Michard by the throat. He composes himself.

"You have grossly miscalculated this case," he says. "It is not simply about a woman who was beaten to a pulp. We are dealing with a gang of experienced armed robbers who left one man dead last January. The leader, Vincent Hafner, is a vicious thug, and the Serbians he's working with are certainly no angels. I may not know why, but Hafner is determined to kill this woman and, though I know you don't want to hear this, I firmly believe he went to the hospital armed with a shotgun. And if this witness is killed, someone is going to have to explain how it happened, and you'll be first in line!"

"Alright, you decide that this woman is of some vital strategic importance, so to neutralise a risk you cannot even prove exists, you round up everyone in Paris born between Belgrade and Sarajevo."

"Sarajevo is in Bosnia, not in Serbia."

"Excuse me?"

Camille closes his eyes.

"O.K.," he concedes, "I haven't followed procedure to the letter, I should have written up a report, I should—"

"Oh, we're well past that, *commandant*."

Verhœven frowns, his internal warning light is flashing faintly, he knows exactly what the *commissaire* can do if she so chooses. She nods towards the room where Ravic's body lies in the glare of spotlights.

"With your little barnstorming operation, you managed to flush Ravic out, *commandant*. In fact, you made things easier for his killer."

"There's nothing to substantiate that."

"Perhaps not, but it's a legitimate question. And a brutal raid targeting a specific immigrant community, conducted without the backing of your superior officers and in breach of the limited authorisation given you by the examining magistrate, that sort of 'operation' has a name, *commandant*."

This is something that Camille honestly did not see coming; his face grows pale.

"It's called racial profiling."

Camille closes his eyes. This is a clusterfuck.

What is Camille doing? Anne has not touched the food on the tray in front of her. The orderly, a woman from Martinique, clears it away: you got to eat, child, you can't go lettin' yourself waste away, it's a cryin' shame to waste good food. Anne suddenly feels a furious anger towards everyone welling in her.

Earlier one of the nurses told her, "It'll all be fine, you wait and see . . ."

And Anne had snapped "I can *see* perfectly well right now!"

The nurse was simply being kind, she was trying to help, it was wrong to dismiss her desire to do good. But even as she tried the classic device of counting to ten, Anne found herself snarling.

"So, you've been beaten up, have you? You've had people pistol whip you, kick you, try to kill you? I suppose people fire shotguns at you all the time? Come on, tell me all about it, I'm sure it'll help . . ."

As Florence made to leave, Anne called her back, in tears.

"I'm sorry," she said, "I'm so sorry."

The nurse gave a little wave. Don't give it another thought. As though people are entitled to say anything they like to nurses.

"You wanted this case, you demanded it be assigned to you on the pretext that you had an informant who, so far, you have been unable to produce. And, while we're on the subject, *commandant*, exactly how did you hear about the robbery?"

"From Guérin."

The name just slipped out. The first name that came into his mind. Racking his brain, he could think of no other solution and so he trusted to providence. But providence is like homeopathy: if you don't believe . . . it is a stupid mistake. Now, he has to call Guérin, who is not likely to help him if it means putting his own head on the block. The *commissaire* looks thoughtful.

"And how did Guérin hear about it?"

She stops herself.

"I mean, why would he have mentioned it to you?"

Verhœven can see what is coming and has no choice but to raise the stakes, something he has been doing since the start.

"It just happened . . ."

He has run out of ideas. The *commissaire* is visibly now curious about this affair. He could find himself removed from the case. Or worse. The prospect of a report to the public prosecutor or an investigation by the *Inspection générale des services* now looms on the horizon.

For a split second, an image of five severed fingers hovers between him and the *commissaire,* they are Anne's fingers, he would know them anywhere. The killer is on the move.

Commissaire Michard manoeuvres her gargantuan derrière out onto the landing, leaving Camille to his thoughts.

His thoughts are much the same as hers: he cannot exclude the possibility that his operation helped the killer find Ravic, but he had no other choice if he was to move quickly. Hafner is determined to dispose of all witnesses and protagonists involved in the Galerie Monier robbery: Ravic, Anne and probably the other stooge, the getaway driver . . .

Anyway, Hafner is the key to the whole case, he is the man in charge.

The I.G.S., the *commissaire,* the examining magistrate – Camille will deal with them in due course. For him, the most important thing is to protect Anne.

He remembers something he was taught at driving school: when you miss a bend, you have two choices. The wrong reaction is to brake, since there is every chance you will skid off the road. Paradoxically, the most effective solution is to accelerate, but to do so, you have to curb the natural survival instinct screaming at you to stop.

Camille decides to accelerate.

It is his only way out of this dangerous bend. He tries not to think about the fact that accelerating is also what someone would do if they were determined to drive off a cliff.

And, besides, his choices are limited.

6.00 p.m.

Every time he sees the man, Camille cannot help but think that Mouloud Faraoui does not look much like someone called Mouloud Faraoui. Though his Moroccan roots survive in his name, any North African traits have been diluted over three generations of unlikely marriages and unexpected couplings, an incongruous melting pot that has produced surprising results. Mouloud's face is a distillate of history: light-brown hair verging on blond, a long nose, a square jaw slashed by a scar that was obviously painful and gives him a bad-boy look, ice-cold, blue-green eyes. He is between thirty and forty, though his age is difficult to guess. Camille checks the police record, where he finds documentary evidence that Mouloud was an exceptionally precocious career criminal. It turns out that he is thirty-seven.

He is relaxed, almost offhand, a man of few words and subtle gestures. He slides into the seat opposite, never taking his eyes off Camille, he seems tense, as though expecting the *commandant* to pull his gun. Mouloud is wary. Not wary enough, perhaps, given that instead of staying safely in his cell, he is here in the prison visiting room. Facing a twenty-year stretch, he was sentenced to ten, he will serve seven and has been inside for two. Despite his arrogant swagger, one look is enough to tell Camille that time has been dragging.

Surprised by this unexpected visit, Faraoui's natural mistrust is on red alert. He sits ramrod straight, arms folded. Neither man has said a word, but already they have exchanged a staggering number of messages.

Verhœven's very presence here constitutes a complicated message in itself.

In prison, word gets around. Hardly has the prisoner set foot in the visiting room than the news has spread along the landings. What would an officer from the *brigade criminelle* want with a small-time pimp like Faraoui? Ultimately, it does not matter what is said at their meeting, the prison, like a giant pinball machine, is already buzzing with rumours that range from sober speculation to wild conspiracy theories, depending on the vested interests of those involved and the relative power of the prison gangs, creating a complex web of misinformation.

And this is precisely why Camille is here, sitting in the visiting room, arms folded, staring silently at Faraoui. He need do nothing else. The work is already being done, he does not even have to lift his little finger.

But the silence is uncomfortable.

Faraoui, still sitting stiffly, watches and waits in silence. Camille does not move. He is thinking about how this little thug's name popped into his head when the *commissaire* asked her point-blank question. Subconsciously, he already knew what he planned to do, but it took a while for Camille's conscious mind to catch up: this is the quickest route to Vincent Hafner.

If he is to reach the end of the path he has chosen, Camille is going to have to tough it out. He feels a suffocating panic well up inside him. If Faraoui were not staring at him so intently, he would get up and open a window. Just walking into the prison gave him the jitters.

Take a deep breath. Another deep breath. And he will have to come back again . . .

He remembers the way he confidently announced that there were "three known suspects". His brain works faster than he can; he only realises what he has said after the fact. He understands now.

The clock ticks off the seconds, the minutes; in the airless visiting room, unspoken words quiver in the air like vibrations.

At first, Faraoui mistakenly thought this was a test to see which of them would crack first, a silent form of arm-wrestling, a cheap police trick. And it surprised him that an officer of Verhœven's reputation would resort to such a ruse. So it must be something else. Camille watches as he bows his head, thinking as fast as he can. And since Faraoui is a smart guy, he comes to the only possible conclusion. He makes to get to his feet.

Camille is expecting this, he tut-tuts softly without even glancing up. Faraoui, who has a keen sense of his own best interests, decides to play along. Still the time ticks away.

They wait. Ten minutes. Fifteen. Twenty.

Then Camille gives the signal. He uncrosses his arms.

"O.K. Well, I wouldn't want you to think I'm bored or any-thing . . ."

He gets up. Faraoui remains seated. The ghost of a smile plays on his lips, he leans back nonchalantly in his chair.

"What do you take me for, a messenger boy?"

Reaching the door, Camille slaps it with the palm of his hand for someone to come and open. He turns back.

"In a sense, yes."

"And what do I get out of it?"

Camille adopts a shocked expression.

"What the . . . ? You get to ensure that justice is served! What do you want, for fuck's sake?"

The door opens, the guard steps aside to allow Camille to pass, but he stands on the threshold for a moment.

"While we're on the subject, Mouloud, tell me something . . . The guy who grassed you up . . . damn, what was his name again? It's on the tip of my tongue . . ."

Faraoui never knew who squealed on him, he did everything he could to find out, but he came up with nothing; he would give four years inside just to know that name, everyone knows that. But no-one can possibly know what Faraoui would do with the guy if he ever found him.

He smiles and nods. Done deal.

This is Camille's first message.

Meeting Faraoui amounts to saying: I've made a deal with a killer.

If I give him the name of the guy who grassed him up, he'll do anything I ask.

In exchange for that name, I can get him to hunt you down and before you have time to catch your breath he will be right behind you.

From now on, you had better start counting the seconds.

7.30 p.m.

Camille is sitting at his desk, colleagues pop their heads round the door, they give a little wave, everyone has heard about his dressing down, it's all anyone can talk about. With the exception of the officers who took part in the "racial profiling", they have nothing

185

to worry about, but still the word gets round, the *commissaire* has already begun to undermine him. It's a nasty business. But what the fuck is Camille playing at? No-one seems to know. Even Louis has hardly said a word, and so rumours are rife – an officer of his reputation, he must have done something, the *commissaire* is livid – to say nothing of the examining magistrate who is preparing to summon everyone involved. Even Contrôleur Général Le Guen has been like a bear with a sore head all afternoon, but pop your head round the door of his office and there's Verhœven, typing up his report for all the world as if this is a storm in a teacup, he hasn't got a care in the world, like this whole business with the robbery and the gang of killers is some personal beef. I don't get it, what do you think? I haven't a clue, but you've got to admit it's pretty weird. But the officers go about their business, they have already been called away to deal with other matters, there is a commotion downstairs, voices are raised in the corridors. No rest for the wicked.

Camille has to sort out this report, do a little damage limitation on the impending disaster. All he needs is to buy himself some time, even just a day or two, because if his strategy pays off, it won't be long before he tracks down Hafner.

This is the purpose of his report: to buy himself two days' grace.

As soon as Hafner has been caught and taken into custody, everything will become clear, the haze of secrecy swirling around the case will dissipate, Camille will explain himself, the disciplinary letter will arrive from his superiors, he could be suspended, have his prospects of promotion permanently quashed, he may even have to request – or accept – a change of post, it does not bother him: with Hafner under lock and key, Anne will be safe. That is all he cares about . . .

As he sits down to compose this difficult and delicate report (Camille is not one for reports at the best of times), he thinks of the piece of paper he tore from his sketchpad earlier and tossed away. He fishes it out of the wastepaper basket. The pencil portrait of Vincent Hafner, a sketch of Anne in her hospital bed. He lays the crumpled page on his desk and smoothes it out, with his free hand he calls Guérin and leaves a message, the third today. If Guérin does not get in touch soon, it means he does not want to talk to Camille. Contrôleur Général Le Guen on the other hand has been trying to get through to Camille for hours. Four messages in a row: "What the fuck are you playing at, Camille? Call me back right now." He is frantic. Understandably so. Hardly has Camille written the first line of his report than his mobile starts to vibrate again. Le Guen. This time, Camille picks up, closes his eyes and prepares himself for the histrionics.

But Le Guen's voice is calm and measured.

"Do you think maybe we should have a chat, Camille?"

Camille could say yes, he could say no. Le Guen is a friend, the one friend who has come through every disaster with him, the one friend capable of changing the course on which he is embarked. But Camille says nothing.

This is one of those decisive moments which may or may not save his life, and yet he says nothing.

Not because he has suddenly become masochistic or suicidal. On the contrary, he feels completely lucid. On a blank corner of the sheet of paper, he sketches Anne's profile in three quick strokes. It is something he used to do with Irène in his idle moments, the way another man might bite his nails.

Adopting his most considerate, his most persuasive tone, Le Guen tries to reason with him.

"You've really stirred up a shitstorm this afternoon, I've got people phoning to ask me if we're tracking international terrorists. This is a complete fuck-up. I've got informants screaming that they've been stabbed in the back. You've fucked over your fellow officers who have to work with these communities day in, day out. In the space of three hours, you've set their work back by a year, and the fact that your man Ravic has been murdered only makes things more complicated. So, right now, I want you to tell me exactly what you're up to."

Still Camille says nothing, he looks down at his drawing. It could have been some other woman, he thinks, but it is Anne. Anne who stepped into his life just as she stepped into the Monier. Why her and not some other woman? Who knows? As he retraces the line of her mouth on the drawing, he can almost feel her soft lips; he accentuates the hollow just below her jawline that he finds so poignant.

"Camille, are you listening?"

"I'm listening, Jean."

"I'm not sure I can bail you out of this one, you do know that? I'm having a hell of a job trying to placate the magistrate. He's a smart guy, so it's not too wise to treat him like an idiot. Needless to say I had a little visit from the top brass less than an hour ago, but I think we can do some damage limitation."

Camille sets his pencil down and bows his head. In trying to perfect Anne's portrait, he has ruined it. It is always the way, a sketch needs to be spontaneous; as soon as you try to change something, it is ruined.

Camille is suddenly stuck by a curious notion, an utterly new thought, a question that, surprising as it seems, he has never asked himself: what is to become of me afterwards? What do I want? And as so often in a dialogue of the deaf, where neither party is prepared to listen or to hear, the two men come to the same conclusion.

"This is personal, isn't it, Camille?" Le Guen says. "You have a relationship with this woman? A personal relationship?"

"Of course not, Jean, what makes you think . . ."

Le Guen lets a painful silence hang over the proceedings. Then he shrugs.

"If this thing blows up in our faces, there are going to be questions . . ."

Camille suddenly realises that this is not simply about love, it is about something else. He has chosen a dark and winding path, not knowing where it will lead, but he knows, he senses that he is not being swept along by his blind passion for Anne.

Something is urging him on, regardless of the cost.

Essentially, he is doing in his life what he has always done in his investigations: doggedly carrying on to the bitter end, so he can understand why things are as they are.

"If you don't come up with something now," Le Guen interrupts the thought, "if you don't give me some kind of explanation, Michard will have no choice but to kick this upstairs to the *procureur*'s office. There'll be no way to avoid an internal investigation . . ."

"What . . . ? An internal investigation into what?"

Le Guen shrugs again.

"O.K. Have it your way."

8.15 p.m.

Camille knocks softly on the door; no answer. He opens it and finds Anne lying on the bed, staring at the ceiling. He sits down next to her.

Neither says a word. Camille reaches out to take her hand and Anne meekly lets him, she is overcome by a crushing sense of resignation, almost a fatalism. But after a few minutes, she says simply:

"I want to leave . . ."

Resting her weight on her elbows, she slowly sits up in bed.

"Well, since they're not going to operate, you should be able to go home soon," Camille says. "In a day or two, maybe."

"No, Camille." She is speaking very slowly. "I want to leave right now, this minute."

He frowns. Anne shakes her head wildly.

"Right now."

"They don't just let people walk out in the middle of the night. A doctor needs to give you the once-over, you'll need to collect your prescriptions, and . . ."

"No! I need to get out of here, Camille, can't you understand?"

Camille gets to his feet, Anne is getting worked up, he needs to think of some way to calm her down. But Anne has already swung her legs over the side of the bed and is struggling to stand.

"I don't want to stay here, and no-one can force me to . . ."

"But no-one is trying to force you to . . ."

Anne suddenly feels dizzy, she has overestimated her strength. She grabs Camille for support, sits back on the bed and bows her head.

"I'm sure he's been here, Camille, he wants to kill me, he'll stop at nothing, I can feel it, I just *know*."

"You don't know anything," Camille says, "you don't know

anything at all!"

It is futile to browbeat her, because the driving force that motivates Anne is a blind terror impervious to reason or to authority. She starts to tremble again.

"There's an officer guarding the door, nothing is going to happen to you . . ."

"Oh, just stop, Camille! When he's not disappearing off to the toilet, he's playing solitaire on his mobile! He doesn't even notice when I leave the room . . ."

"I'll have another officer come and take over. It's just that . . ."

"What? It's just that what?"

Anne tries to blow her nose, but the pain is too great.

"You know how it is . . . Everything seems frightening at night, but I promise you . . ."

"No, Camille, you can't promise. That's just it . . ."

These three simple words are painful to both of them. Anne wants to leave precisely because he cannot promise to keep her safe. It is all his fault. She angrily throws her tissue on the floor. Camille tries to help, but she brushes him off. "Leave me alone, I can manage by myself."

"What do you mean, 'by myself'?"

"Just leave me alone, Camille, I don't need you anymore."

But as she says this, she lies back on the bed exhausted from the simple effort of standing up. Camille pulls up the sheet.

"Leave me alone."

And so he leaves her alone, sits down again, takes her hand in his, but her hand is lifeless, cold. The way she is sprawled across the bed is like an insult.

"You can go now . . ." she says.

She does not look at him. Her face is turned to the window.

DAY 3

Camille has barely slept in two days. Warming his hands on a mug of coffee, he stares out the window of the studio at the forest. It was here in Montfort that his mother painted for years, almost until her death. Afterwards the place lay abandoned, left to squatters and thieves. Camille hardly gave it a thought and yet, for some obscure reason, he never sold it.

Then, some time after Irène's death, he decided not to keep anything of his mother's, not a single canvas, a vestige of an old grudge between them: it is because of her smoking that he is only four foot eleven.

Some of the paintings now hang in foreign museums. Camille had promised himself he would donate all the proceeds of the sale but, of course, he did nothing with the money. Not until some years after Irène's death, when he finally rejoined the world and decided to rebuild and refurbish the little studio on the edge of the forest of Clamart, which had once been the gatekeeper's lodge to a country house that has long since vanished. Back then, the place was more isolated than it is now, when the nearest house is only three hundred metres away. The dirt road goes no further, it stops here.

Camille had the place renovated from top to bottom, replacing every wonky terracotta floor tile, installing a full bathroom and building a mezzanine which became his bedroom. The ground floor is now a huge sitting room with an open-plan kitchen, one entire wall is taken up by a picture window overlooking the edge of the forest.

The forest terrifies him still, just as it did when he spent long afternoons as a child watching his mother work here. These days it is an adult terror, a wistful feeling of mingled pleasure and pain.

The one piece of nostalgia he has allowed himself is the gleaming cast-iron wood-burning stove in the centre of the room which replaced his mother's that was stolen during the years the studio lay derelict.

Unless carefully regulated, all the heat from the stove rises so that the mezzanine is a sauna while downstairs his feet are freezing, but he likes this rustic method of heating because it has to be earned, because it requires as much attentiveness as experience. Camille knows how to stoke and regulate it such that it will run all night. In the depths of winter, there is a chill to the mornings, but he considers this initial hardship – refuelling and relighting the stove – as a little ritual.

He had much of the roof replaced with glass so that the sky is constantly visible and, the moment you look up, the clouds and the rain seem about to tumble on you. When it snows, it is unsettling. This opening onto the sky serves no real purpose. Though it lets in more light, the house had more than enough already. Le Guen, ever the pragmatist, enquired about the skylights on his first visit.

"What do you want?" Camille said. "I might be knee high to a grasshopper, but I can still reach for the stars."

Camille comes as often as he can. He spends days off and weekends here, but he rarely invites guests. Then again, he does not have many people in his life. Louis and Le Guen have visited the studio, as did Armand, but although he made no conscious decision, the studio has become a secret place. Camille spends much of his time here drawing, always from memory. Among the piles of sketches and the hundreds of notepads are portraits of everyone he has ever arrested, of every body whose death he has investigated, of magistrates with whom he has worked and colleagues he barely knows. He has a particular fondness for sketching the witnesses he has questioned, the fleeting shadows who disappear as swiftly as they appeared, troubled bystanders and bewildered onlookers, anguished women, girls overcome by emotion, men distraught by their brush with death, they are all here, there are two, perhaps three thousand sketches, a vast, incomparable gallery of portraits, the daily life of an officer in the *brigade criminelle* as seen by the artist he might have been. Camille's searingly honest portraits reveal a rare talent, he often claims his drawings are more intelligent than he is, and there is something to the idea. Even photographs seem less faithful, less true. Once, at the Hôtel Salé, Anne had seemed so beautiful that he told her not to move and, taking out his mobile, took a snapshot so that he could freeze the moment and have her appear on the screen whenever she called him, though in the end he replaced it with a scan of one of his sketches which seemed to him more true, more expressive.

September has not yet turned cold so when he arrived this evening Camille put only a few logs in the stove to create what he calls a "comfort fire".

He should bring his cat to live here, but Doudouche does not like the countryside; for her it is Paris or nothing. Doudouche has appeared in many of his sketches. As have Louis and Jean, even Maleval once upon a time. Last night, just before going to bed, he dug out all his portraits of Armand, he even found the sketch of Armand in his hospital bed on the day he died, with that placid, peaceful expression that makes all dead bodies look more or less alike.

Outside the cottage, at the far end of what he thinks of as "the yard", is the forest. As night draws in, the humidity rises. This morning he found his car slick with dew.

He has often sketched this forest, has even ventured a watercolour though colour is not his strong suit. He is captivated by emotion, by movement, but he is not a colourist as his mother was.

A 7.15 a.m. precisely, his mobile vibrates. Still cradling his coffee, he picks it up with his free hand. Louis apologises for the early hour.

"Don't worry," Camille says. "So, tell me."

"Madame Forestier, she's left the hospital . . ."

There is a brief silence. If someone should ever write a biography of Camille, much of it would be dedicated to his silences. Louis, who knows this all too well, cannot help but wonder again precisely what role the missing woman plays in Camille's life. Is she the real reason for the curious way he has been behaving? To what extent is his behaviour some sort of exorcism? Whatever the truth, Verhœven's silence is a measure of his distress.

"How long since she left?" he asks.

"We're not sure, sometime during the night. The nurse did her rounds at ten o'clock and talked to her, she seemed calm, but an hour ago the duty nurse found the room empty. She left most of her clothes in the wardrobe which made it seem as though she had just wandered out of the room for a minute, so it took a while before the staff realised she was actually missing."

"What about the guard?"

"He says he has prostate trouble, so when he has to go, it can take a while."

Camille takes a mouthful of coffee.

"I need you to send someone to her apartment immediately."

"I went round myself before I called you," Louis says. "No-one has seen her . . ."

Camille stares out at the forest as though expecting help to arrive.

"Do you know if she has any family?"

No, Camille says, he does not know. Actually, she has a daughter in the States, he remembers. He gropes for a name. Agathe. He decides not to mention her daughter or the brother.

"If she's checked into a hotel, it might take us a while to track her down," Louis says, "but she might have gone to a friend for help. I'll talk to her colleagues."

"No, leave it," Camille sighs. "I'll do it. You focus on Hafner. Is there any news there?"

"Nothing yet, he seems to have completely vanished. There's no-one at his last known address and there's been no sign of him at his usual haunts. His known associates say they haven't seen him since the January . . ."

"Since the robberies?"

"Around that time, yes."

"So he may have left the country?"

"That's what they seem to think. A couple of them even suggested he might be dead, but there's no basis for it. There is talk that he's seriously ill, more than one witness mentioned this, but given his little performance at the Galerie Monier, I'd say he's in fine fettle. We're still looking, but I can't say I'm optimistic . . ."

"The forensics on Ravic's murder, when do we get results?"

"Tomorrow at the earliest."

Louis is silent for a moment, it is a very particular silence – from his own extensive repertoire, one that he observes before broaching the thorniest questions.

"About Madame Forestier . . ." he ventures. "Will you inform the *commissaire* or should I?"

"I'll do it . . ."

The response came unbidden. Too quickly. Camille sets his mug down by the sink. Ever intuitive, Louis waits for the rest of the response.

"Listen, Louis . . . I'd rather look for her myself."

Camille can almost hear Louis nodding cautiously.

"I think I'll be able to find her . . . fairly quickly."

"Understood," Louis concedes.

Camille's message is clear: say nothing to Commissaire Michard.

"I'm heading in now, Louis. I've got a meeting, but I'll be there as soon as I can be."

The razor-sharp rivulet of cold sweat Camille can feel tracing the length of his spine has nothing to do with the temperature of the room.

7.20 a.m.

He quickly pulls on his clothes, but he cannot leave like this, he cannot help but check that everything is locked and bolted, irritated at the thought that somehow everything is down to him.

He creeps up to the mezzanine on tiptoe.

"I'm not asleep. . ."

Reassured, he walks over and sits on the edge of the bed.

"Was I snoring?" Anne asks without turning towards him.

"With a broken nose, it's unavoidable."

He is struck by her position. Even in hospital she turned away from him, lying on her side, staring at the window. *She can't bring herself to look at me, she thinks I can't protect her.*

"You're safe here, nothing can happen to you now."

Anne merely shrugs, and it is difficult to tell whether this means yes or no.

It means no.

"He'll find me. He'll come here."

She rolls onto her back and looks at him. She almost makes him doubt himself.

"That's impossible, Anne. No-one knows you're here."

Anne shrugs again. This time, however, the meaning is clear: say what you like, he's coming here, he's coming to kill me. Her fear is becoming obsessive, becoming hysterical. Camille takes her hand.

"After everything that's happened to you, it's only normal that you should be scared. But I promise you . . ."

Her shrug this time could mean: how can I make you understand? Or it could mean: forget it.

"I have to go," Camille says, checking his watch. "You'll find everything you need downstairs . . ."

She nods. She is still exhausted. Even the half-light of the bedroom can do nothing to hide the ravages of livid bruises and contusions.

He has shown her everything in the studio, the coffeemaker, the bathroom, a veritable pharmacy to deal with her injuries. He was loath for her to leave the hospital – who will look after her, remove her sutures? But there was nothing to be done; frantic and nervous, she could not bear to stay and was threatening to go back to her apartment. He could hardly tell her that someone would be waiting for her, that this was the trap. What could he do? Where could he take her other than here, in the middle of nowhere?

So this is where Anne is.

No woman has ever come here. Camille immediately dismisses this thought, since it was downstairs, by the doorway, that Irène was murdered. In the four years since, everything has changed, everything has been remade and yet everything is the same. He too has been "remade", after a fashion. It never quite works, tattered shreds of a former life still cling; looking around he can see them everywhere.

"I want you to do exactly what I've told you," he tells her, "I want you to shut . . ."

Anne lays her hand on his. Given the splints on her fingers there is nothing romantic about the gesture. It means: you've told me all this already, I've got it, now go.

Camille leaves. He goes down the stairs from the mezzanine, steps out into the yard, locks the door and gets into his car.

If his situation has become much more complicated, Anne's is more secure. All he can do is grin and bear it, take the whole world on his shoulders. If he were of standard height, would he feel such a crushing sense of duty?

8.00 a.m.

Forests are depressing, I've always hated them. This one is worse than most. Clamart, Meudon, welcome to the armpit of the universe. Gloomy as a wet weekend. A sign announces a built-up area. Difficult to know what to call the cluster of houses for the *nouveaux riches*, it's not a part of the city, it's not a suburb, it's not a village. People say "the outskirts", but the outskirts of what? Looking around at the carefully manicured gardens and terraces, I can't decide which is more depressing, the desolate surroundings or the smugness of the inhabitants.

Once past the cluster of houses, there is nothing but forest as far as the eye can see. The G.P.S. system takes an age to find the rue du Pavé-de-Meudon (and, on the left, the rue Morte-Bouteille. Who the fuck comes up with names like Morte-Bouteille?) Obviously,

202

it's impossible to park a car without attracting attention, which means driving deep into the arse-end of nowhere and walking back.

I'm strung out, I haven't been eating properly and I'm exhausted, trying to do too many things at once. And I fucking hate walking. Especially in the forest . . .

The little damsel just needs to sit tight, I'll be there very soon to bring her a little message. And I've got all the tools I need to make myself understood. And when I'm done with her, I plan to take off to where forests are banned, where there's not a single tree within a hundred-kilometre radius. I need sandy beaches, killer cocktails and a few relaxing hands of poker so I can get over all this excitement. I'm getting old. I'd like to make the most of things while there's still time. But if I'm to do that, I need to stay calm, to be cold-blooded as I tramp through this fucking forest, constantly on the alert. It's hard to believe how many people there are traipsing through this desolate wasteland even at this ungodly hour – young people, old people, couples are out rambling, hiking, jogging. I even came across a couple riding horses.

That said, the further I trek, the fewer people I encounter. The shack is set back at least three hundred metres from the road and the dirt track leading there stops abruptly, beyond it there is nothing but forest.

Carrying a sniper rifle – even in its case – is not quite in keeping with the local country attire, so I've stuffed it into a sports bag. Especially as I don't look like some guy out collecting mushrooms.

I haven't seen a soul for several minutes now, the G.P.S. has no reception, but this is the only dirt track around here.

It will just be the two of us. We'll get this little job done.

Every clanging door, every footstep along the hallway, every face peering through the bars, everything weighs on him. Because deep down, Camille is afraid. Long ago, when he first realised that one day he would have to come back here, he dismissed the thought. But it came back to the surface, thrashing like a fish on a riverbank, telling him that sooner or later this meeting would take place. All he needed was some pretext to come here, to give in without shame to this overpowering need.

Before him, behind him, all around, the heavy metal gates of the central prison open and close.

As he moves along the hallways with little, birdlike steps, Camille stifles the urge to vomit, his head is spinning.

The guard escorting him is deferential, almost protective, as though he understands the situation and feels that, given the exceptional circumstances, Camille deserves special consideration. Everywhere Camille looks there are signs.

A hall, another hall and then the waiting room. The door is opened and Camille sits at the metal table bolted to the floor, his heart is hammering fit to burst, his throat is dry. He waits. He lays his hands flat, but seeing them tremble, he hides them under the table.

The second door opens, the one at the far end of the room. At first he can see nothing but a pair of shoes on the footrest of the wheelchair, shiny black leather shoes, then the wheelchair begins to move, infinitely slowly as though wary or suspicious. Two legs appear, fat knees straining at the fabric of the trousers, then the wheelchair comes to a halt halfway across the threshold. Camille can see a pair of fleshy hands, so pale the veins are invisible, gripping the wheels. One metre further, and the man himself appears.

He pauses for an instant. From the moment he enters, his eyes bore into Camille, they never leave him. The guard steps around the table and moves the other metal chair to make room for the wheelchair and then, at Camille's signal, he leaves.

The wheelchair rolls forward, then pivots with unexpected ease.

Finally they are face to face.

For the first time in four years, Camille Verhœven, *commandant* of the *brigade criminelle*, finds himself confronted by the man who butchered his wife.

The man he knew then was tall and lean, with an old-fashioned, almost rakish elegance and a disconcerting sensuality, especially his full lips. The prisoner before him is slovenly and obese. The same physical traits are now half buried in a bloated body. Only his face is the same, like a delicate mask worn by a fat man. His hair is long and lank. His eyes are as sly, as shifty as ever.

"It was written." Buisson's voice is tremulous, too loud, too shrill. "And it is now," he says, as though bringing the interview to an end.

In his glory days, he prided himself on such turns of phrase. In a sense, this was what led him to murder seven times, this taste for the grandiloquent, his ostentatious arrogance. He and Camille despised each other at sight. Later, as so often, history confirmed that their intuitions had been correct. But this is not the time to go over ancient history.

"Yes," Camille says simply. "It is now."

Camille's voice does not tremble. He feels calmer now he is sitting opposite Buisson. He has a lot of experience of face-to-face encounters, he knows he will not rant and rage. The man he so often imagined dead, tortured, suffering in dreams, is not the same, and seeing him now, Camille realises that he feels only a calm, dispassionate animosity. For years, all his hatred, all his rage was heaped on Irène's killer, but that is finished.

Buisson is finished.

But Camille's life, his story, is not.

His culpability in Irène's death is something that will haunt him for ever. He will never be over her, this truth, this simple fact, illuminates everything. Everything else is evasion.

Realising this, Camille looks up, and his eyes well with the tears that instantly bring him closer to Irène as she was, beautifully, eternally young, for him alone. He grows old; she, more radiant than ever, will never change. What Buisson did has no power over his memories, that intimate collection of images, recollections and sensations that comprise his love of Irène.

Something he bears like a scar, imperceptible yet indelible.

Buisson does not move. From the beginning of this encounter he has been afraid.

Camille's brief pang, quickly overcome, creates no awkwardness between the two men. Words will come, but it was necessary that silence be given its due. Camille shakes it off, he does not want Buisson to see this fleeting moment of pain, their mutual silence, as some sort of mute communion. There is nothing he wishes to share with this man. He blows his nose, stuffs the tissue in his pocket, props his elbows on the table, folds his hands under his chin and stares at Buisson.

Buisson has been dreading this moment since yesterday. When he discovered – on the prison grapevine – that Verhœven had paid a visit to Mouloud Faraoui, he knew his time had come. He lay awake all night, tossing and turning, unable to believe it. His death is now a foregone conclusion. Faraoui's gang has spies everywhere in La Centrale, there is not a cockroach that can hide from him. If Camille has found a way of paying for Faraoui's services – by giving up the name of the man who grassed him up, for instance – then an hour from now or two days from now, Buisson will find a shiv embedded in his throat as he comes out of the dining hall or be garrotted from behind while a couple of weight-lifters hold his arms. He may be catapulted in his wheelchair from the third-floor balcony. Or be smothered by his mattress. It will depend on the order given, Verhœven may even insist on a slow, painful death; Buisson might spend a whole night choking on a gag in the fetid toilets, or bleed to death, drop by drop, in the cupboard of one of the workshops . . .

Buisson is scared of dying.

By now, he had convinced himself that Camille would not exact revenge. The fear that he put behind him years ago floods back, all the more violent and terrifying because it feels somehow less justified. The years he has spent in jail, the things he has endured, the respect he has earned, the power he has managed to acquire, instilled in him a sense of impunity that Verhœven has destroyed in a few short hours. Camille had only to visit Faraoui for everyone to realise that the reprieve has been temporary, that Buisson's stay of execution will last only a few hours more. There has been a lot of talk in the corridors, Faraoui was quick to spread the news, part of his deal with Verhœven was to put the fear of God into Buisson. A few of the screws have heard and the inmates have begun to look at Buisson differently.

Why now? That is the question.

"I hear you've become a big shot . . ."

Buisson wonders if this is the answer. But no. Camille is simply stating a fact. Buisson is an exceptionally intelligent man. When he tried to make his escape, Louis lodged the bullet in his spine that put him in this wheelchair, but before that he had been running rings around the police. By the time he arrived in prison, his reputation had preceded him, in fact he became something of a star for having successfully evaded the *brigade criminelle* for so long. With considerable skill, Buisson capitalised on the prisoners' admiration, he managed to remain aloof from the gang wars, he performed small services for other inmates – in prison, an intellectual, a man who knows things, is a rarity. Over the years, he succeeded in forging a small network of contacts, first within the prison and later outside as he continued to do small favours for paroled prisoners, making introductions, arranging meetings, securing interviews. Last year, he successfully intervened in an internecine war between rival gangs in the western suburbs, calmed the situation, proposed terms and expertly negotiated the ceasefire. Within the prison, he does not involve himself in any trafficking, but he knows all the scams. On the outside, Buisson knows all there is to know about high-profile criminals and is remarkably well connected to those who meet his exacting standards; this makes him a powerful man.

But for all that, now that Camille has made his decision, a day from now or perhaps an hour from now, he will be a dead man.

"You look worried . . ." Camille says.

"I'm waiting."

Buisson immediately regrets the phrase which sounds like a challenge and therefore a defeat. Camille raises a hand: no problem, he understands.

"I'll let you explain . . ."

"No," Camille says, "there will be no explanation. I'm simply here to tell you how this is going to go down."

Buisson is deathly pale. Even Verhœven's calmness seems like a threat. He becomes indignant.

"I deserve an explanation!" Buisson roars.

Though physically he is a very different man, inside he has not changed, his titanic ego has survived intact. Camille fumbles in his pocket and lays a photograph on the table.

"Vincent Hafner. He's . . ."

"I know who he is . . ." The remark is curt, as though Buisson feels insulted. But it also betrays his immense relief. In a split second, Buisson realised that he still has a chance.

Camille registers the instinctive exultation in his voice, but he makes no comment. It was to be expected. Buisson immediately goes on the defensive, attempting to confuse the issue.

"I don't know the man personally . . . He's not a major player, but he has his place. He has a reputation for being somewhat . . . savage. A thug."

It would take electrodes attached to his head to record the astonishing speed of firing synapses.

"He disappeared last January," Camille says. "For months, no-one – not even his criminal colleagues – knew where he was. Complete radio silence. Then, suddenly, he reappears and it's like he's got a new lease of life, he's back to his old ways, back on the job, bright as a button."

"And you find this somehow strange?"

"I'm having a little difficulty squaring his sudden disappearance with his spectacular comeback. For a career criminal so close to retirement, it's unusual."

"So, something is not quite right."

Camille's face darkens, he looks worried, almost angry with himself.

"That's one way of putting it: something is not quite right. Something I don't understand."

Seeing the ghost of a smile cross Buisson's face, Camille knows he was right to trust to the man's overweening pride. It was arrogance that led him to kill again and again, even as it led to his arrest. This is the reason that he will die in a prison cell. And still he has learned nothing, his narcissism is like a bottomless well, ever ready to engulf him. "Something I don't understand." Camille's crucial phrase was designed to appeal to that same vanity, because Buisson is convinced that *he* understands. And cannot resist letting Camille know.

"Perhaps he needs money in a hurry . . ."

Camille steels himself, determined not to show how much it pains him to have to stoop to chicanery. He is leading an investigation; the end justifies the means. So he looks up at Buisson as though intrigued.

"Word has it Hafner is seriously ill . . ." Buisson says slowly.

When you choose a stratagem, it is wise to stick with it to the end.

"Good, I hope he dies," Camille says.

"But don't you see?" Buisson triumphantly retorts. "The reason he is acting out of character is *because* he's staring death in the face. He's involved with a slip of a girl . . . A vulgar whore who had copulated with half the city by the time she was nineteen. She obviously likes turning tricks, I can think of no other explanation . . ."

Camille wonders whether Buisson is brave enough – or reckless enough – to see his thought through. And he does.

"But despite her failings, it would appear that Hafner is infatuated with this girl. Love, *commandant*, is a powerful thing, is it not? It is a subject about which you know a thing or two, as I recall . . ."

Though he does not show it, Camille is devastated. He feels utterly broken as he sits here, allowing Buisson to gloat about the murder of Irène. "Love, *commandant* . . ."

Buisson must sense something because a last flicker of self-preservation suddenly extinguishes his exultant smirk.

"If he is terminally ill," he goes on, "perhaps Hafner wants to ensure his paramour is free of financial worries. One comes across the most generous instincts even in the blackest souls . . ."

Louis had already mentioned these rumours to Camille and, though it cost him dearly, the price he paid to confirm them has been worth it. Camille can suddenly see a light at the end of the tunnel. His palpable relief is not lost on Buisson, a man so twisted that he is already trying to work out why this matters so much to Verhœven, why Hafner is so important that the *commandant* has been reduced to coming here. His life has only just been spared and already he is calculating how he might profit from this situation.

Camille does not give him the time.

"I want Hafner, and I want him now. You've got twelve hours."

"Th—that's impossible!" the piteous wail dies in Buisson's throat. As Camille gets to his feet, he sees his last chance of survival disappear. He feverishly pounds his fists on the armrests of his wheelchair. Camille's face is expressionless.

"Twelve hours, not a second more. I find people do their best work when they have a deadline."

He taps on the door. As the guard comes to open it, he turns back to Buisson.

"Even when this is over, I can still have you killed any time I want." It is enough for him to say the words for both men to realise that he needed to say it, but it was not true. That Buisson would already be dead if it were going to happen. That for Camille

Verhœven, ordering a killing is incompatible with who he is.

And now that he knows that his life is no longer in danger, that it was probably never in danger, Buisson decides to find the information Verhœven needs.

As he steps out of the prison, Camille feels both relieved and overwhelmed, like the sole survivor of a shipwreck.

9.00 a.m.
I'm finding the cold almost as tough to cope with as the tiredness. You hardly notice it at first, but unless you keep moving, it seeps into your bones until you're frozen to the marrow. It's not going to make it easy to get a shot. But at least this place is quiet. The studio is a broad, squat building with a high roof, but there's only one storey. There's an unobstructed line of sight in front. I station myself in a tiny lean-to at the far end of the yard that looks like it was once a rabbit hutch or similar.

I stow the sniper rifle, take the Walther and the hunting knife and brave the great outdoors to do a little reconnaissance. It's crucial to know the terrain. Cause only as much collateral damage as necessary. Go for a clean hit. Precise. What do they call it? Oh, yeah, a "surgical strike". Using the Mossberg here would be like using a roller to paint a miniature. Surgical entails making precise holes in very precise places. And since the vast picture window seems resistant to most things, I'm glad I settled on an M40A3 with telescopic sights; it's a very accurate piece of kit. And it takes armour-piercing bullets.

Just to the right of the house there is a sort of hillock. The soil has been partly washed away by the rain, revealing a heap of building rubble, plaster, breeze blocks that builders were probably supposed to clear away but never did. It's not an ideal position for a sniper, but it's the only one I've got. From here, I have a view of most of the main room, though only at an angle. I'll have to stand up at the last minute before I fire.

I've already seen her a couple of times, but she was walking past too quickly. I'm not bothered, no sense rushing things. Better to do it right.

As soon as she got up, Anne went to the door to make sure Camille had double-locked it. The house has been burgled more than once, which is hardly surprising given the isolated location, so he installed reinforced doors. The double-glazed bay window is fitted with toughened glass which could probably take a hammer blow without so much as cracking.

"This is the code for the alarm," Camille had said, handing her a page torn from a notepad. "Press hash, then this number, then hash again. That'll set off the alarm. It's not connected to the local police station and it only lasts a minute, but take my word for it, it's a powerful deterrent."

The numbers are 29091571; Anne did not want to ask what they meant.

"Caravaggio's date of birth . . ." Camille said apologetically. "It seemed like a good idea for a security code. Not many people know it. But as I said, I guarantee you won't need it."

Anne also checked the rear of the building. There is a laundry and a bathroom. The only external door is reinforced with steel, locked and bolted.

Then she went and showered as best she could. It was impossible to wash her hair properly; she considered removing the splints but decided it would be too painful, she had to stop herself crying out merely touching her fingers. She will simply have to make do.

Picking up the slightest thing with these bear paws has become a feat. She does most of the work with her right thumb since the left is sprained.

The shower is a blessed relief after having spent all night feeling grubby and smelling of hospital disinfectant. She allowed the scalding water to enfold her gently for a long moment, then opened a window to feel the delicious, invigorating chill.

Her face seems unchanged. In the mirror, it looks just as it did the previous night, perhaps even uglier, more swollen, the motley blue and yellow bruises, the broken teeth . . .

Camille drives carefully. Too carefully. Too slowly, especially since this stretch of autoroute is short and drivers tend to ignore the speed limits. His mind is elsewhere, he is so preoccupied that even on automatic pilot he slows to a crawl: the car limps towards the Périphérique, dropping from seventy kilometres per hour to sixty, to fifty trailed by the howl of car horns, shouted insults, flashing headlights. His confusion was triggered by a single thought: he has just spent the night with this woman in the most hallowed place in his life, but what does he know about her? What do he and Anne truly know about each other?

He quickly assesses what Anne knows about him. He has told her the most important things: Irène, his mother, his father. His life is a simple one. With Irène's death, he suffered one more tragedy than most people suffer.

He knows little more about Anne: work, marriage, a brother, a divorce, a child.

As he comes to this conclusion, the car veers into the middle lane as Camille takes out his mobile, connects the charger to the dashboard power socket and opens a browser. The screen on the mobile is tiny, and the device slips from his hands as he fumbles for his reading glasses, and he finds himself rummaging for it under the passenger seat – no easy feat for a man who is four foot eleven.

The car drifts into the slow lane, half straddling the hard shoulder and crawls along while Camille recovers the phone, but all the while his brain is working overtime.

What does he know about Anne?

Her daughter. Her brother. Her job at the travel agency.

What else?

His internal alarm manifests itself as a tingling between the shoulder blades.

His mouth is suddenly dry.

Having finally succeeded in retrieving the mobile, Camille keys "Wertig & Schwindel" into the search engine. It is a difficult name to type, but he manages.

He nervously drums his fingers on the steering wheel, waits for the company website to load – a picture of palm trees and beautiful beaches – as an articulated lorry overtakes him with a deafening roar. Camille swerves a little, his eyes still focused on the tiny screen: "ABOUT US, A WORD FROM OUR C.E.O." – who gives a shit? – finally, he comes to a diagram of the company hierarchy. General Manager, Jean-Michel Faye, in his thirties, overweight, balding, but with a typical managerial smugness.

As he joins the Périphérique, Camille is scrolling through the long page of contact details searching for Anne. Thumb pressed firmly on the forward arrow, he flicks through a series of photographs, somehow manages to skip the letter F and by the time he has scrolled back, he can hear a siren behind him. He pulls over as far as he can, the police motorcycle passes and signals for him to turn off the motorway. Camille drops his mobile. Shit.

He pulls over onto the verge. Cops are a fucking pain in the arse.

The studio is a bachelor pad, with none of the accessories a woman might expect: no hairdryer, no mirror. There is no tea, either. Anne finds the mugs and chooses one bearing a Cyrillic inscription:

Мой дядя самых честных правил,
Когда не в шутку занемог

She finds some herbal tea, long past its best-by date and utterly tasteless.

Almost immediately she realises that in this house, she has to rethink every gesture, make a little extra effort in order to do the simplest thing. Because in the home of a man who is four foot eleven, everything is a fraction lower than expected: the door handles, the drawers, the light switches . . . All around her are tools for climbing – stairs, stools, stepladders – because, strangely, nothing is quite at Camille's height either. He has not dismissed the possibility of sharing this space with another person and so everything is positioned midway between what is comfortable for him and what would be acceptable to someone else.

This realisation is like a knife in her heart. She has never pitied Camille – that is not the kind of response he evokes in people – no, she feels moved. She feels guilty, she feels it more here than elsewhere, more now than ever, guilty of monopolising his life, of dragging him into this business. She struggles not to cry; she has decided she is done with tears.

She needs to get a grip. She tips the herbal tea into the sink, angry at herself.

She is wearing her purple tracksuit bottoms and a polo-necked jumper; they are the only things she has here. The blood-stained clothes she was wearing when the paramedics brought her in have been taken away, and Camille decided to leave the things he brought from her apartment in the wardrobe at the hospital so that if anyone noticed her absence, it would look as though she had just popped out for a minute. He had parked next to the emergency exit of the A. & E. department, Anne had slipped out behind the reception desk, got into the car and lay down on the back seat.

He has promised to bring her some clothes tonight. But tonight seems an eternity away. This is the question that must have haunted soldiers who went to war: am I going to die today?

For all Camille's fine promises, she knows the man is coming. The only question is: when? Ever since Camille left, ever since she has been pacing this room, she has been drawn to the looming presence of the forest.

In the dawn light, it looks almost surreal. She turns away, goes into the bathroom, but each time she is drawn back to the forest. A ridiculous image flashes into her mind: Drogo in *The Tartar Steppe,* staring from the remote forward outpost across the desolate wasteland, waiting for the enemy.

How does anyone come out alive?

Cops are not stupid.

When Camille gets out of the car (he has to launch himself, legs extended, like a child getting down from a booster seat), the motorcycle officer immediately recognises him as Commandant

Verhœven. He and his partner are patrolling a specific area but he offers Camille an escort as far as Porte de Saint-Cloud – though not before issuing a warning: "You do realise that using a mobile telephone while driving, regardless of the reason, is extremely dangerous, *commandant*. Being a detective with the *brigade* does not give you licence to endanger other motorists, even in an emergency." The police escort saves Camille almost half an hour. He carries on jabbing at the keypad on his phone, though more discreetly. He is approaching the banks of the Seine when the officer gives him a wave and drives off. Camille immediately puts his glasses on, and though it takes him ten minutes, he discovers that the name Anne Forestier is not on the list of employees at Wertig & Schwindel. Then again, when he looks more closely, he realises that the web page has not been updated since 2005, at which point Anne would still have been living in Lyons.

He pulls into the car park, gets out of the car and is climbing the stairs to his office when his mobile rings

Guérin. Camille turns on his heel and heads back outside to take the call; he does not need anyone overhearing his conversation with Guérin.

"Thanks for getting back to me," he says, trying to sound cheerful.

He is brief and to the point, no need to panic his colleague, but better to be honest: *the reason I called is because I need a favour, let me explain*, but there is no need, Guérin already knows the story, Commissaire Michard has also called and left a message, probably for the same reason. And in a few minutes he will call her back, at which point he will have to tell her that there is no way he could have been the one to tell Camille about the robbery at the Galerie Monier:

"I've been on holiday for the last four days, buddy . . . I'm calling you from Sicily."

Jesus fucking Christ! Camille could kick himself. He says *thanks, no worries, it's nothing serious, yeah, you too*, and hangs up. His mind is already racing ahead, because Guérin's call did nothing to stop the prickling sensation between his shoulder blades or the dry mouth, which in him are clear signs of professional agitation.

"Good morning, *commandant*!" It is the examining magistrate.

Camille comes down to earth with a bump. He feels as though he has spent the past two days inside a giant spinning top whirling at terrifying speed. This morning he is all over the place, the spinning top is behaving like a free electron.

"*Monsieur le juge . . .*"

Camille flashes the broadest smile he can summon. Anyone else in Juge Pereira's shoes might assume that Camille has been desperately trying to get in touch, that he was at this moment coming to find him and that his sudden appearance is a huge relief; flinging his arms wide, Camille nods enthusiastically at this fortuitous meeting of great minds.

The great mind of the judiciary does not seem quite as enthusiastic as Camille. Pereira coldly shakes his hand. Camille is swept along in the wake of the spindle-shanked magistrate, but already it is too late, the *juge* strides solemnly onward and mounts the stairs, it is obvious from his attitude he does not wish to discuss the matter.

"*Monsieur le juge?*"

Pereira stops, turns and feigns surprise.

"Could I speak to you for a moment?" Camille says. "It's about the robbery at the Galerie Monier . . ."

After the balmy heat of the bathroom, the chill air in the living room marks a return to the real world.

Camille reeled off extremely detailed, highly technical instructions about the wood-burning stove which Anne promptly forgot. Picking up a poker, she lifts off the cast-iron lid to toss in more wood, but one of the logs is too big and by the time she has forced it in, the room is filled with acrid smoke. She decides to make a cup of instant coffee.

She cannot seem to get warm, the cold has seeped into her bones. Her eyes are drawn back to the forest as she waits for the water to boil . . .

Then she settles herself on the sofa to leaf through one of Camille's sketchpads – she is spoiled for choice, the room is littered with them. Faces, figures, men in uniform, she is startled to recognise a fat *gendarme* with a bovine expression and dark circles under his eyes, the man who was standing guard outside her hospital room, the one who was snoring loudly as she made her escape. In the drawing, he is on guard duty. With three deft strokes, Camille has captured him perfectly.

The portraits are moving and yet unsentimental. In some, Camille reveals himself to be a gifted caricaturist, sketches that are more cruel than comical and stripped of all illusion.

Suddenly, unexpectedly, in a sketchpad lying on the glass coffee table, she sees herself. Pages and pages of drawings, none of them dated. Her eyes well with tears. For Camille, imagining him alone here, spending whole days recreating from memory the moments they have shared. And for herself. These portraits bear no resemblance to the woman she is now, they are relics of a time when she was beautiful, before the bruises and the broken teeth, before the scars on her cheek and around her mouth, before the vacant eyes. Though Camille merely hints at the setting with a few quick pencil strokes, Anne realises she can remember the circumstances that inspired almost every drawing. Anne having a fit of the giggles at Chez Fernand the day they met; Anne standing on the pavement outside Camille's building: she has only to turn the pages of the sketchbook to retrace the story of their relationship. Here is Anne at Le Verdun, the café where they went that second night. She is wearing a hat and smiling, she looks astonishingly self-assured and – to judge from Camille's thumbnail sketch – she had every reason to be.

Anne sniffles and looks around for a tissue. Here is a full-length portrait, she is walking along a street near the Opéra, coming to meet Camille who has bought tickets for "Madame Butterfly"; she remembers imitating Cio-Cio San in the taxi afterwards. The pages map out their story from the beginning, week by week, month by month. Anne in the shower, or in bed; a series of pages depicts her in tears, she feels ugly, but Camille's glance is loving and gentle. She stretches out her hand to pick up the box of tissues and finds she has to stand to reach them.

Just as she reaches for a tissue, the bullet punctures the picture window and the glass coffee table explodes.

Though she has feared this moment since she woke this morning, still Anne is surprised. Not by the dull crack of the rifle, but by the impact of the bullet which makes a sound as though the whole façade of the house is collapsing. She is petrified as she watches the coffee table shatter beneath her fingers. She lets out a scream and as quickly as her reflexes allow, she curls into a ball like a hedgehog. When she finally glances outside, she sees that the picture window is not shattered. The bullet has made a large, glittering hole from which deep cracks spread. How long can she hold out?

She abruptly realises that she is a sitting target. It is impossible to say where she finds the strength, but with a brutal movement she launches herself over the back of the sofa. The pressure on her fractured ribs as she rolls leaves her winded; she lands heavily, letting out a howl in pain, but her instinct for survival is stronger than the pain and she quickly huddles against the back of the sofa and immediately panics at the thought that a bullet could pass through the upholstery and hit her. Her heart is pounding fit to burst. Her whole body is shivering as though with cold.

The second shot whistles just above her head. The bullet hits the wall and Anne instinctively ducks, feeling fragments of plaster rain down on her face, her neck, her eyes. She lies flat on the ground shielding her head with her hands, almost the same position she adopted in the toilets of the Galerie Monier when he beat her half to death.

A telephone. Call Camille. Right now. Or call the police. She needs someone here. Fast.

Anne knows this is a tricky situation: her mobile is upstairs next to the bed, to get to it she would have to cross the room.

In the open.

A third bullet hits the cast-iron stove with a deafening clang that leaves her half dazed, clapping her hand over her ears as the ricochet shatters one of the pictures on the wall. Anne is so terrified that she cannot seem to focus her thoughts, her mind is swirling with images – the Galerie, her hospital room, Camille's face, his expression grave and reproachful – her whole life flashing past as though she were about to die.

Which she is. The gunman cannot miss for ever. And this time she is utterly alone, with no hope that anyone will come to her rescue.

Anne swallows hard. She cannot stay where she is; the killer will gain entry to the house – she does not know how, but somehow he will. She has to call Camille. He told her to set off the alarm, but the scrap of paper with the scribbled code is next to the control panel on the other side of the living room.

The telephone is up on the mezzanine. She has to get upstairs.

She raises her head and glances around at the floor, at the rug strewn with pieces of plaster, but there is nothing there to help her; she will have to help herself. Her decision is made. She rolls onto her back and, using both hands, pulls off her jumper. The wool becomes caught in the splints on her fingers, she tugs and rips the fabric. She counts to three then sits up, her back against the sofa, clutching the crumpled jumper to her belly. If he fires at the sofa now, she is dead.

There is no time to lose.

Quickly, she looks to her right; the staircase is ten metres away. She looks up and to the left; through the skylight in the roof she can see the branches of a tree – could he climb up there, get in through the skylight? She desperately needs to telephone for help: phone Camille, the police, anyone. She will not get a second chance. She tucks her legs beneath her and throws the rolled-up jumper left, not too hard, she wants it to glide, high and slow, across the room. Hardly has she let it go than she is on her feet and running for the stairs. As she expected, the next bullet explodes behind her.

Alternating fire is a little trick I learned long ago: you have two targets, one on the left, one on the right, and you have to hit them in quick succession. I have the rifle primed and ready. As soon as I see the jumper, I fire – if she plans on wearing it again, she'll need to do some darning because I blew the fucking thing apart. I quickly turn and see her running for the stairs, I aim and my bullet hits the first step just as she reaches the second and disappears into the mezzanine.

Time to up the ante a little. Turns out, it wasn't hard to get her exactly where I wanted her. I thought it would take for ever, but in the end she just needed a little guidance. Now all I need to do is go around. I should probably get a move on though, nothing is ever straightforward, sooner or later she's going to figure things out.

But if everything goes to plan, I'll get there before her.

The first step implodes under her feet.

Anne feels the whole staircase shudder and scrabbles up so fast that she trips and goes flying, hitting her head against the dresser of the cramped bedroom.

Already she is back on her feet. She looks down over the banister to make sure he cannot see her, cannot hit her; she will stay up here. But first she needs to call Camille. He has to come back now, he has to help her. Feverishly, she fumbles for her mobile on the chest of drawers, but it is not there. She tries the nightstand; still nothing. Where the fuck is it? Then she remembers that she plugged it in to recharge before going to bed. She rummages through her discarded clothes, finds the device and turns it on. She is breathless, her heart is hammering so hard in her chest that she feels nauseous, she pounds a fist on her knee, the mobile takes so long to start up. Camille . . . She hits the speed dial.

Come on, Camille, pick up, pick up please . . .

It rings once, twice . . .

Please, Camille, I'm begging you, just tell me what to do . . .

Her hands tremble as they cradle the phone.

"Hello, you've reached Camille Verhœ—"

She hangs up, dials again and gets straight through to voicemail. This time she leaves a message:

"Camille, he's here! Call me back, please . . ."

Pereira is checking his watch. It seems that getting a moment to speak to the magistrate will not be easy. He is a very busy man. To Verhœven, the message is crystal-clear, he is off the case. The *juge* nods his head, exasperated, all these meetings and schedules. Camille finishes his thought: too many irregularities, too much uncertainty, too many doubts, his whole team may have been thrown off the case. To distance herself and cover her arse, Commissaire Michard will file a report with the public prosecutor's office. The looming prospect of an I.G.S. investigation into the actions of Commandant Verhœven is taking shape with an appalling clarity.

Juge Pereira would love to make time, he hesitates, pulls a face, *Let me see*, he checks his watch again, *It's not really a good time, let me think*, he pauses two steps above Camille and stares down, he is faced with a genuine dilemma, avoiding someone is not in his nature. In the end, he capitulates not to Commandant Verhœven, but to a moral imperative.

"Let me get back to you, *commandant*. I'll call you later this morning . . ."

Camille spreads his hands: thank you. Pereira nods gravely: don't mention it.

Camille is very much aware that this is his last chance.

Between Le Guen's friendship and support and the benevolent attitude of the magistrate, there is still a slim chance that he can come through this. He is desperately clinging to this hope, Pereira can see it in his face. And he cannot deny that he is intrigued by what has been going on with Verhœven, the rumours of what has happened over the past two days are so strange that he is curious to know more, to come to his own conclusion.

"Thank you," Camille says.

The words echo like a confession, like an plea, Pereira makes a vague gesture then, embarrassed, he turns and is gone.

Anne suddenly looks up. The man has stopped firing. Where is he?

The back of the house. The window of the ground-floor bathroom is half open. It is far too small for a body to squeeze through, but it is an opening and who knows what this man is capable of. Without considering the risks, and oblivious to the fact he may still be lying in wait outside the picture window, Anne dashes back downstairs, jumps over the shattered bottom step, turns right and almost falls.

By the time she reaches the laundry room he is there, staring at her through the window, his face neatly framed as in a formal portrait. He slips his arm through the opening. A pistol fitted with a silencer is aimed at her. The barrel seems impossibly long.

The moment he sees her, he fires.

After Pereira disappears, Camille rushes upstairs. On the landing he runs into Louis, looking particularly handsome in a Christian Lacroix suit, a pinstripe Savile Row shirt, Forzieri brogues.

"Sorry, Louis, I'll have to catch up with you later . . ."

Louis gives a little wave – *take your time, it can wait* – and steps aside, he will come by later, the guy is diplomacy incarnate.

Camille goes into his office, throws his coat onto a chair, looks up the number for Wertig & Schwindel and as he dials, he checks his watch: 9.15. A voice answers.

"Could I speak to Anne Forestier, please?"

"Hold the line," the voice says. "Let me look . . ."

Deep breath. The vice-like grip constricting his chest loosens. He almost finds himself heaving a sigh of relief.

"I'm sorry . . . what name was that again?" the young woman asks and laughs conspiratorially to get him on side. "I'm really sorry, I'm a temp, so I'm new here."

Camille swallows hard. He feels the noose tighten again, pain shoots through his body and he feels panic rising . . .

"Anne Forestier."

"Do you know which department she's in?"

"Um . . . account management or something like that."

"I'm sorry, I can't see her name in the directory . . . Hold the line, I'll put you through to someone."

Camille can feel his shoulders hunch. A woman's voice comes on the line, probably the one Anne called "a complete bitch", but it can't be her because *No, I'm afraid the name doesn't ring a bell, I've asked around and no-one seems to have heard of her, if you like I can check – are you sure you've got the right name? I can put you through to someone else? Can I ask what you're calling about?*

Camille hangs up.

His throat is dry, he desperately needs a glass of water, but he does not have the time, and besides, his hands are shaking.

He keys in his password, logs on to the system, brings up a search engine: "Anne Forestier." Too many results. Refine the search: "Anne Forestier, date of birth . . ."

He should be able to track down the date, they met early in March and three weeks later, when he found out it was her birthday, he took her to dinner at Chez Nénesse. The invitation had been a spur of the moment thing since he had no time to buy a present; Anne had laughed and said dinner was the perfect gift because she loved desserts. He drew a sketch on the napkin and presented it to her; though he said nothing, he was very pleased with the portrait, it was natural, it was truthful. There are days like that.

He digs out his mobile and brings up the calendar: March 23. Anne is forty-two. 1965. Born in Lyons? Maybe, maybe not. He thinks back to the evening of her birthday, did she say anything about where she was born? He deletes "Lyons" and clicks "submit". The search brings up two Anne Forestiers, which is hardly surprising: type in your date of birth and if you have a common name, you are bound to find you have a twin or even a triplet.

The first Anne Forestier is not his Anne. She died in 1973 at eight years old. Nor is the second. She died two years ago, on 16 October, 2005.

Camille rubs his hands together. He feels the familiar prickle of unease, one of the fundamental tools of a detective, but this is more than merely professional zeal, he has found an anomaly. And as everyone knows, Camille is a past master when it comes to anomalies. Except that in this case, the inconsistency is mirrored by his own inconsistent behaviour, which has been puzzling everyone.

It is beginning to puzzle even him.

Why is he fighting?

Against whom?

Some women lie about their date of birth. It is not Anne's style, but you never know.

Camille gets up and opens the filing cabinet. No-one ever tidies it. He uses his height as a pretext for not doing so – he's happy to exploit his stature when it suits him . . . It takes several minutes for him to find the instruction manual he needs. There is no-one he can ask for help.

"The thing that really takes time after a divorce is the clear-out," Anne said.

Camille lays his hands flat on the table and tries to concentrate. No, it is impossible, he needs a pencil and paper. He sketches. He struggles to remember. They are in Anne's apartment. She is sitting on the sofa bed. "Don't take this the wrong way," he says, "but the place is a little . . . um . . . well, a little dreary." He had tried to come up with a word that was not upsetting, but any sentence that begins "Don't take this the wrong way" and trails off into awkward silence is bound to crash and burn, it is simply a matter of time.

"I don't give a damn," Anne says curtly. "After the divorce, I just wanted to be rid of everything."

The memory becomes clearer. He needs to remember what was said about the divorce. They did not really talk about it, Camille was reluctant to ask questions.

"It was two years ago," Anne says finally.

Camille drops his pencil. He runs a finger down the list of commands in the instruction manual, launches the relevant database and runs a search for information about the marriage and/or divorce of one Anne Forestier in 2005. He goes through the results, filtering out those that do not correspond until he is left with one: "Forestier, Anne, born 20 July, 1970. Age: thirty-seven . . ." Camille clicks on the link: "Arrested for fraud on 27 April, 1998."

Anne has a police record.

This information is so astounding that he cannot quite take it in. Anne has a record. He reads on. Charged with passing fraudulent cheques, with forgery and use of false documents. He is so stunned that it takes several long seconds before he notices that Anne Forestier is incarcerated in the Centre Pénitentiaire de Rennes.

This is not *his* Anne, it is someone else, a different Anne Forestier.

Although . . . The record indicates she was released on parole. When? Is the file up to date? He has to log into a different database to find the official mugshot for the prisoner in question. I'm nervous, he thinks, too nervous. The message onscreen reads: "CTRL+F4 to Submit." A woman appears on the screen, her face front on and also in profile. She is unquestionably of Asian origin.

Place of birth: Da Nang.

He closes the window. Relief. Anne, his Anne, does not have a police record. But she is proving almost impossible to track down.

At last Camille can breathe a little, but his chest still feels constricted, this room is stuffy, he has said it a thousand times.

The moment she saw him staring at her, Anne dropped to the floor. The bullet hits the doorframe a few inches above her head, an almost muffled thud compared to the shriek of the bullet that ricocheted off the cast-iron stove, but the room shudders at the impact.

Crawling on all fours, Anne frantically tries to get out of the room. Terror-stricken. It is madness, but this is precisely the same scene they played out two days ago in the Galerie. Once again, she is scrabbling to escape before he shoots her in the back . . .

She rolls over, the splints on her fingers slipping on the

polished floor, the pain no longer matters, there is no pain now, only instinct.

A bullet grazes her right shoulder and buries itself in the doorframe. Anne scampers wildly like a puppy, manages to roll over the threshold. Suddenly, miraculously, she is safe, sitting with her back against the wall. Can he get into the house? How?

Curiously, she still has her mobile. She rushed down the stairs into the laundry room and crawled out again still clutching it, as a child clutches a teddy bear while bombs and shells rain all around.

What is he doing? She has a desperate urge to take a look, but if he's lying in wait, she would get the next bullet between the eyes.

Think. Fast. She has already redialled Camille. She hangs up; she is alone.

Call the local police? Where's the nearest police station in this godforsaken place? It will take ages to explain, and if they do come how long would it take them to get here? Ten times longer than it will take Anne to die. Because he is there, just on the other side of the wall.

The only person who can help her now is Caravaggio.

Memory is a strange thing. Now that all his senses are sharp as blades, it all comes flooding back. Anne's daughter, Agathe, is studying for an M.B.A. in Boston. Camille is sure of it, he remembers Anne telling him that she visited Boston (she was coming back from Montreal – in fact, it was there that she saw one of his mother's paintings), that the city is very beautiful, very European, "olde worlde" she called it, though Camille did not really know what she meant by the phrase. It vaguely conjured images of Louisiana. Camille does not like travelling.

He needs to consult a different database which requires a different manual. He goes back to the filing cabinet, finds a list of instructions – in principle, nothing he has done so far requires him to request authorisation from a superior. The network connection is fast: Boston University, four thousand professors, thirty thousand students. The list of results is too large. Camille goes through the list of sororities, copies and pastes them into a document where he can do a simple name search.

No-one named Forestier. Maybe Anne's daughter is married? Or maybe she uses her father's surname? Instead he searches by first name. There are several Agathas and a handful of Agatas, but only two Agathes and one Agate. Three C.V.s.

Agathe Thompson, twenty-seven, Canadian. Agathe Lendro, twenty-three, Argentinian. Agathe Jackson, American. No-one from France.

No Anne and now no Agathe.

Camille considers running a search for Anne's father.

"He managed to get himself elected treasurer of about forty different organisations. One day he emptied every one of the accounts, and no-one ever saw him again."

Anne laughed when she told him the story, but it was a strange laugh. With so little information, it would be difficult to track him down. He was a shopkeeper, but what did he sell? Where did he live? When did all this happen? Too many unknowns.

This leaves Anne's brother, Nathan. It is impossible that a researcher (what was his field? – astrophysics, something like that), who by definition has published scientific papers, would not be mentioned somewhere on the internet. Camille struggles to breathe as he waits for the search to complete.

No research scientist named Nathan Forestier, not anywhere. The closest match is Nathan Forest, a New Zealander aged seventy-three.

Camille changes tack again, he scours the travel agencies in Lyons and in Paris . . . By the time he finally runs a trace on Anne's landline number, the tingling between his shoulder blades has stopped. He already knows what he will find. It is a foregone conclusion.

The number is unlisted, he has to circumvent the system, it is time-consuming but not particularly difficult.

The landline is leased to Maryse Roman, 26, rue de la Fontaine-au-roi. In other words, Anne's apartment belongs to her next-door neighbour and everything is in her name, probably because everything belongs to her: the telephone line, the furniture, even the bookcase with its improbable selection of books.

Anne is renting a furnished apartment.

Camille could make further inquiries, he could send a team of officers round, but there is no point. Nothing there belongs to the phantom he knows as Anne Forestier.

Though he considers this fact from every angle, he comes to the same conclusion. Anne Forestier does not exist.

So who is this person Hafner is trying to kill?

Anne sets down her mobile on the tiled floor, she has to crawl, slowly and painfully, using her elbows, longing to be somehow invisible. A grand tour of the living room. Finally she reaches the little sideboard on which Camille left the scrap of paper with the code. The alarm itself is next to the main door.

\# 29091571 \#

As the alarm howls, Anne claps her hands over her ears

and drops to her knees, as though the ear-splitting shriek is a continuation of the murderous attack by other means. She can feel it drilling into her skull.

Where is he? Though everything in her resists, she slowly gets to her feet and peers around the doorframe. No-one. She tries taking away her hands, but the alarm is so deafening she cannot focus, cannot think. Palms pressed to her ears, she crawls towards the window.

Is he gone? Anne's throat is still tight with panic. It cannot be this easy. He cannot have run off. Not just like that.

Camille barely registers Louis' presence when he pops his head round the door of the office – he tried knocking but there was no response.

"Pereira is on his way up . . ."

Camille has still not quite emerged from his daze. To get to the bottom of this will take time, it will take rigorous, rational, dispassionate logic – it will take a whole host of qualities Camille sorely lacks.

"Sorry?"

Louis repeats what he said. "Fine," Camille mutters and gets up. He grabs his jacket.

"Are you O.K. ?" Louis says.

Camille is not listening. He digs out his mobile and sees he has a message. Anne called. Quickly, he punches the keypad and calls his voicemail. "Camille, he's here! Call me back, please . . ." By the time he has heard these words, he is already at the door, he pushes past Louis, races along the corridor, hurtles down the stairs, crashing into a woman on the landing below and almost knocking her over. It is Commissaire Michard. She and Juge Pereira were on their way to meet him. When the magistrate opens his mouth to speak, Camille does not pause even for a millisecond, but as he tears down the stairs, he calls back:

"Later, I'll explain everything later."

"Verhœven!" bellows Commissaire Michard.

But Camille has already left the building. Outside, he scrabbles to open his car, slams the door, throws the vehicle into reverse, rolls down the window and reaches out to stick the police light on the roof. Lights flashing, sirens blaring, headlights on full beam, he roars out of the car park. A beat cop blows his whistle, bringing traffic to a standstill so he can pass.

Camille takes the bus lane. He redials Anne's number, puts the call on speakerphone.

Pick up the phone, Anne.

Pick up the phone!

Anne gets to her feet again. She waits. She cannot understand this absence. It could be a ruse, but the seconds tick past and still nothing happens. The alarm stops, giving way to a throbbing silence.

Anne takes another step towards the window, standing to one side, half hidden, ready to retreat. He cannot simply have run away like that. So swiftly. So suddenly.

At that moment, he materialises right in front of her.

Anne shrinks back in terror.

They are less than two metres apart, on either side of the plate-glass window.

He has no weapons, he stares into her eyes and takes a step forward. If he reached out, he could touch the glass. He smiles and nods his head. Unable to tear her eyes from his, Anne takes a step back. He holds his hands palms out, like Jesus in a painting Camille once showed her. Still gazing into her eyes, he raises his hands above his head and slowly turns around as though she has a gun trained on him.

See? I'm not armed.

And as he comes to face her again, his hands are outstretched in welcome.

Anne cannot move. Like a rabbit sitting in headlights, paralysed with fear, waiting for death.

His eyes still fixed on hers, he takes a step, then another, slowly moving towards the sliding door. Gently, he grasps the handle, he seems anxious not to panic her. And it seems to be working: still Anne does not move, she stares at him, her breathing ragged, her heart pounding, each beat heavy, muffled, painful. The man stops, his smile a rictus, he is waiting.

We might as well get this over with, thinks Anne, we've almost reached the end of the road.

She looks down at the terrace outside the window and notices that he has thrown his leather jacket on the ground. The butt of his pistol is clearly visible and the gleaming handle of a hunting knife sticking out of the other pocket. The man puts his hands into his pockets and turns them inside out.

See? Nothing in my hands, nothing in my pockets.

Just two steps. She has already taken so many. The man does not move a muscle.

She comes to her decision suddenly, as though hurling herself into the flames. One step forward, the splints make it difficult for her fingers to release the latch, especially as she can barely grip it.

The moment the latch slides back, the moment the door is open and he has only to step through, Anne scuttles back, clapping a hand over her mouth, as though suddenly realising what she has just done.

She lets her arms fall limply to her sides. The man steps into the room. In the end, she cannot contain herself.

"Bastard!" she shrieks. "Bastard, bastard, bastard . . ."

Slowly edging backwards, she unleashes a torrent of insults mingled with sobs that come from deep within her belly, *bastard, bastard . . .*

"Oh, dear, oh dear . . ."

He clearly finds this tedious. He steps further into the studio, looking around curiously like a visitor or an estate agent – the mezzanine is a nice touch, and there is a lot of light . . . Panting for breath, Anne is cowering next to the stairs.

"All better now?" the man says, finally turning to her. "Feeling a bit calmer?"

"Why are you trying to kill me?" Anne wails.

"What the . . . what on earth makes you think I'm trying to kill you?"

He sounds genuinely upset, almost outraged.

Anne's hand falls away from her mouth and in a sudden frenzy, all her rage, all her fear comes pouring out, her voice is high and shrill, she has lost all self-control, she feels nothing now but pure hatred. But she is still afraid, afraid that he will beat her, she shrinks back . . .

"You're trying to kill me!"

The man sighs . . . This whole situation is tiresome. He listens wearily as Anne rages on.

"That wasn't part of the plan!"

This time he nods his head, disappointed in the face of such naivety.

"Oh, but it was."

Clearly, she needs to have everything spelled out for her. But Anne has not finished.

"No, it wasn't! You were only supposed to push me aside! That's what you said, 'I'll just give you a little push'!"

"But . . ." He is dumbfounded to find he has to explain something so basic. "But it needed to be convincing. Don't you get it? Con-vin-cing!"

"You've been stalking me!"

"Well, yeah, but bear in mind it's all in a good cause . . ."

He laughs, which further fuels Anne's rage.

"That's not what we agreed, you fucking bastard!"

"O.K., so there are a couple of details I didn't fill you in on . . . And don't call me a bastard or I'll give you a fucking slap."

"Right from the start you've been planning to kill me."

This time, he snaps.

"To kill you?" he growls, "No, no, no, darling. Because if I really wanted to kill you, you wouldn't be here to bitch about it now. [He raises his index finger to emphasise the point.] With you, I was just trying to make an impression, there's a difference! And let me tell you it's a lot harder than you think. Even that little performance at the hospital where I had to scare that runty little boyfriend of yours without him calling in an armed response unit took restraint, it took talent."

The argument hits home. Anne is beside herself.

"You ruined my face! You smashed my teeth! You . . ."

"O.K., I'll admit you're no oil painting right now. [He struggles to suppress a smile.] But it can be fixed, plastic surgeons these days can work miracles. Tell you what, I'll pay for two gold teeth out of my share if I hit the jackpot. Or silver if you prefer. You

238

choose. But if you're hoping to find a husband, for the front teeth I'd recommend gold, it's classier . . ."

Slumped on the floor, curled into a ball, Anne has no more tears, only hatred.

"I'll kill you one of these days . . ."

"So, not bitter, then . . ." The man laughs, wandering around the room as though he owns the place. "But you're only saying that because you're angry. No, no, no . . ." he says, his tone deadly serious now. "If all goes well, you'll have your stitches removed, you'll have a couple of plastic teeth fitted and you'll go home like a good little girl."

He stops and looks up at the staircase, the mezzanine.

"It's not bad, this place. I like what he's done with it. [He looks at his watch.] Right, you'll have to excuse me, but I can't hang around."

He steps towards her and she presses herself against the wall.

"I'm not going to touch you!"

"Get the fuck out!" she shrieks.

The man nods, but he is distracted by something else. Standing at the foot of the stairs he looks down at the shattered step, then back at the bullet hole in the window.

"Pretty good, don't you think?" He turns back to Anne, eager to persuade her.

"Get out . . . !"

"Yeah, you're right. [He glances around. Satisfied.] I think we've put in a good day's work. We make a good team, don't we? And now [he gestures to the bullet holes around the room], everything should go smoothly, unless I'm very much mistaken."

He strides over to the windows.

"I have to say, the neighbours aren't exactly fearless! That alarm could have gone on all day and no-one would come over to see what was up. Still, it's hardly surprising. It's the same everywhere these days. Right, better run . . ."

He steps out onto the terrace, picks up his jacket, slips a hand into one of the pockets and comes back.

"There," he says, tossing an envelope towards Anne. "You use this only if everything goes according to plan. And you better hope for your sake that it does. Whatever happens, you don't leave here without my permission, understood? Because otherwise, what you've suffered so far will just be a down payment."

He does not wait for an answer. He disappears.

A few metres from where she is sitting, Anne's mobile starts to ring, vibrating against the tiled floor. After the piercing howl of the alarm, it sounds tinny, like a child's toy telephone.

It is Camille. She has to answer.

"Do exactly what I tell you and everything will be fine."

Anne presses the answer button. She does not need to pretend to be devastated.

"He's gone . . ." she says.

"Anne?" Camille roars. "I can't hear what you're saying. Anne?"

Camille is panicked, his voice is colourless.

"He came to the house," Anne says, "I set off the alarm, he panicked and ran off . . ."

Camille can barely hear her. He turns off his siren.

"Are you alright? I'm on my way there now, just tell me you're alright . . ."

"I'm O.K., Camille," she speaks a little louder. "Everything's fine now."

Camille slows the car, takes a breath. His terror gives way to agitation. He wants to be there now.

"What exactly happened? Tell me everything . . ."

Cradling her knees with her arms, Anne starts to sob.

She wishes she were dead.

10.30 a.m.

Camille feels a little calmer, having turned off the siren. He turns it on again now. There are so many elements of the case to consider, but his mind is still a jumble of emotions and he is incapable of ordering his thoughts . . .

For the past two days, he has been inching forward on a rickety plank with an abyss on either side. Now Anne has dug another chasm right beneath his feet.

Despite the fact that his career is at stake, that three times in the past two days someone has attempted to kill the woman in his life, that this woman he is involved with has been living under a false name, that he no longer knows exactly what her role is in this case, Camille needs to think strategically, to think logically, but his mind is consumed by a single thought that trumps all others: what is Anne doing in his life?

In fact, he has not one question, but two: if it turns out that Anne is not Anne, what does that change?

He goes back over the time they have spent together, the evenings spent finding each other, hardly daring to touch, and the nights they spent between the sheets . . . In August, she dumps him and an hour later he finds her still outside in the stairwell – was this simply a ploy on her part? A clever ruse? The whispered words, the tender embraces, the hours, the days, was it all just deliberate manipulation?

In a few minutes, he will find himself face to face with a woman who calls herself Anne Forestier, a woman he has been sleeping with for months, a woman who has been lying to him since the day they met. He does not know what to think, he is completely drained, put through a wringer.

What is the connection between Anne's false identity and the robbery at the Galerie?

And what exactly is his role in this story?

But the most important thing is that someone is trying to kill this woman.

He no longer knows who she is, but he knows one thing It is his responsibility to protect her.

When he walks into the studio, Anne is still sitting on the floor, her back against the sink, her arms wrapped around her knees.

In all the confusion, Camille had forgotten what she looks like now. On the long drive here, it was the other Anne he was picturing, the pretty, smiling Anne he fell for, with her green eyes and her dimples. Seeing her mutilated face, the yellow bruises, the bandages, the grubby splints, he is shocked – almost as shocked as he was two days ago when he saw her in the casualty department.

Overcome by a wave of compassion, he feels himself founder. Anne does not move, does not look at him, she is staring into the middle distance as though hypnotised.

"Are you alright, darling?" Camille creeps towards her as if attempting to tame an animal. He kneels and clumsily takes her in his arms – not easy given his size. He touches her chin and turns her face towards his. She stares at him as though only now registering his presence.

"Oh, Camille . . ."

She lays her head in the hollow of his shoulder.

The world could end right now.

But the world is not destined to end just yet.

"Tell me."

Anne looks left, then right, it is difficult to tell if she is distraught or if she simply does not know where to begin.

"Was he alone? Was the whole gang here?"

"No, just him . . ."

Her voice is low and resonant.

"Hafner? The man you identified from the photo array?"

Anne simply nods. Yes, it was him.

"Tell me what happened."

As Anne struggles to describe the events (her words come in halting, ragged fragments, never complete sentences), Camille pieces together the scene. The first shot. He turns towards the shards of glass strewn across the floor where the coffee table was, the splintered cherrywood that looks as though it came through a tornado. As he listens, he gets to his feet and walks over to the window, the bullet hole is too high for him to reach, he visualises the trajectory.

"Go on . . ." he says.

He moves to the wall, then back to the cast-iron stove, lays a finger on the spot where the bullet ricocheted then scans the back wall and sees the gaping hole. He walks to the staircase and crouches there for some time, one hand resting on the splintered fragments of the first step, glances thoughtfully towards the top of the stairs, then turns back to the spot from which the shot was fired. He stands on the second stair.

"What happened next?" he says, stepping down.

He walks into the bathroom; from here, Anne's voice is faint, barely audible. Camille continues his reconstruction; this may be his house, but just now it is a crime scene. Conjecture, observation, conclusion.

The window is half open. Anne comes into the room, Hafner is waiting, he pushes his arm through the gap and aims the pistol fitted with a silencer. Camille finds the bullet lodged in the doorframe above his head. He goes back into the living room.

Anne has fallen silent.

Camille fetches a broom from under the stairs and quickly sweeps the remains of the coffee table against the wall, dusts off the sofa, then goes to boil some water.

"Come on . . ." he says at length. "It's over now . . ."

Anne huddles next to him on the sofa and they sip something Camille insists is tea – it tastes horrid, but Anne does not complain.

"I'll take you somewhere else."

Anne shakes her head.

"Why not?"

It little matters why, Anne flatly refuses to leave though the folly of her decision is evidenced by the ruined coffee table, the bullet holes in the window, the door, the staircase, by every object in this room.

"I think th—"

"No," Anne cuts him off.

This settles the matter. Camille decides that if Hafner did not manage to gain access to the house, he is unlikely to try again today. There will be time to think again tomorrow. Over the past three days, whole years have elapsed so tomorrow seems very far away.

Besides, Camille has finally decided on his next move.

It has taken him a little time, just as long as a boxer might need to scrape himself up off the canvas and get back into the fight.

Camille is almost there.

He needs an hour or two. Maybe a little longer. In the meantime, he will lock up the house, check all the exits and leave Anne here.

They sit together in silence, their thoughts interrupted only by the vibrations from Camille's mobile which rings constantly. He does not need to check, he knows who is calling.

It feels strange to sit here holding this unknown woman he knows so well. He knows he should ask questions, but that can wait until after. First he needs to unravel the thread.

Camille feels suddenly exhausted. Lulled by the leaden sky, the shadowy forest, this squat, slow house transformed into a blockhouse, cradling this mystery to his chest, he could sleep all day if he allowed himself. Instead, he listens to Anne, her ragged breathing, to the soft gulp as she drains her tea, to the heavy silence that has come between them.

"Are you going to find him?" Anne whispers after a moment.

"Oh yes."

The answer comes immediately, instinctively; Camille sounds so certain, so convinced, that even Anne is surprised.

"You will let me know as soon as you find him, won't you?"

To Camille, the subtext to Anne's every question could be a whole novel. He frowns quizzically: why?

"I just need to feel safe, you can understand that, can't you?"

Her voice is no longer a whisper, her hand falls away from her mouth and he can see her gums, her broken teeth.

"Of course . . ."

He almost apologises.

Finally, their separate silences merge. Anne has dozed off. Camille can find no words. If he had a pencil, in a few strokes he could sketch their twin solitudes; they are each coming to the end of a story, they are together yet alone. Curiously, Camille has never felt closer to her, a mysterious solidarity binds him to this woman. Gently, he withdraws his arm, lays Anne's head against the back of the sofa and gets to his feet.

Time to go. Time to find out the real story.

He creeps up the stairs like a hunter tracking prey, he moves soundlessly, being intimately familiar with every stair, every creaking board, and besides, he does not weigh much.

The roof upstairs slopes steeply, at its lowest point the room is only a metre or so high. Camille lays down on the floor and crawls to the far side of the bed to a trapdoor that swings open to provide access to the narrow crawlspace. The cubbyhole is filthy with dust and cobwebs. Camille reaches inside and gropes around, finds the plastic bag and pulls it towards him. A black bin-liner containing a thick folder. A file he has not opened since . . .

He cannot help but see that everything about this case has forced him to confront his greatest fears.

He looks around, finds a pillowcase and carefully slips the file inside. With every little movement, the film of dust creates clouds of ash. Camille gets up and steals back downstairs.

Some minutes later, he is writing a note to Anne.

"Get some rest. Call anytime. I'll be back as soon as I can be."

I'll keep you safe – no, this is something he cannot bring himself to write.

When he is finished, he makes a tour of the house, checking all the door handles, ensuring everything is locked. Before he leaves, he stands and stares at the sleeping form of Anne on the sofa. It pains him to think of leaving her alone. It is difficult to leave, but impossible to stay.

Time to go. Carrying the thick folder in the striped pillowcase under one arm, Camille crosses the yard and heads through the forest to where he parked the car.

He stops and looks back. From here, surrounded by the forest, the silent house looks as though it is built on a plinth like a casket or a still-life painting, a *vanitas*. He thinks of Anne asleep inside.

But by the time his car slowly moves away into the forest, Anne's eyes are wide open.

11.30 a.m.

As the car speeds towards Paris, Camille's mental landscape becomes simplified. He may not know what happened, but he knows the questions to ask.

The key thing now is to ask the right questions.

In the course of an armed robbery, a killer assaults a woman who calls herself Anne Forestier. He hunts her down, he is determined to kill her, he tracks her all the way to Camille's isolated studio.

What is the link between the robbery and the fact of Anne's false identity?

Everything would suggest that the woman was simply in the wrong place at the wrong time, having come to collect a watch being engraved for Camille, but though they seem utterly unrelated, the two events are connected. Intimately connected.

Are there any two things that are not connected?

Camille has not been able to find out the truth from Anne, he does not even know who she really is. So now he must look elsewhere. At the other end of the thread.

Three missed calls from Louis who, typically, has not left a voicemail. Instead he sent a text message: "Need help?" Some day, when this is all over, Camille plans to adopt Louis.

Three voicemails from Le Guen. In fact, the message is the same, only the tone changes. With every call, Jean's voice is calmer, his message shorter and more circumspect. "Listen, I really need you to call me b—" *Message deleted*. "Um . . . why haven't you ca—" *Message deleted*. In the third message, Le Guen sounds grim. In fact, he is simply sad. "If you don't help me, I can't help you." *Message deleted*.

Camille empties his mind of every obstacle and pursues his train of thought. He needs to stay focused.

Everything has become more complicated.

He has had to radically rethink the situation after the mayhem at the studio. The damage caused is undeniably dramatic, but though he is not a ballistics expert, Camille cannot help but wonder.

Anne is behind a picture window twenty metres wide. Outside, there is a skilled, determined, heavily armed killer. It is not impossible that missing Anne was sheer misfortune. But failing to put a bullet in her head when he had his arm thrust through an open window and was less than six metres away is suspicious. It is as though, since the Galerie Monier, he has been cursed. Unless this has all been carefully planned from the start. Such a spectacular run of bad luck is scarcely credible . . .

In fact, one might think that to avoid killing Anne, given the number of opportunities there have been, would take an exceptional marksman. Camille has not known many people equal to such a task.

This question inevitably prompts others.

How did he track Anne down to the studio in Montfort?

Last night, Camille drove this same route from Paris. Anne, exhausted, fell asleep almost immediately and did not wake until they arrived.

There is a lot of traffic on the motorway and on the Périphérique even at night, but Camille stopped the car twice and waited for several minutes, watching the traffic, and took a roundabout route on the last leg of the journey, along byroads where the headlights of another would have been visible from a considerable distance.

He has a chilling sense of *déjà vu*: by launching a raid on the Serbian community, he led the killers straight to Ravic; now he has led them to Anne in Montfort.

This is the most plausible hypothesis. It is obviously the one he is supposed to accept. But now that he knows that Anne is not Anne, that everything he assumed about the case until now is in doubt, the most plausible theories become the least likely.

Camille is certain that he was not followed. Which means that someone came looking for Anne in Montfort because they knew she would be there.

He needs to come up with a different theory. And this time, the possibilities are limited.

Each solution is a name, the name of someone close to Camille, someone close enough to know about his mother's studio. To know that he is in a relationship with the woman who was brutally beaten during the raid on the jeweller's.

To know that he was planning to take her there for safety.

Camille racks his brain, but try as he might he can barely come up with a handful of names. If he excludes Armand, who he watched go up in smoke two days ago, the short list is very short indeed.

And it does not include Vincent Hafner, a man he has never met in his life.

The only possible conclusion sends Camille into a tailspin.

He already knows that Anne is not Anne. Now he is convinced that Hafner is not Hafner.

It means starting the investigation over.

It means: back to square one.

And given everything that Camille has done so far, it may mean: *Go to jail. Go directly to jail. Do not pass Go . . .*

There he goes again, the runty little cop, making the trip between Paris and his country estate, like a hamster in a wheel. Like a rat. Always scuttling around. I just hope it pays off. Not for him, obviously, at this point he's up shit creek, he's well and truly screwed as he'll find out very soon. No, I hope it pays off for me.

I'm not about to give up now.

The girl has done what she needed to, you might reckon she paid her pound of flesh, I can't complain. It's going to be a close-run thing, but right now everything seems to be going like clockwork.

Now it's my move. My good friend Ravic and I did a perfect dummy run. If the guy were still alive, he'd testify to that, though with all those missing fingers, he'd have a job swearing on the Bible.

Thinking back, I went easy on him, in fact I think I was pretty lenient. Putting a bullet in his head was almost an act of kindness. I swear, the Serbs are like the Turks, they're a thankless bunch. It's their culture. They have no sense of gratitude. And then they come bitching about how they've got problems.

But it's time to get down to some serious business. I know that wherever he is – I don't know if there's a heaven for Serbian thugs, after all there's definitely one for terrorists – Ravic will be happy. He'll have his revenge served *post mortem* because I have a powerful urge to flay someone alive. I'm going to need a bit of luck. But since I haven't had to call on her so far, I figure the goddess Fortuna owes me a favour.

And if Verhœven does his job, things should move pretty fast.

Right now, I'm heading back to my fortress of solitude to rest up a bit, because when this kicks off, I'm going to have to move fast.

My reflexes might be a little blunted, but my motivation is intact, and that's what counts.

12.00 noon

In the bathroom mirror, Anne examines her gums, stares at the ugly, gaping hole. Since she was admitted to hospital under a false name, she will not be able to access her medical file – the X-rays, the test results – she will have to start over. Start again from scratch – though the word hardly does justice to her injuries.

He says he wasn't trying to kill her because he needs her. But he can say what he likes, she does not believe a word. Dead or alive, Anne would have served her purpose. He beat her so brutally, so savagely . . . He might claim that it had to look authentic, but she knows that he actually enjoyed beating her, that he would have done more damage if he could have.

In the medicine cabinet, she finds nails scissors and a pair of tweezers. The young Indian doctor assured her that the gash on her cheek was not deep. He suggested removing the stitches after ten days. She wants to do it now. In one of the drawers in Camille's desk she finds a magnifying glass. Working with makeshift instruments in a dimly lit bathroom is not ideal. But she cannot bear to wait any longer. And this is not simply about her obsession with neatness. This is what she used to say to Camille when they were together, that she was a neat freak. Not this time. Contrary to what he might think when all this is over, she did not tell him many lies. The bare minimum. Because it is difficult to lie to Camille. Or because it is too easy. It amounts to the same thing.

Anne wipes her eyes with her sleeve. It is hard enough to remove the sutures by herself; with tears in her eyes, it is impossible . . . There are eleven stitches. She holds the magnifying glass in her left hand and the scissors in her right. Close up, the little black threads look like insects. She slides the tip of the scissors under the first knot and immediately she feels a sharp pain as though she has stabbed herself. Under normal circumstances, the procedure would be painless, obviously the wound is not yet healed. Or perhaps it is infected. She has to slide the blade quite far to cut the stitch, she screws up her face and goes for it. The first insect is dead, now all she has to do is pull it out. Her hands are trembling. Still trapped beneath her skin, she has to tug with the tweezers, struggling to keep her hands from shaking. Finally it begins to move, leaving an ugly mark as it emerges. Anne peers at the wound but can see no difference. She is about to start on the next suture, but she feels so tense, so unsteady, that she has to sit down and take a breath . . .

Coming back to the mirror, she presses on the gash and winces, she snips the second suture, and the third. She pulls them out too quickly. Looking through the magnifying glass, the wound is still red, it has not closed up. The fourth stitch is more troublesome, it feels almost welded to her skin. But Anne is determined. She grits her teeth, digs the tip of the scissors into her flesh, tries to cut the thread and fails, the wound gapes and oozes a little blood. Finally the thread snaps, but great drops as big as tears are now trickling from the cut. She deals with the next few sutures quickly, sliding them out and flicking the corpses into the sink, but for the last few Anne has to work blindly because as she wipes away the blood, more gushes to the surface. She does not stop until all the stitches have been removed. Still the blood flows. Without thinking, she rummages in the medicine cabinet for the bottle of surgical spirit and, having no compress, pours some onto her palm and dabs it on.

The pain is excruciating . . . Anne howls and pounds her fist on the washbasin, the splints on her fingers come loose making her scream even louder. But this scream is hers and hers alone, no-one has ripped it from her body.

She dabs more alcohol directly onto the wound, then grips the sink with both hands, she feels as though she might pass out, but she stands firm. When the pain finally subsides, she finds a compress, soaks it in surgical spirit and applies it against her cheek. When finally she looks, the bandage does little to hide the ugly, swollen gash which is still bleeding a little.

There will be a scar. A straight line slashed across her cheek. On a man, people would call it a "war wound". She cannot tell how big the scar will be, but she knows it will never go away.

It is permanent.

And if she had to dig out the wound with a knife she would have done it. Because this is something that she wants to remember. For ever.

12.30 p.m.

The car park at the casualty department is always full. This time, Camille has to flash his warrant card just to get in.

The receptionist is blooming like a rose. A slightly wilted rose, but she lays the concern on thick.

"So, I hear she disappeared?"

She makes a sad pout, as though she understands how difficult this is for Verhœven – *what happened, it must have come as a shock, it doesn't say much for the police, does it?* Camille walks on, desperate to be rid of her, but this is not as easy as he might have expected.

"What about that admission form?"

He retraces his steps.

"I mean, it's not really my department, but when a patient does a runner and we don't even have a social security number, there's ructions upstairs. And the big shots are quick to pass the buck, they don't care who's responsible, they come down on us like a ton of bricks. It's happened to me often enough, that's the only reason I'm asking."

Camille nods – I get the picture – as though he sympathises while the receptionist fields a series of telephone calls. Obviously, since Anne was admitted under a false name, she could not have produced a social security number. This is why he found no papers in her apartment. She has no papers, or none under that name.

Suddenly he feels the urgent need to call, for no reason, as though he is afraid he cannot handle the situation without her, without Anne . . .

And once again he remembers that she is not Anne. Everything that name once signified is meaningless. Camille feels distraught, he has lost everything, even her name.

"You O.K. ?"

"Yes, I'm fine," Camille tries to look preoccupied, it is the best thing to do when you need to throw someone off the scent.

"Her file, her medical file," he says, "where is it?"

Anne disappeared the night before, so all the paperwork is still up on the ward.

Camille thanks the receptionist. When he gets upstairs, he realises he has no idea how to play this, so he takes a moment to think. He stands at one end of the corridor, next to the waiting room that is now a junk room where he and Louis did their first debriefing on the case. He watches as the handle slowly turns and the door reluctantly opens as though a child is afraid to come out.

When he appears, the child turns out to be close to retirement: it is Hubert Dainville, the consultant, the big boss. His grey mane is perfectly blow-dried, it looks as though he has only just removed his curlers. He flushes scarlet when he sees Camille. Usually, there is no-one in the junk room, it has no purpose and leads nowhere.

"What the devil are you doing there?" he snaps officiously, ready to bite.

I could ask the same of you. The retort is on the tip of Camille's tongue, but he knows that is not the way to go about things. He looks around distractedly.

"I'm lost . . . [Then, resigned:] I must have taken the wrong corridor."

The surgeon's blush has faded to pale pink, his awkwardness forgotten, his personality reasserts itself. He strides off as though he has just been summoned to an urgent case.

"You no longer have any business here, *commandant*."

Camille trots after him, having been caught off-guard, his brain is whirring feverishly.

"Your witness absconded from this hospital last night!" Dainville growls as though he blames Verhœven personally.

"So I heard."

Camille can think of no other solution, he thrusts a hand into his pocket, takes out his mobile and drops it. It clatters across the tiled floor.

"Shit!"

Dainville, who has already reached the lifts, turns and sees the *commandant*, his back towards him, scrabbling to pick up the pieces of his mobile. Stupid prick. The lift doors open; Dainville steps inside.

Camille gathers up his mobile, which is actually in one piece, and pretends to put it back together it as he walks back towards the junk room.

Seconds pass. A minute. He cannot bring himself to open the door, something is holding him back. Another few seconds tick by. He must have been mistaken. He waits. Nothing. Oh, well. He is about to turn on his heel, but changes his mind.

The handle turns again, and this time the door is briskly opened.

The woman who bustles out, pretending to be preoccupied, is Florence, the nurse. Now it is her turn to blush as she sees Camille. Her plump lips form a perfect O, he hesitates for a second and by then it is too late to create a diversion. Her embarrassment is clear as she pushes a stray lock of hair behind her ear and, staring at Camille, she closes the door calmly, deliberately – *I'm a busy woman, I'm focused on my job, I have nothing to feel guilty about.* Nobody believes her little performance, not even Florence herself. Camille does not have to press his advantage, it is not really in his nature . . . He hates himself for doing it, but he must. He stares at Florence, tilts his head quizzically, increasing the pressure – *I didn't want to interrupt you during your little tryst, see how tactful I am?* He pretends he has just been standing here fixing his mobile, waiting for her to conclude her *tête-à-tête* with Dr Dainville.

"I need Madame Forestier's medical file," he says.

Florence walks ahead of him, but makes no attempt to lengthen her stride as Dr Dainville did so blatantly. She is not mistrustful. And there is not an spiteful bone in her body.

"I'm not sure . . ." she says.

Camille squeezes his eyes shut, silently imploring her not to make him say it: *maybe I should have word with Dr Dainville, I suspect he . . .*

They have come to the nurses' station

"I'm not sure . . . if the file is still here."

Not once does she turn to look at him, she pulls opens a drawer of patient files and promptly takes out one marked "FORESTIER", a large manila folder containing the C.A.T. scan, the X-rays, the doctor's notes. To hand this over to someone, even a policeman, is a serious breach of nursing protocol . . .

"I'll bring over the warrant from the *juge d'instruction* this afternoon," Camille says. "In the meantime, I can issue a receipt."

"That won't be necessary," she says hurriedly, "I mean, as long as the *juge* . . ."

Camille takes the file. Thank you. They look at each other. Camille feels an almost physical pain, not simply because he has resorted to such an ignoble ploy, extorting information to which he has no right, but because he understands this woman. He knows that her botoxed lips are not an attempt to remain young, but stem from an overpowering need to be loved.

1.00 p.m.

You go through the wrought-iron gates, along the long path. The imposing pink building rises up before you, tall trees tower above your head. You might be forgiven for thinking you have arrived at a mansion; it is difficult to believe that behind the graceful windows, bodies are lined up and dissected. Here, livers and hearts are weighed, skulls are sawn open. Camille knows this building like the back of his hand and cordially loathes it. It is the people he likes, the staff, the assistants, the pathologists, Nguyên above all. The many shared memories, most of them painful, have created a bond between them.

Camille makes his usual entrance, waving to this person or

that. He can tell there is a certain chill in the air, that rumours about the case have preceded him, it is obvious from the awkward smiles, the diffident handshakes.

Nguyên, inscrutable as a sphinx as always. He is not much taller than Camille, thin as a rail and last smiled in 1984. He shakes Camille's hand, listens attentively, takes Anne's medical file and reads it. Guardedly.

"Just a quick once-over," Camille says, "in your spare time."

In this context, "Just a quick once-over" means: *I need your advice, something doesn't feel right, I want your honest opinion, I won't say any more because I don't want to influence your opinion, oh, and if you could do it a.s.a.p.*

"In your spare time" means: *this is not official, it's personal* – implying that the rumours that Verhœven is up shit creek are true. Nguyên nods, he has never been able to refuse Camille. Besides, he is not in any trouble and cannot resist a mystery, he has a nose for inconsistencies, an eye for detail – he is a pathologist.

"Give me a call around five o'clock," Nguyên says and locks the file in his desk drawer; this is personal.

1.30 p.m.

Time to head back to the office. Knowing what awaits him at the *brigade*, Camille is reluctant to go, but he has no choice.

From the way his fellow officers greet him in the hallway, it's obvious the atmosphere is fraught. At the morgue, the tension was muted; here it is palpable. As in any other office, three days is more than enough time for a rumour to circulate widely. And it is a natural law that the more vague the rumour, the more it is blown out of proportion. His colleagues' expressions of sympathy sound more like condolences.

Even if he were asked point-blank, Camille has no desire to explain himself, to anyone; besides, he would not know what to say, where to start. Luckily, only two of his team are there, the other officers are all out working on cases. Camille gives a vague wave. One of his colleagues is busy on the telephone, the other barely has time to turn around before Camille disappears into his office.

Minutes later, Louis appears and, without bothering to knock, steps into the *commandant*'s office. The two men look at each other.

"A lot of people are looking for you . . ."

Camille looks down at his desk. An order to appear before Commissaire Michard.

"I can see that . . ."

The meeting is scheduled for 7.30 p.m. In the meeting room. Neutral territory. The memo does not state who else will be in attendance. It is an unusual request. An officer suspected of misconduct is not generally summoned to explain himself, since this would be tantamount to acknowledging that his actions might warrant investigation by the I.G.S. This means that it does not matter who will be there, it means that Michard has got tangible evidence of misconduct that Camille no longer has time to neutralise.

He does not try to anticipate what might happen. It is not exactly pressing. 7.30 seems a thousand years away.

He hangs up his coat, slips a hand into one of the pockets and extracts a plastic bag which he handles as delicately as if it were nitroglycerine, careful not to touch the contents with his bare fingers. He sets the mug down on his desk. Louis walks over and, bending down, reads the inscription in a low voice: Мой дядя самых честных правил . . .

"It's the first line of 'Eugene Onegin', isn't it?"

For once, Camille knows the answer. Yes. The mug belonged to Irène. He does not say this to Louis.

"I need you to have it dusted for prints. Quickly."

Louis nods and re-seals the plastic bag.

"On the docket, I could say it's evidence in . . . the Pergolin case?"

Claude Pergolin, the transvestite found strangled in his own home.

"That sort of thing."

It is increasingly difficult for him to carry on without explaining the situation to Louis, but Camille is reluctant, partly because it is a long and complicated story, but mostly because if he knows nothing, Louis cannot be accused of misconduct.

"Right," Louis says. "Well, if you want these results immediately, maybe I should take advantage of the fact that Madame Lambert is still in the lab."

Madame Lambert has a little crush on Louis; like Verhœven, if she could, she would adopt him. She is a militant trade unionist committed to fighting mandatory retirement at sixty. Madame Lambert is sixty-eight, and every year she finds some new ruse to carry on working. She will carry on the struggle for another thirty years unless someone defenestrates her.

Despite the urgency of the job, Louis has not moved. Holding the plastic evidence bag, he stands in the doorway brooding, like a young man steeling himself to propose.

"I think I may have missed a few episodes . . ."

"Don't worry," Camille smiles. "So did I . . ."

"You decided to keep me out of the loop . . . [Louis raises his hand in submission.] That's not a criticism."

"Oh, but it is a criticism, Louis. And you're bloody right to point it out. But right now . . ."

"It's too late?"

"Exactly."

"Too late for criticism or too late for explanations?"

"Worse than that, Louis. It's too late for anything. Too late to understand, to react, to explain . . . And probably too late for me to emerge with my honour intact. It's pretty grim."

Louis nods towards the ceiling, towards the powers that be.

"Not everyone seems to have my long-suffering patience."

"I promise you, Louis, you'll get the scoop," Camille says. "I owe you that at least. And if everything goes according to plan, I might have a little surprise for you up my sleeve. The greatest honour any serving officer can dream of: the chance to shine in front of your superiors."

"'Honour is . . .'"

"Oh, come on, Louis! Give me a quote!"

Louis smiles.

"No, don't tell me, let me guess," Camille says. "Saint-John Perse! Or even better, Noam Chomsky!"

Louis turns to leave.

"Oh, by the way . . ." He turns back. "I'm not sure, but I think there's a message for you under your desk blotter."

Yeah, right.

A Post-it note bearing the unmistakable scrawl of Jean Le Guen: "Bastille *métro* station, rue de la Roquette exit, 3.00 p.m.", which is much more than simply a meeting.

When the *contrôleur général* feels obliged to leave an anonymous message under a desk blotter rather than calling him on his mobile, it is a bad sign. Le Guen is unambiguously saying: I'm being careful. He is also saying: As your friend, I care about you enough to take the risk, but meeting with you could put an end to my career, so let's try and be discreet.

Given his height, Camille is well used to being shunned, sometimes he only has to take the *métro* . . . But finding himself under suspicion by his own colleagues – though hardly a surprise, given everything that has happened in the past three days – comes as a bitter blow.

2.00 p.m.

Fernand is a decent guy. He may be a fuckwit, but he's biddable. The restaurant was closed, but he opened up again just for me. I'm hungry, so he whips up an omelette with some wild mushrooms. He's a good cook. He should have stayed in the kitchen, but what can you do, a little guy always dreams of being the big boss. Now he's up to his eyes in debt, and for what? For the pleasure of being "*le patron*". Fucking moron. Not that I'm complaining; morons are very useful. Given the exorbitant interest rate I'm charging him, he owes me more money than he will ever be able to repay. For the first year and a half, I bailed out the business almost every month. I'm not sure that Fernand realises it, but his restaurant belongs to me. I can click my fingers and "*le patron*" will find himself penniless and on the streets. Not that I ever mention this to him. He is much too useful. I use him as an alibi, a mailbox, an office, a witness, a guarantor, a cash machine, I'm slowly drinking his wine cellar and he feeds me when the need arises. Last spring, when we staged Camille Verhœven's brief encounter, Fernand was perfect. In fact everyone was perfect. The scene went off without a hitch. In the nick of time, my favourite *commandant* stepped in, he got up from his dinner and did what he does best. My only worry was that someone else would try to intervene, because she's a very beautiful woman. Well, not anymore, obviously, what with the scars and the broken teeth and her face swollen up like a beach ball. If we staged the scene in the restaurant today, there wouldn't be many men rushing to rescue her, but back then she was pretty enough to make a man want to take on Fernand. Pretty, and cunning, she managed to give just the right looks to just the right person. She reeled Verhœven in without him even knowing.

The reason I'm thinking about all this is because I've got time on my hands. And because this is where it all began.

I've left my mobile on the table, but I can't help checking it every five minutes. Subject to the end results, I'm pretty happy with the way things have gone so far. I'm just hoping the pay-off is big enough, because otherwise I'm liable to get a little angry and to rip the nearest person limb from limb.

In the meantime, I savour the first breather I've had in the past three days. God knows, I deserve it.

Fundamentally, manipulation is a lot like armed robbery. It takes a lot of preparation and a skilled team to carry it off. I don't know how she managed to manipulate Verhœven into letting her leave the hospital and taking her to his little house in the country, but she pulled it off.

She probably went with the hysterical crying routine. That's always a winner with the more sensitive man.

I check my mobile.

When it rings, I'll have my answer.

Either I've done all this work for nothing, in which case we might as well all go home.

Or, I've hit the jackpot, and if that's the case, I don't know how much time I'll have. Not much, certainly, I'll need to act fast. But now I'm so close to the finish line, I have no intention of missing my prey. I ask Fernand for a glass of mineral water, this is no time to piss about.

In the medicine cabinet, Anne found some plasters. She needed to use two to cover the scar. The pain from the wound is still excruciating. But she doesn't regret removing the stitches.

Next, she picks up the envelope he tossed her, the way a keeper might throw a circus animal a hunk of meat. She can feel it burning her fingers. Carefully, she opens it.

Inside is a wad of notes – two hundred euros – a list of phone numbers for local taxi companies, a map of the area and an aerial photograph in which she can make out Camille's house, the path, the outskirts of Montfort village.

In full and final settlement.

She sets her mobile on the sofa next to her.

And waits.

3.00 p.m.

Camille is expecting Le Guen to be foaming at the mouth, instead he finds him shell-shocked. Sitting on a bench outside Bastille *métro*, he is staring at his shoes, looking utterly despondent. There is no bollocking. The only criticism sounds more like a plea.

"You could have asked for my help . . ."

Camille notes the use of the past tense. For Le Guen, some part of this case is already over.

"For an intelligent man," he goes on, "you really know how to pick them."

And he doesn't even know the half of it, Camille thinks.

"Asking for the case to be assigned to you was pretty suspicious. Because I don't believe this story you cooked up about having an informer, it's bullshit . . ."

And that's not all. Le Guen is about to find out that Camille personally helped the key witness in this case to leave the hospital and thereby to evade justice.

Camille does not even know the real identity of the witness, but if it turns out that "Anne" is guilty of a crime, he could well be charged with aiding and abetting . . . If that happens, he could be charged with anything: armed robbery, kidnapping, accessory to murder . . . And he will have a hard time convincing anyone of his innocence.

Camille swallows hard but says nothing.

"As for your dealings with the *juge*," Le Guen goes on, "you've been a bloody idiot: you went over his head, you told me as much, you set up this raid. And the dumb thing is that Pereira is the kind of guy you can talk to."

Very soon, Le Guen will find out that Camille has done much worse since: he has illegally obtained medical documents relating to the witness. A witness he has harboured in his own home.

"Your little raid yesterday has stirred up a shitstorm! You must have known it would! Do you have any idea what you're doing? You've been completely irresponsible."

The *contrôleur général* does not even know that Camille's name appears on an invoice, a crucial piece of evidence that went missing from the jeweller's, and that he gave a false name at the station. And it is too late now to do anything.

"As far as Commissaire Michard is concerned," Le Guen continues, "you manipulated her to get this case because you're trying to protect this woman."

"That's bullshit!" Camille snaps.

"I'm sure it is. But you've spent the past three days behaving like a loose cannon. So, obviously . . ."

"Obviously," Camille acknowledges.

The trains continue to disgorge crowds. Le Guen studies every woman who passes, every single one, there is nothing salacious about his gaze, he admires them all, he owes his many marriages to womankind. Camille has always been his best man.

"But what I want to know is why you're turning this investigation into a personal vendetta!"

"I think it might be the other way round, Jean. This is a personal vendetta that became an investigation."

As he articulates the thought, Camille realises just how true it is. He is plunged into turmoil, it will take some time for him to work out all the ramifications. He tries to engrave the words in his mind: a personal vendetta that became an investigation.

Le Guen is bewildered by what Camille has said.

"A personal vendetta . . . Who exactly do you know in this case?"

A good question. A few hours ago, Camille would have said Anne Forestier. But everything has changed.

"The robber," Camille says unthinkingly, his mind still struggling with what he has just realised.

Le Guen is no longer bewildered, he is panicked.

"You were *in business* with one or more of these thugs? With an armed robber who at the very least was an accomplice to murder? [His tone is concerned, in fact he is utterly hysterical.] You know this Hafner guy *personally*?"

Camille shakes his head. No. It is too complicated to explain.

"I'm not sure," Camille says evasively, "I can't explain it right now . . ."

Le Guen brings his index fingers to his lips, a sign that he is in deep thought.

"You don't really seem to understand what I'm doing here."

"Of course I understand, Jean."

"Michard is going to want to call in the public prosecutor. She's well within her rights, she has to protect herself, she can't turn a blind eye to what you've done, and I don't see how I can possibly object. The very fact that I'm telling you this means that I'm also implicated. Just being here implicates me."

"I know, Jean, and I'm grateful . . ."

"That's not why I came here, Camille! I don't give a fuck about your gratitude! You may not have the I.G.S. breathing down your neck yet, but believe me, they're coming for you. Your phone will be tapped, if it isn't already, you're probably being followed, your every move will be scrutinised . . . And from what you've just told me, Camille, it's not just your job on the line, you could be banged up!"

Le Guen falls silent for a moment, a few brief seconds in which he is hoping against hope that Camille will get a grip. Or explain himself. But he has no ace up his sleeve to force his friend to talk.

"Listen," he says, "I don't think Michard will call in the *procureur* without talking to me. She's just been promoted, she needs my support, but your fuck-up has given her some serious leverage . . . This is why I'm getting in first. I was the one who organised for you to meet with her at 7.30."

When sorrows come, they come not single spies . . . Camille stares at Le Guen questioningly.

"That will be your last chance, Camille. It will be a small, informal meeting. You tell us the whole story and we'll see about damage limitation. I can't promise it will end there. It all depends on what you tell us. So what are you planning to tell us, Camille?"

"I don't know yet, Jean."

He has an idea, but no words to explain it; first he has to set his doubts at rest. Le Guen is annoyed. In fact, he says as much.

"I'm pissed off, Camille. My friendship obviously doesn't mean much to you."

Camille lays a hand on his friend's enormous knee, he pats it as though trying to console Le Guen, to show his support.

It is the world turned upside down.

5.15. p.m.

"What do you want me to say? She was beaten up, that's all there is to it."

Over the telephone, Nguyên's voice has a nasal twang. He sounds as though he is calling from a large, high-ceilinged room, his voice reverberates, he sounds like an oracle. Which, to Camille, he is. Hence his next question:

"Was there any attempt to kill her?"

"No . . . No, I don't think so. The intention was to hurt, to punish, even to scar, but not to kill . . ."

"Are you sure about that?"

"Have you ever known a doctor to be sure about anything? All I can say is that, unless someone physically stopped him, if the guy had really wanted to, he could have burst this woman's skull like a ripe melon."

And since that did not happen, Camille thinks, he had to exercise great self-control. He had to calculate. He pictures the thug raising his shotgun and bringing the butt down on her cheekbone and her jaw, rather than her skull, easing up at the last second. This man is cool-headed.

"Same goes for the kicks," the pathologist says. "The hospital report documented eight separate blows, I found nine, but that's not the most important discrepancy. The guy is aiming to break her ribs or fracture them, he's aiming to cause damage, but given the location of the bruises and the shoes he was wearing, it would have been easy for him to kill the woman had he wanted to. With three swift kicks he could have ruptured her spleen and she would have died of internal bleeding. She could have died, but it would have been an accident: everything points to him intending to leave her alive."

As Nguyên describes it, it sounds like a warning. A sort of punishment beating intended as a show of force. Brutal enough to make the point, but not so brutal that it jeopardises the future.

If her attacker (there's no way that it was Hafner now, he's ancient history) did not intend to kill Anne (there's no way, now, that it was Anne either), this raises the question of her involvement in the robbery, which now seems not just probable, but almost certain.

But in that case, the real target is not Anne, it is Camille.

5.45 p.m.

There is nothing to do now but wait. The deadline of Camille's ultimatum to Buisson expires at 8.00 p.m., but these are just words, a mere fiction. Buisson gave his orders, he made a few telephone calls. He shook down his networks, his contacts, the fences, the middle-men, the traffickers in forged papers, all Hafner's known accomplices. He has to squander all the favours they owe him to get what he wants. He might come through in the next two hours, but it might as easily take him two days and, however long it takes, Camille will just have to wait: he has no other choice.

It is a terrible irony to know that his salvation, when it comes, if it comes, is in the hands of Buisson.

Camille's whole life depends on the success of the man who murdered his wife.

Anne, meanwhile, is sitting on the sofa in Montfort, she has not bothered to turn on the light, the forest shadows have gradually invaded the house. The only light comes from the flickering L.E.D.s on the alarm and on her mobile, as they count off the seconds. Anne sits motionless, silently rehearsing the words that she will say. She worries that she might not have the strength, but she cannot fail, it is a matter of life and death.

If it were simply a question of her own life, she would give up now.

She does not want to die, but she would accept it.

But this is the last step, and she has to succeed.

Fernand plays cards much the way he lives his life in general – scared of his own shadow. He's so terrified, he's deliberately losing to me. The dumb fuck he thinks he's humouring me. He doesn't say anything, but he's scared shitless. In less than an hour, the staff will start turning up and he'll have to sort things before the restaurant opens for dinner. The chef has already arrived – *Bonjour, patron!* – Fernand is so proud to be called *patron*, he's sold his soul for it and he still believes it was bargain.

I'm thinking about other things.

I watch as the hours roll by, I can keep it up all day and all night. I hope Verhœven lives up to his reputation, I've taken a gamble on his ability, so he'd better not disappoint me.

According to my calculations, the cut-off time is noon tomorrow.

If I haven't got what I want by then, I think the deal is dead.

In every sense of the word.

6.00 p.m.

Rue Durestier. The headquarters of Wertig & Schwindel. The ground floor is divided in two. On the right is the lobby and lifts up to the offices, on the left is a travel agency. In old buildings like this, the lobby is vast. To make the reception area seem less forbidding, the ceilings have been lowered and everywhere there are potted plants, comfy chairs, coffee tables and display stands full of colourful travel brochures.

Camille stands in the doorway. He can easily picture Anne sitting in one of those chairs, checking her watch, waiting for the moment when she can leave and be with him.

When she emerged, she was always a little flustered, always a little late and she always give an apologetic shrug – sorry, I did my best to get away – and the smile that accompanied that shrug would have made any man say: don't worry, it's fine.

Seeing a courier suddenly appear by the lifts, a motorcycle helmet tucked under his arm, Camille realises that the plan was even more cunning than he thought. Stepping forward, he sees that there is a separate entrance on the rue Lessard so that, if Anne arrived after he did, she could sneak into the lobby and come out onto the rue Durestier.

Camille would be standing there, thrilled to see her; a win-win situation.

He wanders off the boulevard and finds a table on the covered terrace of La Roseraie at the corner of the rue de Faubourg-Laffite. If he has time to kill, he might as well keep busy; when you feel your life spiralling out of control, doing nothing is a killer.

Camille checks his mobile. Nothing.

The office workers are beginning to head home. Camille sips his coffee, peering at the bustle of people over the rim of his cup, watching as they say their goodbyes, as they smile and wave or hurry towards the *métro*. People of all races, colours, creeds. He spots a boy whose face connects him to another hundred faces imprinted on Camille's memory, the self-satisfied paunch of a middle-aged man, the graceful silhouette of a young girl awkwardly holding a handbag, not because she likes it, nor because she needs it, but because a girl must have a handbag. If he observes it for too long, life pierces Camille to the core.

Then, suddenly, she appears at the corner of the rue Bleue and stops, sensibly standing back from the pedestrian crossing. She is wearing a navy-blue coat. Her face is eerily similar to the woman in Holbein's "The Artist's Family", but without the squint; it is because of this mental association that he remembers her so perfectly. He pushes open the glass door to the street as she crosses and waits by the traffic lights. She hesitates for a moment, looking at him with an expression of mingled concern and curiosity. Camille's height often has this effect on people. He is staring at her, but she goes on her way, walks past as though she has already forgotten him.

"Excuse me . . ."

She turns and looks down at him. Camille calculates she is about five foot seven.

"I'm sorry," he says. "You don't know me . . ."

She seems about to contradict him, but says nothing. Her smile is not as sad as her eyes, but it has that same pained, compassionate air.

"Madame . . . Charroi?"

"No," she says with a smile of relief, "I'm afraid you must be mistaken . . ."

But she does not move, she realises that the conversation is not yet over.

"We bumped into each other here once or twice before . . ." Camille continues, nodding towards the pedestrian crossing. If he carries on like this, he will get bogged down in protracted explanations; he decides it is easier to take out his mobile, he clicks, the woman leans down, curious to see what he is doing, to understand what it is he wants.

He had not noticed that there is a message from Louis. Concise: "Fingerprints: N.O.F."

N.O.F: not on file. Anne does not have a police record. A false lead.

One by one, the doors are closing. An hour and a half from now, the last door will slam, the one he least imagined would ever close, and with it his career.

He will be thrown off the force after a long and humiliating process. It will be up to him to decide how long it takes. He tells himself he has no choice though he knows that whether or not one chooses is in itself a choice. Caught up in a maelstrom, he no longer knows what he wants, this swirling vortex is terrifying.

He looks up, the woman is still standing there, curious, attentive.

"Excuse me . . ."

Camille looks down at his mobile, closes one app and opens another – the wrong one – then manages to open his contacts, scrolls down and holds out a picture of Anne towards the woman.

"You don't work with her, do you?"

It is not really a question. But the woman's face brightens.

"No, but I know her."

Happy to be of help. But the misunderstanding does not last long. She has been working in the area for the past fifteen years, so the number of people with whom she is on nodding acquaintance is vast.

"We waved to each other on the street one day. After that, whenever we ran into each other, we'd say hello, but we never actually spoke."

"A complete bitch," Anne had said.

6.55 p.m.

Anne has decided that she cannot wait much longer. Regardless of the consequences. It's been too long. And the house is beginning to frighten her, as though as the night draws in, the forest has begun to close in around her.

When they were together, she noticed Camille had a number of irrational rituals; they were alike in that they were both prone to superstition. Tonight, for example, in order to ward off misfortune (though it seems scarcely possible that anything worse might befall her), she does not turn on the lights. She moves around by the faint glow of the nightlight at the foot of the stairs above the shattered step where Camille lingered for so long.

How long before he comes back and spits in my face? she wonders.

She cannot bring herself to wait any longer. It seems irrational now that she is so close to the end, but it seems impossible that she will ever achieve her goal. She has to leave. Leave now.

She picks up her mobile and calls for a taxi.

Doudouche is sulking, but she will get over it. The moment she senses that Camille is in no mood to indulge her, she slinks off.

274

Camille once dreamed of getting a housekeeper, a crabby old biddy who would come in every day, clean the flat from top to bottom and cook him boiled potatoes as flabby as her buttocks. Instead he got himself a cat, which amounted to the same thing. He adores Doudouche. He scratches her back, opens a tin of cat food and sets a bowl on the window ledge so she can sit and watch the comings and going along the canal outside.

Then he goes into the bathroom where he carefully extracts the file from the dusty plastic bag, careful not to get dirt everywhere, comes back into the living room and sets the file down on the coffee table.

From her perch at the window, Doudouche glares at him reproachfully. *You shouldn't be doing that.*

"What else can I do?" Camille says aloud.

He opens the file and reaches immediately for the envelope containing the photographs.

The first is a large, slightly over-exposed colour snapshot showing the remains of an eviscerated corpse, broken ribs protruding through a crimson pouch – probably the stomach – and a woman's severed breast, covered in bite marks. The second photograph shows a woman's head which has been severed from her body and nailed to a wall . . .

Camille gets to his feet, walks to the window to get a breath of air. It is not that these images are more appalling than many of the squalid murders he has seen in the course of his career, it is the fact that, in a sense, these are his murders. Those that are closest to him, those he has constantly struggled to keep at arms' length. He stands for a moment, stroking Doudouche and staring down at the canal.

It has been years since he opened this file.

This, then, was how it began, with the discovery of the bodies of two women in a loft apartment in Courbevoie. It ended with the murder of Irène. Camille goes back to the table.

He needs to skim-read the file, find what he is looking for quickly so that he can close it. And this time he will not stow it in the attic space of the Montfort studio . . . He is startled to realise that he has spent months sleeping in the same room as this file without giving it a second thought, that it was almost within reach last night, while Anne lay next to him and he held her hand, tried to calm her as she tossed and turned.

Camille flips through the sheaf of photographs, stops at random. This one shows the body of a different woman. The lower half of her mutilated body, to be precise. A large section of the left thigh has been ripped away and black clotted blood marks out a long deep gash that extends to her vagina. From the way they are positioned, it is clear that both legs have been broken at the knees. One toe bears a fingerprint, carefully applied using a rubber stamp.

These corpses were Camille's first glimpse into the vicious mind of Philippe Buisson.

Inexorably, this series of sadistic murders led to the murder of Irène, though Camille could not have known that when he first saw the bodies.

Camille remembers Maryse Perrin, the young woman in the next photograph. Buisson clubbed her to death with a hammer. Camille moves on.

The young foreign girl who was strangled. It had taken some time to identify her. The body was discovered by a man called Blanchet or Blanchard, the name escapes him, though, as always, Camille perfectly remembers the face: the grey thinning hair, the rheumy eyes, the mouth thin-lipped as a knife wound, the pink neck beaded with sweat. The girl had been found half buried in mud, her body had been unceremoniously dropped onto the canal bank from the bucket of the dredging machine in which it had been dumped. A dozen people were watching from the pedestrian bridge – among them Buisson, who was determined to see the show – and, in a sudden surge of compassion, Buisson had covered the naked body with his coat. Camille cannot help but linger on the picture. He has sketched the pale, thin hand of the girl emerging from beneath the coat a dozen times.

You need to stop this, he tells himself, just find what it is you're looking for.

He randomly grabs a large sheaf of papers, but fate, though it does not exist, is tenacious: he comes up with the picture of Grace Hobson. Though he has not thought about the case for years, he still remembers almost every word, every comma of the text: "She was partly covered by foliage . . . Her head was skewed at a funny angle on her neck, as if she was listening for something . . . On her left temple he saw a beauty spot, the one she had thought would spoil her chances." A passage from a novel by William McIlvanney. A Scotsman. The young woman had been raped, sodomised. She had been found with every item of clothing intact, except one.

This time, Camille is determined; he picks up the file with both hands, turns it over and, starting at the end, begins to work his way backwards.

What he does not want is to happen on the photographs of Irène. He has never been able to face them. Moments after she died, Camille glimpsed the body of Irène in the blue flash of a police light for one flickering instant before he passed out, he remembers nothing more, this is the one image that has remained with him. The file contains other images, those taken by the forensics team, the photographs taken during the autopsy, but he has never looked at them. Never.

And he is not going to now.

In his long career as a serial murderer, Buisson had needed no help from anyone. He was terrifyingly efficient. But in order to kill Irène, in order to conclude his murderous spree with a grand finale, he had needed reliable information. Information he had obtained from Camille himself, after a fashion. From those closest to him, and from one of the members of his team.

Camille comes back to reality, he glances at his watch, picks up his mobile.

"You still at the office?"

"Of course I am . . ."

It is rare that Louis would say such a thing, it is almost a rebuke. His concern is usually expressed with a half-smile. Camille only has twenty minutes to get to his meeting with Michard and the *contrôleur general,* and from Camille's first words, Louis realises that he is far away. Very far away.

"I don't want to take advantage, Louis."

"What can I do for you?"

"I need Maleval's file."

"Maleval . . . Jean-Claude Maleval?"

"You know another one?"

Camille stares at the photograph on the coffee table.

Jean-Claude Maleval, a big man, heavyset but athletic, a former judoka.

"I need you to send everything we've got on him. To my personal e-mail."

The photograph was taken when Maleval was arrested. His face is sensual, he must be thirty-five, perhaps a little older, Camille finds it hard to tell a person's age.

"Can I ask what Maleval has got to do with any of this?" Louis says.

Dismissed from the police force after Irène's death for feeding information to Buisson, Maleval had been unaware that the man was a murderer and so was not technically an accessory, something that was reflected in the verdict. But that did not change the fact that Irène was dead. Camille has dreamed of killing both Buisson and Maleval, but he has never killed anyone. Not until today.

Maleval is behind all this. Camille is convinced of it. He has studied every detail of the case from the robberies in January to the raid at the Galerie. The only thing he does not know is how Anne fits into it.

"Will it take long for you to pull the stuff together?"

"No, about half an hour. It's all on the system."

"Good . . . Can you keep your mobile on in case I need to get in touch?"

"Of course."

"And take a look at the duty roster, you might be needing back-up."

"Me?"

"Who else, Louis?"

In saying this, Camille is admitting that he is out of the running. Louis is shocked. He has no idea what is going on.

Meanwhile, it is not difficult to imagine the scene in the fourth-floor meeting room. Slumped in an armchair, Le Guen is drumming his fingers on the table and trying not to look at his watch. On his right, half hidden behind a vast pile of paperwork, Commissaire Michard is hurriedly reading files, signing, initialling, underlining, annotating, her whole attitude declares that she is a very busy woman, that every second counts, that she is utterly in control of her . . . Shit!

"I'd better go, Louis . . ."

Camille spends the rest of the time sitting on the sofa with Doudouche on his lap. Waiting.

The case file is now closed.

Camille simply snapped a picture of Jean-Claude Maleval with his mobile, then stuffed everything back into the folder and closed it. He even left it by the front door, by the exit.

In Montfort and in Paris, Anne and Camille are both sitting in the gathering dusk, waiting.

Because Anne did not call a taxi; the moment the telephone was answered, she hung up.

She has always known that she would not leave. There is still a faint glow. Anne is stretched out on the sofa, clutching her mobile, every now and then checking the charge left in the battery, checking that she has not missed a call, checking she has a signal.

Nothing.

Le Guen crosses his legs, his right foot idly kicking at the empty air. He seems to recall that Freud believed this nervous tic was merely a substitute for masturbation. What a fucking idiot, thinks Le Guen, who has racked up eleven years on the couch and twenty years of marriage. Surreptitiously, he glances at Michard who is rapidly checking her e-mail. Trapped between Freud and Michard, Le Guen does not rate his chances of surviving the evening.

He feels terribly upset about Camille. There is no-one with whom he can share this feeling. What is the use of six marriages if you have no-one to talk to about such things?

No-one will call Camille to ask whether he is simply running late. No-one will help him now. It is all such a waste.

7.00 p.m.

"Turn it off, for fuck's sake!"

Fernand apologises, runs back and flicks off the light, mutters some excuse, he's obviously relieved I'm letting him go back and help out in the restaurant.

I'm sitting on my own in the little room where we were playing cards earlier. I prefer to sit in the dark. It helps me think.

It's waiting and not being able to do anything that I find exhausting. I need to be in the thick of the action. Idleness just makes me angry. I was like this even as a kid. And it's not something that has improved with age. I guess I'll have to die young.

A shrill *beep* rouses Camille from his thoughts. A flashing message on his computer screen informs him that he has an e-mail from Louis.

The Maleval file.

Camille slips on his glasses, takes a deep breath and opens the attachment.

At first, Jean-Claude Maleval had a distinguished service record. He graduated top of his class from the police academy, rapidly proved to be a promising officer and this led, within a few short years, to him being transferred to the section of the *brigade criminelle* led by Commandant Verhœven.

This was the high point, working on important cases, doing rewarding work.

What Camille remembers is not in the file. Maleval working

relentlessly, constantly on the go, always coming up with ideas, an ambitious, intuitive officer who works hard and plays hard. He goes out a lot, begins to drink a little too much, becomes a womaniser, though it is not the women he loves so much as the act of seduction. Camille has often thought that working on the force, like working in politics, is a form of sexually transmitted disease. Maleval is a player, he is constantly seducing women, a sure sign of a deep-rooted anxiety about which Camille can do nothing; it is not his responsibility, and besides, they do not have that kind of relationship. Maleval is forever chasing women, including witnesses if they are female and under thirty. He begins to show up for his shift looking as though he has not slept a wink. Camille becomes a little worried about his rather dissolute lifestyle. Louis lends him money that is never repaid. Then the rumours start. Maleval is shaking down drug dealers a little more often than necessary and not always turning in all the evidence. A prostitute claims he robbed her, no-one listens, but Camille overhears. He takes Maleval aside, invites him out for dinner, talks to him. But by now it is too late. Maleval swears blind that he's clean, but already he's on the fast track to dismissal. The bars, the late nights, the whisky, the girls, the clubs, the dodgy company, the ecstasy.

Most officers, when they are on this slippery slope, slide slowly and steadily, giving those around them time to adjust, to compensate. Maleval does not do things by half; his descent is meteoric.

He is arrested for aiding and abetting Buisson, who has been charged with seven murders, but the authorities manage to contain the scandal. Buisson's story is so bizarre, so baroque that it completely dominates the press coverage, it burns up all the oxygen, like a forest fire. Maleval's arrest all but disappears behind the curtain of flames.

Immediately after Irène's death, Camille is hospitalised with severe depression. He spends several months in a psychiatric clinic staring out of the window, sketching in silence, refusing to see anyone. Everyone assumes he will never come back to the *brigade*.

At the trial, Maleval is found guilty, but his sentence is covered by the time he has spent on remand, and he is immediately released. Camille does not know this because no-one dares tell him. When he finally does find out, he says nothing, as if too much time has passed, as if Maleval's fate is no longer important, as if it does not concern him personally.

Released on parole and dismissed from the force, Maleval vanishes. And then he begins to reappear, briefly, unremarkably. Camille comes across his name here and there in the dossier that Louis has compiled.

For Maleval, the end of his career in the force coincides with the beginning of his career as a thug, something for which he displays a remarkable aptitude, which is perhaps why he had previously made such a good officer.

As Camille quickly scrolls through the document, a picture begins to take shape. Here are Maleval's first charge sheets: misdemeanours, minor offences. An investigation turns up nothing particularly serious, but it is clear that he has made his choice. Not for him the usual route of parlaying his time on the force into a job with a security firm, working in a shopping centre or driving an armoured van. Three times he is questioned and released without charge. Which takes Camille up to the summer of last year.

This time, Maleval's name crops up in another case.

Nathan Monestier.

Now we're getting there, Camille sighs. Monestier/Forestier, it's not much of a leap. It's an old technique: the best lie is a half-truth. Camille needs to find out whether Anne had the same surname as her brother. Anne Monestier? Maybe. Why not?

Reading on, Camille sees how closely they have stuck to the truth: Anne's brother Nathan is indeed a promising scientist, a child prodigy with a whole alphabet of letters after his name, though he seems to have a nervous disposition.

Nathan's first arrest is for possession with intent to supply. Thirty-three grams of cocaine can hardly be dismissed as personal use. Nathan first denies everything, then he panics, then he claims that Jean-Claude Maleval supplied the drugs or introduced him to the dealer, in a vague and inconsistent statement which he quickly retracts. Pending trial, he is released on bail. And almost immediately turns up in hospital having been beaten to a bloody pulp. Unsurprisingly, he declines to press charges . . . It is obvious that Maleval's solution to his problems is brute force. His penchant for violence foreshadows his taste for armed robbery.

Camille does not have all the details, but he can guess. Maleval and Nathan Monestier are in business together. How does Nathan come to be indebted to Maleval? Does he owe him money? And how does Maleval go about blackmailing the young man?

Other names begin to turn up in Maleval's wake. Among them, a number of vicious thugs. Guido Guarnieri, for example. Camille, like everyone on the force, knows the man by reputation. Guarnieri is a loan shark who buys up debt cheaply and uses strong-arm tactics to recover the money. A year ago, he was questioned about a body discovered on a building site. The pathologist confirmed that the victim had been buried alive, had taken days to die and endured unimaginable suffering. Guarnieri knows how to make himself feared. Did Maleval threaten to sell on Nathan's debt to Guarnieri? It's possible.

It hardly matters since Camille does not care about Nathan, he has never even met the man.

What matters is that all this leads to Anne.

Whatever the nature of her brother's debt to Maleval, it is Anne who pays.

She bails him out. Like a mother. "Actually, that's what I've always been to him," she told Camille.

She has always bailed him out.

Sometimes, just when you most need something, it appears.

"Monsieur Bourgeois?"

Number withheld. Camille had allowed the mobile to ring several times until finally Doudouche looked up at him. On the other end, a woman's voice. Fortyish. Working-class.

"I think you've got the wrong number," Camille says calmly. But he does not even think of hanging up.

"Really?"

She sounds surprised. He almost expects her to ask if he is sure. She reads something from a piece of paper.

"It says here, 'Monsieur Éric Bourgeois, 15, rue Escudier, Gagny.'"

"As I said, you have a wrong number."

"Oh . . ." the woman says. "So sorry."

He hears her mutter something he cannot make out. She hangs up angrily.

It has finally happened. Buisson has done the favour Camille requested. Camille can now have him killed at his leisure.

But right now, this new information has opened a single door. Hafner has changed his name. He is now Monsieur Bourgeois. Not a bad name for a retired crook.

Behind every decision lurks another decision waiting to be made. Camille stares at his mobile.

He could rush to the meeting with Michard and Le Guen, tell them: this is Hafner's address, if he's there we can have him banged up by morning, let me explain the whole thing. Le Guen heaves a sigh of relief, though not too loudly, careful not to make Camille's confession to Commissaire Michard sound like a triumph, he glances at Camille, gives an almost imperceptible nod – *you did well, you had me scared for a minute* – then says testily: "That hardly constitutes a full explanation, Camille, I'm sorry."

But he is not sorry, and no-one present is fooled. Commissaire Michard feels cheated, she was so happy at the prospect of hauling Verhœven over the coals, she paid for her ticket and now the show has been cancelled. Now it is her turn to speak; her tone is poised, disciplined. Sententious. She has a fondness for categorical truths, she did not choose this profession for the good of her health, at heart she is a deeply moral woman. "Whatever your explanations might be, Commandant Verhœven, I should warn you that I am not going to turn a blind eye . . . To anything."

Camille holds up his hands. No problem. He explains the whole story.

The whole scam.

Yes, he is personally connected to the person who was attacked in the raid on the Galerie Monier, that is where it all started. There is a barrage of questions: how exactly do you know this woman? Is she implicated in the robbery? Why did you not immediately . . . ?

The rest is predictable. The most important thing now is to go and pick up Hafner a.k.a. Monsieur Bourgeois from his hideout, and charge him with grievous bodily harm, armed robbery and murder. They cannot spend all night quibbling about the details of Verhœven's story, there will be time for that later. Right now, Michard agrees, they need to be pragmatic – it is one of her favourite words, "pragmatic". In the meantime, Commandant Verhœven, you will remain here.

He will not be involved, he will be merely a spectator. He has already provided the evidence and it is damning. When Le Guen and Michard get back, they will decide whether he is to be sanctioned, suspended or transferred . . . It is all so predictable that it is hardly worth the effort.

This is what he could do. But Camille has long since known that this is not how things are going to play out.

He has already made his decision, though he is not quite sure when.

It relates to Anne, to this case, to his life, to everything. There is nothing anyone else can do.

He thought he was being tossed about by circumstance, but that is not true.

We are masters of our own fate.

7.45 p.m.

France has almost as many rues Escudier as it has inhabitants, all leafy suburban streets lined with stone-clad houses featuring identical gardens, identical railings, and identical patio furniture bought from the same branch of IKEA. Number 15 is no exception: stone cladding, patio furniture, wrought-iron railings, garden, all present and correct.

Camille has driven past two or three times in each direction and at different speeds. The last time he drove past, one of the lights on the first floor is turned off. No point waiting any longer.

He parks at the far end of the street. On the corner is a mini-market, the only shop for miles around in this deserted wasteland. Standing on the doorstep, an Arab man of about thirty who looks as though he has just stepped out of a Hopper painting is chewing a toothpick.

Camille turns off the engine at precisely 7.35 p.m. He slams the car door. The grocer raises a hand in greeting. Camille waves back and heads down the rue Escudier, past identikit houses differentiated only by an occasional dog growling half-heartedly or a cat curled up on the wall. The streetlights cast a yellow glow on the potholed pavement, the dustbins have been put out for collection and other cats – the waifs and strays – are fighting over the spoils.

The steps leading up to number 15 are about fifteen metres from the wrought-iron gate. A garage door on the right is padlocked.

Since he passed, another light on the first floor has been turned out. Only two windows are lit up, both on the ground floor. Camille presses the buzzer to the right of the gate. But for the time of day, he could be a sales rep hoping to find a warm welcome. The door opens a fraction and the figure of a woman appears. With the light behind, it is impossible to tell what she looks like, but her voice sounds young.

"Can I help you?"

As though she does not know, as though the ballet of lights flickering on and off is not clear evidence that he has been spotted, that he is being watched. If this woman were in an interrogation room, he would tell her: you're not very good at lying, you're not going to get very far. She turns back to someone inside, vanishes for a moment, then reappears.

"I'll be right there."

She comes down the steps. She is young, but she has the sagging belly of an old woman and her face is slightly swollen. She opens the gate. "A vulgar whore who had copulated with half the city by the time she was nineteen," was how Buisson described her. To Camille she seems ageless and yet the one thing that is beautiful about her is her fear, he can see it in the way she walks, in the way she keeps her eyes lowered, there is nothing submissive about her, it is pure calculation because her fear is courageous, defiant, almost aggressive, capable of withstanding anything. This woman could stab you in the back without a moment's hesitation.

She walks away without a word, her every movement radiating hostility and determination. Camille crosses the patio, climbs the steps and pushes the door which has begun to close. The hallway is bare, with only an empty coat rack on the wall. In the living room to the right, sitting in an armchair, his back to the window, is a terrifyingly gaunt man, his eyes are sunken, feverish. Even indoors, he wears a woollen cap that accentuates the perfect roundness of his head. His face is pale and drawn. Camille immediately notices how much he looks like Armand.

Between two men of long experience, there are many things that go unsaid, to voice them would almost be an insult. Hafner knows who Verhœven is; there are not many policemen of his height. He also knows that if Camille were coming to arrest him, he would have done it differently. So it must be something else. Something difficult. Best to wait and see.

Behind Camille, the young woman stands wringing her hands, she is accustomed to waiting. "*She must get off on being beaten, I can't see why else she would stay . . ."*

Camille hovers in the hall, caught in a vice between Hafner, sitting, staring at him, and the woman behind. The heavy, pointed silence makes it clear that they will not easily be taken in. But he also knows that to them, the unprepossessing little officer has brought chaos into their midst. And given the lives they lead, chaos means death.

"We need to talk . . ." Hafner says finally in a low voice.

Is he talking to Camille, to the woman, perhaps only to himself?

Camille takes a few steps, never taking his eyes off Hafner. He can see none of the savagery described in the police reports. This is not unusual, Camille has often noticed that, excepting those few minutes when they are intent on their violent activities, robbers, thugs and gangsters are much like everyone else. Murderers are just like you and me. But there is something else too: disease and the looming spectre of death. And this silence, this mute menace.

Camille takes another step into the room, which is lit only by the dim bluish glow of a standard lamp. He is not particularly surprised to find the room tastelessly furnished with a large flat-screen T.V., a sofa covered with a throw, a few knick-knacks and a round table covered with a patterned oilcloth. Organised crime often goes hand in hand with very middle-class tastes.

The woman has disappeared; Camille did not notice her leave the room. For an instant he pictures her sitting on the stairs holding a pump-action shotgun. Hafner does not move from his chair, he is waiting to see how things will go. For the first time, Camille wonders if the man is armed – the thought had not occurred to him before. It doesn't matter, he thinks, but even so, he moves slowly and deliberately. You never know.

He takes his mobile from the pocket of his coat, turns it on, brings up the picture of Maleval and, stepping forward, hands the device to Hafner who simply grimaces, clears his throat and nods – *I get it now* – then gestures to the sofa. Camille chooses a chair instead, pulls it towards him, lays his hat on the table. The two men sit facing each other as though waiting to be served.

"Someone told you I would be coming . . ."

"In a way . . ."

Logical. Whoever Buisson forced to give up Hafner's address and his new identity will have wanted to cover his own back. But this does not change anything.

"Shall I recap?" Camille says.

From another part of the house, he hears a distant, high-pitched wail and then hurried footsteps upstairs and the crooning voice of the woman. Camille wonders whether this new factor will complicate matters or simplify them. He jerks his chin at the ceiling.

"How old?"

"Six months."

"Boy?"

"Girl."

Someone else might have asked the girl's name, but the situation hardly lends itself to such familiarity.

"So, last January, your wife was six months pregnant."

"Seven."

Camille indicates the woollen cap.

"It must make being on the run more difficult. And on that subject, do you mind if I ask where you've been having your chemo?"

Hafner pauses for a moment.

"In Belgium, but I've stopped treatment."

"Too expensive?"

"No. Too late."

"And therefore too expensive."

Hafner gives the ghost of a smile, it is almost imperceptible, just a shadow that plays on his lips.

"So back in January," Camille continues, "you knew you didn't have much time to make sure your family were provided for. And so you organised the Big Stick-Up. Four armed robberies in a single day. The jackpot. Most of your usual partners were out of circulation – and maybe you even had qualms about fucking your old friends over – so you hired Ravic, the Serb, and Maleval, the ex-cop. I have to say, I didn't know armed robbery was Maleval's thing."

Hafner takes his time.

"He spent a long time trying to find his way after your lot tossed him out," he says at length, "He was doing a lot of cocaine."

"So I heard . . ."

"But, actually, he's really taken to armed robbery. It suits his personality."

Ever since the penny finally dropped, Camille has been trying to picture Maleval holding up a shop, but he cannot seem to manage. His powers of imagination are limited. And besides, Maleval and Louis will always be part of his team, he cannot picture them in any other context. Like many men who will never have children, Camille has a paternal instinct. His height has a lot to do with it. And he created two sons for himself: Louis, the perfect son, diligent, faultless, who makes everything worthwhile, and Maleval, violent, generous, sinister, the son who betrayed him, the one who cost him his wife. The son who carried evil in his very name.

Hafner waits for Camille to finish. Upstairs, the woman falls silent, she is probably rocking the baby.

"In January," Camille goes on, "everything goes according to plan – but for the niggling exception of a murder. [Camille is not so naive as to expect a reaction from a man like Hafner.] You planned to double-cross everyone and disappear with the cash. All the cash. [Once again, Camille points to the ceiling.] Hardly surprising, a man with a sense of responsibility would want to ensure his loved ones are provided for. In a sense, the proceeds from the four armed robberies were to be your legacy. I'm no lawyer, so tell me, would that be taxable?"

Hafner does not so much as blink. Nothing will shift him from his planned course. He is not about to vouchsafe a smile, a confession, to the harbinger of doom who has finally flushed him out.

"Morally, I suppose, your position is unassailable. You're doing what any good father would do, making sure that your family don't go without. But for some reason, your partners in crime are unlikely to see it that way. Not that it matters, since you have everything planned. They may try to find you, but you have anticipated their every move, you've bought yourself a new identity, cut all ties with your old life. I'm a little surprised that you didn't decide to go abroad."

At first, Hafner says nothing but, sensing that he may well need Camille's help, he throws him a crumb.

"I stayed for her sake . . ." he mutters.

Camille is not sure whether he is referring to his wife or his child. It comes to the same thing.

Outside, the streetlights suddenly flicker off; they must be on timers, or there has been a power cut. The light in the living room dims a little. Hafner is framed in silhouette like an empty carcass, spectral, menacing. Upstairs the baby begins to cry quietly, there is another patter of footsteps and whispered words and the wailing stops. Camille would be happy to stay here, in this half-light, in this silence. What is there waiting for him elsewhere, after all? He thinks of Anne. *Come on, Camille.*

Hafner crosses and uncrosses his legs, he does so infinitely slowly as though wary of frightening Camille. Or else he is in pain. *Come on.*

"Ravic . . ". As Camille says the name he realises that he has dropped his voice to a muffled whisper, in tune with the atmosphere of the house. "I didn't know Ravic personally, but I'm guessing he didn't much appreciate being double-crossed and left without a red cent. Especially since he came away from the robberies with a murder charge hanging over him. I know, I know, it's his own fault, he should have held his nerve. But even so, he'd earned his share of the loot and you just took off with it. Did you hear what happened to Ravic?"

Camille thinks he sees Hafner stiffen slightly.

"He's dead. His girlfriend – or whatever she was – got off lightly: a bullet to the head. But before he died, Ravic saw his fingers hacked off one by one. With a hunting knife. Personally, I think a guy who would do something like that is a savage. I know Ravic was a Serb, but France has always been a safe haven for refugees. And chopping up foreigners is hardly good for tourism, wouldn't you say?"

"I would say you're a pain in the arse, Verhœven."

Camille inwardly heaves a sigh of relief. Unless he can jolt Hafner out of his self-imposed silence, he will not get any information out of him. He will be forced to listen to his own soliloquy when what he needs is dialogue.

"You're right," he says. "Now is no time for recriminations.

Tourism is one thing, armed robbery is something very different. But then again . . . So let's talk about Maleval. Now he's someone I used to know very well, in the days before he went in for dismemberment."

"If I were you, I'd have killed the fucker."

"That would have suited you, wouldn't it? Because even if Maleval has become a brutal, bloodthirsty bastard, he's still as cunning as he ever was. He didn't appreciate being double-crossed either, and he's been doing his best to hunt you down . . ."

Hafner nods slowly. He has his own informants, he will have been following the progress of Maleval's search from a distance.

"But you managed to change your identity, you cut yourself off completely from everyone and everything, you had a little help from those who still admire you – or fear you – and although Maleval has moved heaven and earth to find you, he doesn't have your contacts, your resources, your reputation. Eventually he was forced to accept that he might never find you. And then he came up with a brilliant idea . . ."

Hafner looks at Camille, puzzled, waiting for the other shoe to drop.

"He got the police to do his searching for him." Camille spread his hands wide. "He entrusted the task to your humble servant. And he was right to, because I'm a pretty decent cop. It would take me less than twenty-four hours to track down someone like you, if I was motivated. And what better to motivate a man than a woman? And a battered woman at that, I mean I'm such a sensitive soul, it was bound to work. And so, a few months ago, he arranged an introduction, and at the time I was flattered."

Hafner nods. Though he realises that his time is up, and senses that very soon he may have to fight for his life, he cannot but admire Maleval's ingenuity. Perhaps, half hidden in the shadows, he is smiling.

"In order to persuade me to track you down, Maleval organised an armed robbery, being sure to give it your M.O., your panache, for want of a better word: a jeweller's, a sawn-off shotgun and a helping of brute force. Everyone at the *brigade criminelle* was convinced that the raid on the Galerie Monier was your work. And I panicked. I was bound to – the woman I cared about was beaten half to death on her way to pick up a present for me, the whole set-up was designed to ensure I would be a loose cannon. I did what I had to do to ensure I was assigned the case, and since I'm not as dumb as I look, I succeeded. My suspicions were confirmed when this woman, the only witness, formally identified you, though she had only ever seen you in a photograph Maleval showed her. You and Ravic. She even claimed to have recognised a few Serbian words. So now we're certain that you were behind the job at the Galerie, there's not a shadow of a doubt."

Hafner slowly nods again, seemingly impressed by the preparation that has gone into the plan. And realising that in Maleval he has found a formidable adversary.

"And so I set out looking for you on Maleval's behalf," Camille says. "Unwittingly, I become his private detective. The more he piles on the pressure, the faster I work. He appears to try to kill the witness, so I redouble my efforts. You have to admit, he made the right choice. I'm a good cop. To find you, I had to make a particularly painful sacrifice, a . . ."

"What sacrifice?" Hafner interrupts.

Camille looks up. How can he put it into words? He thinks for a long moment – Buisson, Irène, Maleval – then gives up.

"I . . ." Camille says almost to himself, "I had no score to settle with anyone."

"That's not true. Everyone has . . ."

"You're right. Because Maleval has an old score to settle with me. In feeding information to Buisson, he was guilty of serious professional misconduct. So he was arrested, humiliated, banished, his name was all over the papers, the scandal, the trial, the verdict. And he spent time in prison. Not long, I'll grant you, but can you imagine what it's like for an officer to be inside? And so this is the perfect opportunity to get his revenge. Two birds with one stone. He gets me to track you down and in doing so he makes sure that I will be fired."

"You did it because you wanted to."

"Partly . . . It's too complicated to explain."

"And I don't give a flying fuck."

"Well, you're wrong there. Because now I've found you, Maleval will be paying you a visit. And he's not just going to want his share. He's going to want everything."

"I've got nothing left."

Camille pretends to weigh up the merits of this answer.

"Yes," he says. "You could try that, I mean, nothing ventured . . . I'm guessing Ravic tried the same spiel: I've nothing left, I spent it all, I might have a little left, but not much . . ." Camille smiles broadly. "But let's be serious. You've put that money aside for the time when you won't be here to provide for your family. You've still got it. The question isn't whether Maleval will find your savings, only how long it will take him to do so. And, incidentally, what methods he's prepared to use to get that information."

Hafner turns towards the window as though expecting Maleval to appear wielding a hunting knife. He says nothing.

"He'll pay you a visit. If and when I decide. All I have to do is give your address to his accomplice and Maleval will be on his way. I'd give it an hour before he blasts your front door open with his Mossberg."

Hafner tilts his head to one side.

"I know what you're thinking," Camille says. "You're thinking that you'll be waiting, that you'll take him down. Well, no offence, but you don't seem in such great shape right now. Maleval has got twenty years on you, he's trained and he's cunning. You made the mistake of underestimating him once before. You might get a lucky shot in, of course, but that's your only hope. And if you want my advice, make sure you don't miss. Because he's not exactly your biggest fan right now. If you do, you'll regret it, because after he's put a bullet between the eyes of that pretty little wife of yours, he's liable to take a knife to your kid, to her little hands, her little feet . . ."

"Don't talk shit, Verhœven, I've dealt with guys like him dozen of times."

"That was the past, Hafner, even your future is behind you now. You could try to send your family into hiding with the cash – assuming I give you enough time – but it won't make any difference. If Maleval tracked you down for all your cunning, finding them will be child's play. [Silence.] I'm you're only hope."

"Go fuck yourself!"

Camille nods, reaches for his hat. His face neatly sums up the paradox, a combination of feigned resignation and frustration – *Oh well, I did what I could.* Reluctantly, he gets to his feet. Hafner does not move.

"O.K.," Camille says, "I'll leave you to spend some time with your family. Make the most of it."

He heads into the hallway.

He has no doubt that this is the right strategy. It will take as long as it takes: he might get to the front door, the steps, the garden, maybe even as far as the gate, but Hafner will call him back. The streetlights come on again, casting a pale-yellow glow over the far end of the garden.

Camille stands for a moment in the doorway, staring out at the tranquil street, then he turns and jerks his chin towards the ceiling.

"What's her name?"

"Ève."

Camille nods. A pretty name.

"It's a good start," he says, turning away again, "I just hope it lasts."

He walks out.

"Verhœven!"

Camille closes his eyes.

He retraces his steps.

9.00 p.m.

Anne is still in the studio. She does not know whether this is bravery or cowardice, but she is still here, waiting. The hours tick by and the exhaustion has become a crushing weight. She feels as though she has survived an ordeal, as though she has come through: she is no longer in control, she is an empty shell, she can do no more.

It was her ghost who, twenty minutes earlier, packed up her few belongings. Her jacket, the money, the piece of paper with the map and the telephone numbers. She heads for the sliding glass door, then turns back.

The taxi driver from Montfort has just called to say he has been driving around but cannot find the lane. He sounds Asian. Anne is forced to turn on the living-room light so she can study the scribbled map and try to guide him, but it is no use. "Just past the rue de la Loge, you said?" "Yes, on the right," she says, though she does not know which direction he is coming from. She will come to meet him, she says, *Park next to the church and wait for me there, alright*? The driver agrees, he is happier with this solution, he apologises but his G.P.S. . . . Anne hangs up. Then goes and sits on the sofa.

Just a few minutes, she promises herself. If the telephone rings in the next five minutes . . . But what if the call does not come?

In the darkness, she runs her finger over her scarred cheek, over her gums, picks up one of Camille's sketchpads. She could do this a hundred times and not happen on the same drawing.

Just a few minutes. The taxi driver calls back, he is impatient, unsure whether to stay or go.

"Wait for me," she says, "I'm on my way."

He tells her the meter is running.

"Give me ten minutes. Just ten minutes . . ."

Ten minutes. Then, whether Camille calls or not, she will leave. All this for nothing?

What then? What will happen then?

At that moment, her mobile rings.

It is Camille.

Jesus, I fucking hate waiting. I opened up the futon, ordered a bottle of Bowmore Mariner and some food, but I know I won't get a wink of sleep.

On the other side of the wall, I can hear the bustle of a busy restaurant. Fernand is raking it in, which will add to my bank balance. That should make me happy, but it's not what I want, what I'm waiting for. After all the effort I've put in . . .

But the more time passes, the less chance I have of pulling this thing off. The biggest risk is that Hafner fucked off to the Bahamas with his tart. Word on the street is that he's terminally ill, but who knows, maybe he's decided to do his convalescing on the beach. With my cash! It really pisses me off to think that right now he could be living it up on the money he owes me.

But if he *is* still in France, then the moment I find out where he's holed up I'll be all over him before the cops even have time to get their boots on, I'll drag him down to his cellar and we'll have a nice little chat, just me, him and a blowtorch.

In the meantime, I sip my fifteen-year-old malt, think about the girl, about Verhœven – I've got the little fucker by the short and curlies – and I think about what I'll do when I find Hafner . . .

Deep breath.

In his car again, Camille sits motionless behind the steering wheel. Is it the fact that it still has not sunk in? That he can finally see light at the end of the tunnel? He feels cold as a snake, prepared for anything. He has everything set up for a finale that will be done by the book. He has only one doubt: will he be strong enough?

Standing in the doorway of his shop, the Arab grocer smiles cordially and goes on chewing his toothpick. In his head, Camille tries to replay the footage of his relationship with Anne, but nothing comes, the film is caught in the sprockets. He is too preoccupied by what is about to happen.

It is not that Camille is incapable of lying, far from it, but he always hesitates when the end is in sight.

Anne needs to get away from Maleval, this is why she agreed to spy on Camille's investigation. She has promised to pass on

Hafner's address.

Camille is the only person who can help her, but his actions will signal the end of their relationship. Just as it has already signalled the end of his career. Camille feels a great weariness.

Let's do this, he thinks. He shakes himself, takes his mobile and calls Anne. She picks up immediately.

"Camille . . . ?"

Silence. Then the words come.

"We've found Hafner. You don't have to worry anymore . . ."

There. It is done.

His calm tone is intended to persuade her that he is completely in control.

"Are you sure?" she says.

"Absolutely." He hears a sound in the background, like a breath. "Where are you?"

"On the terrace."

"I told you not to leave the house!"

Anne does not seem to understand. Her voice is quavering, her words come in a rush.

"Have you arrested him?"

"No, Anne, that's not how it works. We've only just tracked him down, but I wanted to let you know as soon as possible. You asked me to call, you insisted. Look, I can't stay long on the phone. The important thing is th—"

"Where is he, Camille?"

Camille hesitates, for the last time no doubt.

"We found him in a safe house . . ."

The forest around Anne begins to rustle. The wind whips through the treetops, the light on the terrace flickers. She does not move. She should bombard Camille with questions, gather all her strength and say: *I need to know where he is.* This is one of the lines she has been rehearsing. Or: *I'm scared, can't you understand I'm scared?* She needs to make herself shrill, hysterical, she needs to insist, *What safe house? Where?* And if that does not work, she needs to be aggressive: *You say you've found him, but do you even know he's there? Why can't you just tell me?* Or she might try a little emotional blackmail: *I'm still worried, Camille, surely you can understand that?* Or remind him of the facts: *That man beat me half to death, Camille, he tried to kill me, I have a right to know!*

Instead there is silence, she cannot bring herself to say any of these things.

She had precisely the same feeling three days ago as she stood in the street, covered in blood, clinging to a parked car, and saw the robbers' jeep round the corner, saw the man aim the shotgun at her, the barrel only inches away, and yet, drained, exhausted, ready to die, unable to summon a last ounce of strength, she did nothing. And now, once again, she finds she can say nothing.

Camille will come to her rescue one last time.

"We tracked him down to the suburbs, to 15, rue Escudier in Gagny. It's a quiet residential neighbourhood. I've only just found out, I don't know how long he's been there. He's going by the name Éric Bourgeois, that's all I know."

Another silence.

Camille is thinking: That was the last time I will hear her voice, but it is not true because she continues to press him.

"So, what happens now?"

"He's a dangerous man, Anne, you know that. We'll stake out the area, work out exactly where he is, try to find out if there is anyone there with him. There may be several of them. We can't just go storming a Paris suburb as if it's the Alamo, we'll need to bring in a tactical unit. And we'll need to make sure the timing is right. But we know where to find him, and we have the resources to make sure he doesn't do any more harm. [He forces himself to smile.] You feel better?"

"I'm fine."

"Listen, I have to go now. I'll see you later.

Silence.

"See you later."

9.45 p.m.

I'd more or less given up hope, but we got our result! Hafner has been found.

It's not surprising he was impossible to track down if he's going by the name "Monsieur Bourgeois". I knew this man, this ruthless gangster, when he was at the height of his powers, so it's kind of pathetic to discover he's saddled himself with such a name.

But Verhœven is convinced it's him. So I'm convinced.

The reports that he was ill are true, I just hope he hasn't pissed away all of that cash on chemo. There'd better be a decent wad left to compensate me for all my efforts, because otherwise cancer will be nothing compared to what I have in store for him. Logically, he'll need to eke out the money, keep it handy in case he needs it.

Now I just jump in the car, head down the Périphérique, pedal to the metal, and before you know it I'll be in Gagny.

Difficult to picture Vincent Hafner in a dump like that. Have to hand it to him, it's a clever place to hide out, but I can't help thinking that if he's slumming it in a cosy little suburban house, there's probably a woman in the picture. Probably the woman I've heard about on the grapevine, the sort of torrid May–December romance that can persuade a man to become Monsieur Bourgeois to impress the neighbours.

It's the kind of thing that makes you think about life: Hafner spends half his life bumping off his neighbours, then he falls in love and all of a sudden he's totally pussy-whipped.

It suits me. If there's a girl involved, I can use it to my advantage. Women make for good leverage. Break her fingers and he'll hand over his life savings, gouge out her eye and he'll throw in the family silver. I tend to think of a woman as an organ donor, and every piece is worth its weight in gold.

Obviously, nothing beats a kid. If you really need to get your hands on something, the best weapon you can have is a kid.

When I get to Gagny, I drive around for a bit, take a tour of the neighbourhood, steering clear of the rue Escudier. Cordoning off the area won't be a problem, the police just need to set up a couple of roadblocks, but raiding the house will be a lot more complicated. First they have to be sure that Hafner is in there, and that he's alone. That won't be easy because there's nowhere for a G.I.G.N. Special Ops team to park in this neighbourhood, and given there's almost no traffic in the area, a car prowling around would be noticed straight away. Best would be to bring in a couple of plain-clothes to keep a watch on the place, but even that can take half a day.

Right now, the boys at G.I.G.N. are probably devising complicated strategies, poring over aerial maps, marking out zones, sectors, trajectories. They're in no hurry. They've got the whole night to think about it, they can't do anything before about 6 a.m. and even then it's all about surveillance, surveillance, surveillance . . . The operation could take two days, maybe three. And by then, their target will be no threat at all, I'll see to that.

I parked the car two hundred metres from the rue Escudier,

shouldered my bag and walked past the gardens, bludgeoned a few dogs that tried to play the tough guy, crept past the hedges and the railings and here I am, sitting in a garden under a pine tree. The residents are in the living room watching television. On the other side of the railing separating the gardens, I have a perfect view of the back of number 15, thirty metres away.

The only light is a bluish glow from an upstairs window, obviously a T.V. The rest of the house is in darkness. There are only three possibilities: either Hafner is watching T.V. upstairs, or he's out, or he's in bed and the girl is watching educational programmes on T.F.1.

If he's gone out, I'll be the welcome committee when he gets back.

If he's in bed, I'll be his alarm clock.

And if he's watching television, he's going to miss the ad break because I've got my own entertainment planned.

I study the place through my binoculars, then I'll creep over and slip inside. Make the most of the element of surprise. I'm having fun already.

A garden is the ideal place for meditation. I assess the situation. Realising that everything is going smoothly, almost better than I had expected, I force myself to be patient – by nature I tend to be impulsive. When I got here, I felt like firing shots in the air and charging into the house, screaming like a lunatic. But just getting to this point has taken a lot of work, a lot of thought and effort, I'm so close to the money I can almost smell it, so it's important that I keep a cool head. When nothing happens after half an hour, I pack up my things and do a recce of the house. No burglar alarm. Hafner wouldn't have wanted to attract attention by turning his little haven into a bunker. He's a crafty bastard, that Monsieur Bourgeois, he just blends into the background.

I go back to the tree and sit down, zip up my parka and again look through the binoculars.

Finally, at about half past ten, the T.V. upstairs is turned off. The small window in the middle lights up briefly. Narrower than the others, it must be the toilet. I couldn't have wished for a better set-up. I get to my feet. Time for action.

It's a standard '30s house with the kitchen at the rear of the ground floor. The back door leads onto a small flight of steps and down to the garden. I move silently. The lock is so old you could open it with a tin-opener.

On the other side is the great unknown.

I leave my bag by the door, taking only the Walther fitted with a silencer and the hunting knife tucked into a leather sheath on my belt.

Inside, the silence is pounding; there's always something nerve-racking about a house at night. I need to calm my heart rate, otherwise I won't hear a thing.

I stand for a long time, watching, listening.

Not a sound.

I steal across the tiled floor, moving slowly because here and there the tiles creak. I emerge from the kitchen into a narrow hall. The stairs are on my right, the front door straight ahead and on my left is an archway that probably leads to the living or the dining room.

Everyone is upstairs. As a precaution, I hug the walls, gripping the Walther with both hands, the barrel pointed downwards.

As I pad across the hall towards the stairs, something catches my eye: the living room on my left is in pitch darkness, but at the far end, bathed in the faint glow of the streetlights, I see Hafner sitting, staring at me. I'm so shocked that I'm literally rooted to the spot.

I just have time to make out a woollen cap pulled down to his eyebrows, his bulging eyes. Hafner sitting in an armchair, I swear, like Ma Barker in her rocking chair.

He has his Mossberg trained on me.

The moment he sees me, he fires.

The noise fills the whole house, a blast like that is enough to stun anyone. I move fast. In a split second, I throw myself to the ground behind the door. Not fast enough to avoid the buckshot peppering the hallway, I'm hit in the leg, but it feels like a flesh wound.

Hafner has been waiting for me, I've been hit, but I'm not dead. I scrabble to my knees, feeling blood trickling down my shin.

Everything is happening so fast my mind is having trouble processing it. Luckily, my reflexes are focused in the reptilian brain, they come straight from my spinal cord. And I do what no-one would anticipate: even though I'm startled, shot and wounded, I snap into action.

Without taking time to assess the situation, I swing round to face him. From the expression on Hafner's face I can tell he wasn't expecting me to reappear in the doorway where he just shot at me. I am hunkered on the ground, my outstretched arm gripping the Walther.

The first bullet slices through his throat, the second hits him right between the eyes, he doesn't even have time to squeeze the trigger. His body jerks wildly as the last five bullets leave a cavernous crater in his chest.

I have scarcely processed the fact that there's lead in my leg, that Hafner is dead and all my hard work has resulted in an epic failure, when I dimly become aware of something else: I am kneeling in the hall holding an empty gun and the barrel of another gun is pressed against my temple.

I freeze. I set the Walther down on the ground.

The hand holding the pistol is steady. I feel the barrel dig into my flesh. The message is clear: I push the Walther away from me, it skids two metres and comes to a stop.

I've just been well and truly screwed. I spread my arms to indicate that I don't plan to resist, I turn slowly, head down, careful not to make any sudden movements.

It doesn't take long for me to work out who would want to kill me, and my suspicions are confirmed when I see the tiny shoes. My brain is still racing, trying to come up with some way out, but all I can think is: How did he get here before me?

But I don't waste time trying to analyse what went wrong, because before I figure it out, he'll have put a bullet in my brain with complete impunity. In fact I can feel the barrel drag across my skin and stop in the middle of my forehead, precisely where Hafner took the second bullet. I look up.

"Good evening, Maleval," Verhœven says.

He's wearing a hat and has one hand stuffed into the pocket of his overcoat. He looks as though he's about to leave.

More worryingly, I notice that he's wearing a glove on the other hand, the one holding the gun. I can feel the panic rising. No matter how fast I move, if he manages to get a shot off, I'm dead. Especially since there's lead in my calf already, I'm losing a lot of blood and I'm not sure what will happen if I try to put any weight on it.

Verhœven knows this all too well.

Cautiously, he takes a step back, but his arm is steady, his hand doesn't tremble, he's not afraid, he's determined, his bony face is grave, serene.

I'm on my knees, he's standing, our faces aren't quite at the same level, but there's not much in it. This could be my last chance. He's almost within reach. If I can just gain a few centimetres, stall for a few minutes . . .

"I see you've still got the same quick reflexes, son."

"Son" . . . Verhœven has always been protective, paternalistic. Given his height, it's ridiculous. But he's a clever runt, I'll give him that. And I know him well enough to recognise that this hasn't been one of his good days.

"Well, I say 'quick' . . ." he says, "but tonight you're missing something. And you were so close to pulling it off, it must be galling." His eyes never leave mine. "If you came looking for a suitcase full of cash, you'll be thrilled to know that it was right here. Hafner's wife left with it an hour ago. In fact, I even called her a taxi. You know me, I never could resist a damsel in distress, whether she's carrying a heavy suitcase or causing a scene in a restaurant. I'm always willing to step in."

He can't miss, the gun is cocked, and it's not his service revolver . . .

"Well spotted," he says, as though he can read my mind. "The gun is Hafner's. You wouldn't believe the arsenal he's got upstairs. But he recommended this one. Personally, I don't much care, in a situation like this, one gun is as good as the next . . ."

His eyes are still fixed on mine, it's almost hypnotic. It's something I remember from when I worked with him, that icy, razor-sharp stare.

"You're wondering how I got here before you, but mostly you're trying to think of a way out. Because you must know that I'm feeling fucking furious."

From his strange stillness I can tell that any second now . . .

"And insulted," Verhœven says. "Above all, insulted. And for a man like me, that's much worse. Fury is something you live with, sooner or later you calm down, you get things in perspective, but when a man's pride is injured he's capable of terrible things. Especially a man who has nothing left to lose, a man who has nothing left at all. A guy like me, for example. Right now, I'm capable of anything."

I swallow hard and say nothing.

"Any minute now, you're going to try and rush me. I can tell." He smiles. "It's what I would do in your position. Double or quits, that's the way we work. When it comes down to it, we're very alike, don't you think? That's what made this whole thing possible."

He blethers on, but he's still perfectly focused.

I tense.

He takes his left hand from his pocket.

Without moving my eyes, I calculate the angle of attack.

He's gripping the gun with both hands now, pointing it directly between my eyes. I'll take him by surprise, he's expecting me to rush him or to dodge sideways, but I'll dive backwards.

"Tsk tsk tsk . . ."

He takes one hand from the gun and brings it to his ear.

"Listen . . ."

I listen. Sirens. They're approaching fast, Verhœven doesn't smile, he doesn't savour his triumph, he just looks sad.

If I weren't in this fucked-up situation, I'd almost pity him.

I always knew I loved this man.

"Three counts of murder," he whispers, his voice so low I have to strain to hear. "Armed robbery, accessory to murder in the January raid . . . In Ravic's case, malicious wounding and murder, for his girlfriend, you might get off with second-degree. You're going to be banged up for a very long time, and that upsets me, it really does."

He's completely sincere.

The sirens converge on the house, there are at least five cars, maybe more. Through the windows, the flashing lights illuminate the rooms like a blaze of neon at a fairground. Slumped in the armchair at the far end of the living room, Hafner's face flickers blue and red.

I hear running footsteps. The front door seems to explode into splinters. I turn to look.

Louis, my old friend Louis, is the first on the scene. His suit is pressed, not a hair out of place, he looks like an altar boy.

"Hey, Louis . . ."

I'd like to sound indifferent, cynical, to go on playing the role, but seeing Louis again after all this time brings everything flooding back, the terrible waste is heartbreaking.

"Hi, Jean-Claude . . ." Louis steps closer.

I turn back to Verhœven, but he has disappeared.

10.30 p.m.

Every house in the street is lit up, every garden, too. The residents are standing in their doorways, shouting to each other, some have crept out to their railings and a few brave souls are standing in the middle of the road, reluctant to come any closer. Uniformed officers are posted on either side of the house to deter rubberneckers.

Commandant Verhœven, hat pulled down, hands buried in the pockets of his overcoat, stares down the street which is lit up like a Christmas scene.

"I want to apologise, Louis." He speaks slowly, like a man

overcome by fatigue. "I'm sorry for not confiding in you, for giving the impression I didn't trust you. That's not why I did it, you know that, don't you?"

The question requires no answer.

"Of course," Louis says.

He is about to protest, but Verhœven has already turned away. This is how it has always been between them, they start a conversation but rarely finish. But this time is different. Each feels he is seeing the other for the last time.

This thought prompts Louis to be particularly reckless.

"That woman . . ." he says.

For Louis to utter these two words is momentous. Camille quickly turns back.

"No, Louis, please don't think that!" He seems not angry, but indignant. As though he is being unjustly accused. "When you say 'that woman', you make it sound as though I am the injured party in a tragic love story."

For a long moment, he stares down the street again.

"It wasn't love that made me do it, it was the situation."

There is a steady clamour from outside the house, idling engines, sporadic voices, shouted orders. The atmosphere is not frenzied but calm, almost peaceful.

"After all this time," Camille goes on, "I thought I'd got over Irène's death. But actually, though I didn't realise it, the embers were still smouldering. Maleval fuelled the fire at the crucial moment, that's all. In fact 'that woman', as you call her, had very little to do with it."

"But still," Louis says. "The lies, the betrayal . . ."

"Oh, Louis, they're just words . . . When I realised what was happening, I could have stopped it, there would have been no more lies, there would have been no betrayal."

Louis' silence is a deafening: *So?*

"The truth is . . ."

Camille turns back to Louis, he seems to be searching for his words in the young man's face.

". . . I didn't want to stop, I wanted to see it through, I wanted it over with once and for all. I think . . . I think I did it out of loyalty. [Camille himself seems surprised by the word. He smiles.] And this woman . . . I never thought her intentions were evil. If I'd thought that, I would have arrested her on the spot. By the time I realised what was happening, it was a bit late, but I could live with the damage done, I could still do my job. Actually, it's more than that. I knew that she wouldn't have suffered everything she suffered . . . for some selfish reason. [He shakes his head, as though waking from a trance. He smiles again.] And I was right. She was sacrificing herself for her brother. Yes, I realise the word 'sacrifice' is a bit much. People don't use the word so often these days, it's old-fashioned. Look at Hafner, he was no angel, but he sacrificed himself for the woman and her child. Anne did it for her brother . . . People like that still exist."

"And you?"

"And me."

Camille hesitates.

"When I hit rock bottom, I realised that maybe it wasn't so bad to have someone for whom I was prepared to sacrifice something important. [He smiles.] A little luxury in these selfish times, don't you think?"

He turns up the collar of his coat.

"Well, that's that, I'm done for the day. And I've got a resignation letter to write. I haven't slept since . . ."

Still he does not move.

"Hey, Louis!"

Louis turns. One of the forensics officers on the pavement outside Hafner's house is calling him.

Camille waves: go on Louis, don't keep the man waiting.

"I'll just be a minute."

But when he comes back, Camille has already gone.

1.30 a.m.

Camille felt his heart pound when he saw there was a light on in the studio. He stopped the car, switched off the engine and sat in the darkness, considering what to do.

Anne is here.

This is an additional disappointment he could have done without. He needs to be alone.

He sighs, grabs his coat and hat, the package with the thick file held together by elastic bands, then trudges up the path wondering how she will react, wondering what he is going to tell her, *how* he is going to tell her. He pictures her as he last saw her, sitting on the floor next to the sink.

The terrace door is ajar.

The faint glow in the studio comes from the night-light under the stairs, it is too dark to see where Anne might be. Camille sets his package on the terrace, reaches for the handle and slides the door open.

He is alone. He hardly needs to ask, but he does.

"Anne . . . are you there?"

He already knows the answer.

He walks over to the stove, this is what he always does. He

throws in a log. Opens the flue.

He takes off his coat, switches on the kettle as he passes, then immediately turns it off, wanders to the cupboard where he keeps the liquor and hesitates: whisky, cognac?

Let's go for cognac.

Just a snifter.

Then he goes outside and fetches the package from the terrace and closes the patio door.

He will take his time, sip the brandy. He loves this house. Up above, the skylight is darkened by the shifting shadows of the leaves. Inside he cannot hear the wind, but he can see it.

It is strange, but in this moment – though he is a big boy now – he misses his mother. Misses her terribly. He could cry if he let go.

But he resists. There is no point to crying alone.

Then he sets down his glass, kneels next to the coffee table and opens the thick file of papers, photographs, official reports and newspaper clippings; somewhere amongst them are the last pictures ever taken of Irène.

He does not search, he does not look, methodically he takes fistfuls of documents and feeds them into the gaping maw of the stove, which is now humming peacefully, at cruising speed.

Acknowledgements

My thanks to my wife, Pascaline, to Gérald Aubert for his advice and to my friend Sam, a constant presence and a constant help. Thanks also to Pierre Scipion for his care and his kindness, and to all the staff at Albin Michel.

And of course I would like to express my gratitude to those authors from whom I have borrowed (in alphabetical order): Marcel Aymé, Thomas Bernhard, Nicholas Boileau, Heinrich Böll, William Faulkner, Shelby Foote, William Gaddis, John le Carré, Jules Michelet, Antonio Muñoz Molina, Marcel Proust, Olivier Remaud, Jean-Paul Sartre, Thomas Wolfe.

PIERRE LEMAITRE was born in Paris in 1951. He worked for many years as a teacher of literature and now writes novels and screenplays. In 2013 he was awarded the C.W.A. International Dagger for *Alex*, the second in a crime series known as the Commandant Camille Verhoeven trilogy that began with *Irène*, and concludes with *Camille*. That year he was also winner of the Prix Goncourt, France's most prestigious literary award, for his novel *Au revoir là-haut*.

FRANK WYNNE is a translator from French and Spanish of works by Michel Houellebecq, Boualem Sansal, Antonin Varenne, Arturo Pérez-Reverte, Carlos Accosta and Hervé le Corre. He was the winner of the *Independent* Foreign Fiction Prize for his translation of Frédéric Beigbeder's *Windows on the World*.